Praise for Umar Turaki

"*Every Drop of Blood Is Red* marries a thrilling, twisty premise with a moral inquiry about where we're taken once we reach the end point of vengeance. Umar Turaki is among the most dazzling and inventive novelists I've come upon in years."

—Kevin Chong, *The Double Life of Benson Yu*

"A mysterious disease sweeps through an African village in Umar Turaki's debut novel. Estranged siblings reunite to band against this insidious illness, highlighting the power of the everyday in this terrifying yet elegant read."

—*Good Morning America*

"*Such a Beautiful Thing to Behold* is ultimately a redemptive and uplifting text about what family means. The characters draw apart and come together again, showing an astonishing and moving amount of resilience. Though some of the characters commit unimaginable acts, their determination to prevail perfectly matches our own, and that brings great solace."

—*Fredericksburg Free Lance-Star*

"No matter how terrible the circumstances . . . Umar Turaki isn't glossing over the reality of how bad this situation could get—the changing perspectives kick in at exactly the right times to break the tension and allow a little hope back for the reader . . . It's a beautiful book, and even more impressive as a debut."

—*Mystery & Suspense*

"*Such a Beautiful Thing to Behold* is dark and gloomy, but also packed with tiny moments of joy and curious revelations that show life is always worth living. This is a pandemic book that shows the ugliness of the world and the way we can turn against those who need our help the most, but it also shows the power of love and the importance of forging bonds when everything seems lost. Turaki has taken the classic pandemic novel and infused it with his own brand of hope, and that makes this a must-read novel."

—LOCUS

"There is an aching beauty woven into the lyrical prose of this novel that lingers with the reader beyond the last page. Against the richly drawn canvas of a landscape rendered vividly and with meticulous detail, a story unfolds of a family and community faced with both outward and inner desolation. Compelled to untangle the difficult questions of what it means to be both human and humane in the face of unspeakable cruelty and horror, one is drawn in and held by their resilience, courage, vulnerability, and tenderness and the inimitable power of the ties that bind."

—Colleen van Niekerk, author of *A Conspiracy of Mothers*

"*Such a Beautiful Thing to Behold* is a stark, powerful novel about family, resilience, and survival in the face of nearly insurmountable odds. Turaki's engrossing storytelling will draw you in from the very first page, and the siblings' determination to escape their grim fates is as harrowing as it is hopeful, reminding us that even when faced with all matters of adversity and tragedy, humanity will still seek a way to forge ahead and prevail."

—Kirthana Ramisetti, author of *Dava Shastri's Last Day*

"Grim, beautiful—a stunning novel."

—T. L. Huchu, author of *The Library of the Dead*

Every Drop of Blood Is Red

OTHER TITLES BY UMAR TURAKI

Such a Beautiful Thing to Behold

Every Drop of Blood Is Red

a novel

UMAR TURAKI

This is a work of fiction. Names, characters, organizations, places, events, and incidents are either products of the author's imagination or are used fictitiously. Otherwise, any resemblance to actual persons, living or dead, is purely coincidental.

Published by Little A, New York

www.apub.com

Transliterations of the Holy Qur'an taken from Auran411.com.

ISBN-13: 9781662508110 (hardcover)
ISBN-13: 9781662508103 (paperback)
ISBN-13: 9781662508127 (digital)

Cover design by Erin Fitzsimmons
Cover image: © Golubovy / Shutterstock; © Benjamin Harte / ArcAngel; © Azigbo Waves Photography

Printed in the United States of America

First edition

For Tong & Salma

And I the believer was also the doubter; For often have I put my finger in my own wound that I might have the greater belief in you and the greater knowledge of you.

—Kahlil Gibran, The Prophet

Stirring into the morning and sitting up in bed. It is still raining. The light curls weakly around the edges of the curtain, strangled by the deluge. No bar of light under the bathroom door to suggest it is occupied, but still going to it and knocking. After looking inside, padding to the living room. She isn't there either. She isn't in the kitchen. She isn't in the dining room. Opening the front door and standing on the verandah, watching the rain shatter against the Honda.

Going to rouse the boy, but his bed is empty. Checking every room in the house. Then searching the compound, circling the house multiple times. Not caring for an umbrella and getting soaked through within seconds. At the gate, clutching the padlock and shaking it. Unyielding as ever.

At night, he raises a lamp in the dark and stares at the cake. He had forgotten how large it is, how much space it takes up. In the harsh white gaze of the electric lamp, the cake's light-green coating takes on a bluish, ghostly haze. He is struck by the level of detail in the work. Little lines of golden yellow gild the edges of all three tiers. He gets a knife from the kitchen and stabs it. Carves out a wedge the size of his thumb. The butter icing isn't too sweet; the cakes tastes rather good. Cutting a triangular slice that fills his hand, weighs it down. Raising it to his mouth and taking bite after large bite. Grainy, like sandpaper against his throat as he swallows, but it is a good cake. A very good cake. Another slice. There is suddenly salt in his mouth. Where did it come from? He sniffs loudly.

Putting what remains of the second slice on the table, going outside through the kitchen. The lamp held aloft, its white light a beacon sweeping the path before him. His steps are calm, purposeful. He finds a metal rod in the generator room. It fills his grip nicely. Smooth and light like aluminium. Raising it over the cake, bringing it down like a final judgement. A dull, thick smack. Like a palm connecting loudly with a great expanse of skin. Raising the rod again, bringing it down. It sinks deeper into the cake each time it falls. Placing the lamp on the floor for the ease of both hands. Sweat springs forth, irrigating his skin. He swings from every conceivable angle. Stops only because his heart will if he doesn't. His chest heaves like a strange animal that's trying to break away from him. There are flecks of cake and icing on the walls, like a child's version of a fresco. The cake looks like a building whose top two floors have been bombed, laterally and from above, the roof blown off. There is a deep, uneven gash in its side, revealing a layer of golden-orange tissue. The ground floor is all but intact where her name had been fiercely inscribed with careful, trembling hands.

BEFORE

1

Jos during the rainy season is mischievous and merciless. The weather changes on a dime. The rainwater unlocks deep scents trapped in the ground for half a year. Everything is lush. The rocks are clean, each pockmark a perfect blemish in the grey igneous faces. The sky and the landscape beneath it have a scrubbed appearance, as if someone took a brush and some soapy water to a dusty relief. At dusk, bats living in the grand trees around the old zoo and museum leap into the air, filling the sky.

When it rains—particularly on Fridays, it seems—the city descends into traffic chaos. Pamson had noticed this. Gridlocks ensuing at major intersections. Farin Gada Roundabout, Hill Station Junction Roundabout, even Old Airport Junction Roundabout. Especially Old Airport Junction. Pamson knew this, which was why he took a long detour from Farin Gada through Rukuba Road. The buildings fell away as he drove up the incline, replaced by bush, planted fields, and rock-crusted hills. Every now and then, a fleet of houses would erupt out of the wilderness, reminding him of unrelenting change. On this Friday, the raindrops were big as they rolled down his windshield. By the time he had waved to the soldiers at the Miango Road–intersection checkpoint, the bumpy road had fully conceded to a smooth coating of asphalt. He floored the pedal and the BMW cruised on, passing more fields and properties in development, more change, all the way home.

Rahila was lying on the sofa, dozing to the sounds of the TV. He stood there for a moment, dripping lightly with rainwater, and watched her. She had always been a stomach sleeper, but since her pregnancy bump had grown too big, she'd learned to sleep on her side. He watched the rise and fall of her breathing. In her six months of pregnancy, he hadn't been allowed to touch the bump once, hadn't felt the tremors of the life that was growing there.

When he came out of the bathroom, Rahila was in the room, making the bed. He had tried not to comment on her housekeeping in recent months, how sloppy it had become. Every time he was tempted to complain, his tongue would be stilled by the rift that lay between them, the rift he had made.

"Your food will get cold," she said in Hausa.

"I had to take a bath. This rain."

The rain continued to pound the roof as he ate his dinner. He'd cleared half the plate of yam pottage when Paul entered the dining room from the kitchen. His hair gleamed with water.

"Uncle, there's a girl at the gate. She says she's here to see you."

Pamson paused in his chewing. "A girl?"

"Yes."

"What girl?"

"I don't know her. She just said she wants to see you."

"Me?"

"Yes."

"Who did she say she wants to see?"

Paul looked at him, confused. "You."

Pamson rolled his eyes and spoke patiently. "Which name did she give?"

"Mr. Dareng Pamson."

Pamson turned his head and looked out the window. The raindrops crashed on Rahila's CRV a million pellets at a time. Rather than risk getting wet from going to the gate, he told Paul to bring the girl to the front door. He stood on the porch and waited. He could feel the spray of the rain on his feet, endless tiny pinpricks. He moved back until he was flush against the wall. Could a woman like Mary, well into her thirties, objectively be described as a girl? Would she dare come here? How would she have gotten his address? But the figure that stepped through the curtain of rain wasn't Mary. She was drenched through even though she was standing under Paul's umbrella. She was probably in her late teens or early twenties. Her clothes were plastered to her body, her blouse, her hijab. She had a nose ring and henna-adorned hands. But more than anything else, it was her eyes that arrested him, the way they landed on him and moved over him, combing, knowing.

"You go about without an umbrella at this time of the year?" Pamson said in Hausa. "You don't know Jos?"

She wiped water from her face and shook her head. "The sun was shining when I went out. Not even up to an hour ago. Are you Mr. Dareng Pamson?"

He waited for her to say more, but she stood there with her arms folded around her, shivering. Her eyes boomeranged over the house itself, the compound, then returned to him.

"Yes," Pamson said at last. Paul was watching him. He nudged his head a fraction toward the door, indicating that Pamson should invite her inside.

Once they were inside, she asked if she could use the bathroom to dry herself. Paul said she could use the one in his room and led her away. Pamson stood there, wondering if he might have met her somewhere before. Her slim figure made her look quite young. He wouldn't have put her past twenty-three. But nothing in her features was familiar to him. What would Rahila think if she saw her? It didn't help either that the girl was so good-looking. The best thing was to dismiss her quickly. Before Rahila came out of the bedroom.

When the girl stepped in, she was wearing black sports trousers and a bright-blue T-shirt that said SAY YES TO THE HUSTLE in international currency symbols. Paul's clothes. Pamson had always hated the irony that the shirt's owner was anything but a hustler, but the sight of the shirt had never irked him more than it did now.

"You've changed," he said, as though she wasn't aware of this.

"He offered to dry my clothes for me," she said, throwing a grateful look in the direction of Paul's room. Her hair was now exposed—natural hair gathered into a frizzy ponytail.

Pamson showed her the love seat across the room, as far away from him as possible. As she sat down, Paul passed through behind her and into the kitchen. Pamson followed him.

"What do you think you're doing?"

Paul had taken an iron from one of the overhead cabinets. He raised it in defence. "I just want to dry her clothes for her."

"I wanted her to leave quickly."

"But, Uncle . . ." Paul indicated the window, where raindrops angrily met their end against the panes.

"Do it quickly. She shouldn't stay long," Pamson said. He returned to the living room and retook his seat. The girl's face was now clear and open, like the poorly lit page of a book placed under fresh illumination. She had large almond-shaped eyes, a small nose like the tip of an arrow, and slender lips. Her eyes seemed to exist in counterpoint with the rest of her face. He could imagine how innocent, even pure, she would seem when she closed them. But as long as they were open, they gave her face a cunning and piercing beauty.

"What can I do for you?" he said.

"Please forgive me for coming to your house like this," she said. "You don't even know me. I went to your garage, but they said you didn't come to work today. They showed me where you live, and when I went out today I promised myself—"

"Who?"

"Sir?" she said in English.

"Who showed you where I live?"

"The woman who sells food there."

Pamson nearly hissed. If anyone would give up his privacy, of course it would be Maman Ivie. Paul, who had been going back and forth through the living room, entered from the kitchen with a steaming mug and passed it to the girl. Pamson threw him a lethal look as he withdrew from the room, then turned back to the girl.

"What do you want?"

The girl blew on the cup of tea before taking a sip. She opened her mouth to speak and was again interrupted, this time by Rahila's entrance. Pamson watched his wife's reaction out of the corner of his eye. She looked at the girl, back at Pamson, back at the girl.

The girl stood up and curtsied. "Good afternoon, ma," she said in English.

"Good afternoon," Rahila said. "How are you?"

"I'm fine, ma."

"Sit down."

Rahila looked at Pamson. He knew she was waiting for an explanation right there and then, never mind that the object to be explained was sitting in front of them.

"Darling," he began, "this is . . . What's your name?"

"Murmula, sir."

"This is Murmula. She was just about to tell me what has brought her here in this rain."

Rahila sat next to Pamson and took his hand in hers, looked at the girl. "Don't mind me, my dear. Please continue."

Pamson's hand began to feel like a foreign object in his wife's grasp. When was the last time they had touched like this? When was the last time they had touched at all? She was only marking her territory, effectively declaring that he was taken, wasn't she? Could he dare hope that there might be more to it?

"In all truth, I'm looking for work," the girl said.

"Work?" Pamson said.

The girl nodded.

"What makes you think I can give you work?" Pamson asked. "I'm a mechanic."

"I want to learn about cars," the girl answered.

Pamson waited for her face to crack into a smile, waited for her voice to tinkle with laughter. But her eyes remained calm, unamused.

"Why?" Pamson said.

"Because I've always loved cars. Since I was little."

"Why me? I'm sure I'm not the only mechanic in Jos."

The girl sighed and placed the mug on the coffee table. "I'm new in this town. I started by going one by one to garages on Domkat Bali Road, then on Tudun Wada Road. None of them wanted a girl to work for them. The woman that sent me here said you're a very nice man who helps people all the time."

"I doubt I'm that nice."

He felt like the girl could see through him when she nodded and said, "The nicest people don't always know that they're nice." He found himself unable to respond, frozen by the gravity of her gaze. Once again, he felt like he was being x-rayed, as though she were seeing through him and into the deep of his past.

"Tell me about your interest in cars," Rahila said suddenly in English. "Why cars?"

The girl sighed again, then launched into her speech. "I'll never forget the first time I entered a car. I was six years old. It was my uncle's car. A maroon Honda Accord. Eighty-four model. It had maroon seats, maroon everything. Even the steering was maroon. Inside, the car had a new smell, like no one had used it before. But my uncle bought it Tokunbo. He put me on his legs and let me hold the steering. The car started to move. When I turned it, it felt very soft. The car smelled so nice; it sounded so quiet when it moved, like a cat walking. When I turned the wheel left, the car went left. When I turned it right, the car went right. I didn't understand why it was like that, but I knew it was magic. I promised myself I was going to learn the magic. I haven't stopped desiring it since that time."

Pamson continued to watch the girl. He didn't know what to make of it. Her speech sounded convincing, and she spoke English very well for a Hausa girl—assuming she was Hausa. Yet something about the situation wasn't adding up. He looked at Rahila, but she also seemed to be studying the girl, trying to make up her mind about her.

"It sounds like you want to make cars," Pamson said, "and I don't make cars. I only repair them."

"I have to start somewhere," the girl said. "I can start by learning how they work and how to repair them."

"How old are you?" Rahila asked.

"Twenty-five."

"Where are you from?" Pamson said.

"I was born here, but I've lived in Ilorin for the last ten years."

"Why did you come back?" Rahila said.

"There are better opportunities here. No mechanic in Ilorin will let a woman work in his shop. Jos is special."

"Aren't those Paul's clothes?" Rahila asked in Hausa.

"Yes, ma. I got wet. Your son let me wear this while my clothes get dry."

Pamson feared for a moment that Rahila would correct her and say that Paul wasn't their son. But Rahila said, "Where did you say you went to school?"

"University of Ilorin. I studied mechanical engineering. I graduated with a two-one."

"And you want to work for me as what?" Pamson said.

"An apprentice, in the beginning."

"And what after that?"

"If you like my work, you can promote me. Maybe one day I'll be helping you to run the workshop."

Pamson chuckled away his incredulity. The nerve on this girl. "Let us not get ahead of ourselves."

The girl smiled.

"That means you don't expect to get paid," Pamson said.

"I'm staying with my uncle. I'm not paying rent or buying food. But it would be nice to have some pocket money for my toiletries and to buy something for the house from time to time."

Pamson looked at Rahila. He had already made up his mind. And he could sense from her coiled-up posture—and the fact that she still hadn't relinquished his hand—she wasn't up for it either.

"Let me think about it for a day or two."

"Should I come back in three days?"

"You don't have to come back."

"How will I know what you decide?"

Pamson realised there was no way of completely severing links with the girl without appearing callous.

"You can give your number to Paul," he said.

The girl nodded. She picked up the mug. "Can I finish drinking my tea before I go?"

"Take your time, my dear," Rahila said.

Pamson excused himself and went to the bedroom. He sat at the foot of the bed and called Yunusa, his panel beater, first, asking about the girl. Then he realised he didn't know her surname. He called Abdulsalam, the AC repair guy. He called Mallam Tanko, the seat-cover supplier. No one seemed to know a girl who went by the unusual name of Murmula.

2

She had stood in front of Number 27 after alighting from the keke, staring at the black gate. She forgot for a time that she was in the rain and had no umbrella, that she was supposed to knock. Her hand, when she finally raised it, was as heavy as a brick. It slammed into the metal three times before falling again to her side. Once she was inside the compound, she stared at the house, deaf to all but the thunder of her heart. It was a modest bungalow, with richly painted white walls and an aluminium roof, whose deep maroon was still vivid to look at, even in the downpour. The stretch of ground in front of the house had been paved, but the backyard hadn't, surrendering to wild-growing weeds and bushes. All these details, she had clocked between the gate and the front door. She took a deep breath. Her chest felt like paper against the emotions that were churning inside her: regret, a brilliant lightning fork of anger. She exhaled, and with that, her sense of control returned. When she laid her eyes on the man for the first time, she had felt a little disappointed. How could this portly, ordinary-looking man be the author of her suffering? He was a younger, slimmer version of Papa Ajasco. She had expected someone more imposing and brooding, someone who looked like the villain he actually was. She had scanned his body for any incriminating detail, but there was nothing to indicate his villainy. No scar, no deformity, no disfigurement of note.

What she hadn't expected: to be welcomed into the house by a handsome young man her age, who seemed so intent on prolonging her visit he had practically given her access to his room, his clothes, and a cup of tea. Getting soaked right through hadn't been part of her plan either, but it had worked in her favour.

Now, seated in the car next to him, she continued to study his movements, interested in the way he seemed to respond to her needs without her having to say them. He had offered to drive her home without her asking. When she wrapped her arms around herself, shivering from the cold of the AC, he automatically turned a dial on the dashboard. The car started to heat up after a minute or so.

She looked out the window. The rain showed no sign of letting up. She was nearly a week back in this city, and yet her memories of it remained fuzzy. Some things she remembered, like the unforgiving rain. But she had forgotten this heavy scent of it, which almost felt like drowning. And the way the clouds gathered around the sun like an angry mob and erased its existence. The city was dark today, grey, a slab of concrete pressing down on her, reminding her at every turn of why she had left it in the first place and why she was now back.

Paul had both hands on the steering wheel. He shared a striking resemblance with his mother. Their lips were the same shape and had the same darkness around them that gave them the appearance of smokers. But she knew he didn't smoke; she would have smelled it on his clothes. He turned the car off Miango Road and slithered up a dark road guarded by tall trees. The wipers swished powerfully against the windshield, periodic thuds that punctuated the silence. She realised how quiet it was, and that he could have put on the radio but didn't.

When he pulled up at her neighbourhood junction in Dadin Kowa, he offered to drive her in.

"The road is very bad and narrow," she said. "You don't want to spoil your mother's car."

"Then take the umbrella," he said, and snatched it up from where it leaned against the door.

She collected the umbrella, but he didn't release it, and it remained suspended between them like a bridge. She saw his throat move before he spoke. "They said I should take your number." He whipped out his phone and punched in the digits as she called them out, then asked for her full name.

"Murmula Denge," she said quietly.

"Murmula is a strange name. I've never heard it before."

"My father chose it," she said. "I'm the only person with that name, as far as I know."

"Your father sounds like a genius."

Murmula nodded, then took a breath to stem the flood of emotion that threatened to breach her composure. Her father, a genius. She smiled, then erased the smile. He had existed for so long in the past tense that hearing someone refer to him as though he were still around was a small gift. But it was a gift from unsuitable quarters. She couldn't accept it. "He had an imagination."

"Is he . . . I'm sorry." Paul paused. "Can I ask how he died?"

"He disappeared during the crisis of 2008. We never saw him again."

Paul turned his face away and looked out the windshield. She could tell he was searching for the right words. She forced herself to release a small chuckle, to change the dour tone of the conversation.

"What's funny?" Paul said.

"We drove from your house to this place without saying anything. Now we suddenly have so much to talk about it."

"I'm sorry to be keeping you."

"No, it's fine. I don't mind. Maybe we can carry on the conversation next time."

"Yes, next time," he said, wearing a small smile.

"I hope your father will consider my request," she said with an earnestness that surprised even her. "It would mean so much if he agrees."

Paul smiled again and shook his head.

"Is it my turn to ask what's funny?" she said.

"He's not my father. They're not my parents. Aunty Rahila is my cousin. Our fathers were brothers."

"Oh, I see," Murmula said. "Sorry for assuming."

"Everybody assumes it. You can't blame them. Aunty and I look very alike. But I'll see what I can do."

"Thank you."

She opened the door to the roaring rain and popped the umbrella. A river of rainwater barrelled down the gutter by the side of the road. One wrong step and she would slide into it. She wondered how far it would take her, *where* it would take her. The drops were countless tiny angry fists pounding on the umbrella. She reached the house half-drenched and kicked off her shoes inside the door of the living room. The rumble of the generator was audible from the backyard despite the din on the roof. Baba Karami and Ishat were on the sofa, watching an action film. Her uncle was reclining in his white undershirt, his caftan draped on the back of the sofa and iridescently green in the white fluorescent light. He was back early from the shop today.

"Good evening, Baba," she said.

Baba Karami moved his feet and patted the space for Murmula to sit beside him. Ishat shifted closer to her father.

"How was the job search?" he said. His eyes were still on the screen. Sylvester Stallone had a machine gun the size of a tree. Bullet shells poured from it like a metallic version of the downpour outside.

"Fine," she said. She had told them she was looking for an apprenticeship in a tailoring shop in Bukuru. Her uncle and aunt were not intrusive. Their children had almost complete autonomy in their lives, even Ishat at sixteen. Baba Karami and Gogo Hauwawu could have been like some other parents she knew, who wouldn't even let their adult daughters outside without a male relative escorting them, but they weren't—they seemed to trust their children by default, even though it hadn't been earned. This trust had automatically expanded to include Murmula. She had told them her first lie earlier that week, and it was only now, as she was seated beside Ishat and her uncle, that she saw the lie had been a door into a new way of being with them. She didn't know what she would find in this new room. She looked at her uncle, with his lean face that was her father's, right down to the bridged nose, his eyes that reflected the spectacle of the bloodbath unfolding on the television screen. When she had called him two months earlier to ask if she could move back to Jos and live with them, he had said simply, "This is your house; we're waiting." He was her father's younger twin, and their resemblance still tripped her up. Since her arrival she had been repeatedly taken by a fleeting impression, each time she entered a room and saw her uncle, that her father had walked right back into her life as abruptly as he had left.

"The shop owner wasn't around, and I had to wait for the rain to stop," she explained. "Thank God there was a customer who was coming this way and gave me a lift."

"But if it's tailoring, you don't even have to go that far," Baba Karami said. "Hajiya Ladi's shop is just here by First Gate. You can learn there."

"Baba, the woman I went to meet has the best finishing I've ever seen. It's women's fashion, you won't understand it," Murmula said, smiling. "Besides, Bukuru isn't even that far."

"Hajiya Ladi's finishing is also very good," Ishat said without taking her eyes off the screen.

Murmula stood up and went into the kitchen. Her cousin—with her sashes, sequins, and shoes—was a fashion expert. It was best to avoid any sustained conversations on the matter of her apprenticeship with her. Gogo Hauwawu was seated on a low stool, making masa over the kerosene stove. She flipped the white discs of rice batter one after the other without missing a beat. The freshly turned faces were burnished and pristine in their holes. Murmula greeted her aunt, then took over the cooking. When she had cleared away the freshly done masa, she spooned fresh batter into each hole slowly, taking her time. Her hands weren't as deft as her aunt's and would probably never be.

"I wish that sister of yours was more like you," Gogo Hauwawu said from the gas stove, where she had started making the miyan taushe that would go with the masa. "She's sitting there watching a film, and her father doesn't even have the sense to tell her to come and help me. If I talk, they'll say I'm being hard on her. One day she'll go to her husband's house and not be able to lift even a spoon. And who will people blame?"

Murmula said nothing. When her aunt complained to her like this about her children, she was torn between agreeing with her that both Ishat and Musty were lazy when it came to house chores—which they were—and pointing out that children didn't just get spoiled by themselves: somebody had to have done the spoiling. But she mostly maintained a cordial silence that allowed her aunt's complaints to hang between them without unease.

"And Mustapha," Gogo Hauwawu said, "who even knows what that boy is up to? University, he has refused to go. Work, he isn't interested. 'Come and work for your father,' no. It's always one scheme or another. Yesterday he wanted to go into tin mining—or was it tantalite? Allah knows what it'll be today."

Musty was three years older than Murmula. It wasn't lost on her that his mother still called him a boy. The other day, he had brought a he-goat and tried to sell it to the neighbour for some quick cash. It was a large and healthy goat, to be fair, and the neighbour, Mallam Aliyu, had been tempted to buy it. But he ultimately declined. Murmula had secretly watched the exchange from the window of her and Ishat's room, which opened onto the street. Musty walked away trailing the goat, lanky and forlorn looking, and returned hours later without it. It wasn't clear whether he'd managed to sell it or not.

Musty entered the kitchen through the backdoor after maghrib prayers. Murmula was at the sink, doing the dishes. She felt his eyes sliding over her. He was small and narrow in frame, but Murmula's memories of him overflowed with energy, contention. What he lacked in stature, he made up for in other ways. She remembered his temper well. He seemed a bit unsteady on his feet now, swaying by the door. The smell of weed crossed the kitchen brazenly.

"What about Mama?" he said.

"She's in her room. I think she's still praying. Your food is there." Murmula pointed at the covered aluminium plate on the counter, just by the door where he was standing.

Musty touched the cover, then lifted it to see what was underneath. "Masa. It's cold. Can you warm it for me?"

"The generator can't carry the microwave," Murmula said.

Musty nodded, as if he had never known this until now. He picked up the food.

"I heard you went to look for work today," he said.

"Yes."

"Where?"

"A tailoring shop."

"Did you get it?"

"No."

"Didn't you study engineering or something like that? What was it?"

"Mechanical."

"And you want to work for a tailor?"

Murmula looked at him for a moment, then averted her face. She didn't move, but he did. He closed the space between them until he was right next to her. He used his fingers to gently tip her chin so that she faced him again. He didn't remove his hand. She realised she had stopped breathing. This was another thing that had crept into their relationship since her return: a leering quality in her cousin's eyes and speech that was either lascivious or malicious. She couldn't decide which. It made her uncomfortable, and she hadn't yet figured out a way to make him stop.

Musty removed his finger from her chin at last and waved it around as he spoke. "This city. If you don't know what you're doing, you won't get what you want. You should come and talk to me. I know people who can help you. With a proper job, not some tailoring rubbish. Do you understand?"

Murmula nodded. After he left, she took the empty bucket to the drum at the end of the counter and filled it with water again, then brought it back and rinsed the remaining dishes. As she dried her hands on a towel, she leaned against the counter, thinking about what had just happened. He was clearly attracted to her. What unnerved her was his boldness, his certainty that it was okay to act on that attraction.

"Murmula."

She turned her head. Baba Karami was by the door to the living room. She hadn't heard him enter.

"Are you okay?"

"I am. Do you need anything?"

He came closer and looked at her properly even though there was enough light to see by.

"Are you worried about getting a job?" he said.

"I'm trying not to be."

"You know, you've only been here a week. Give it time. Something will come through. Your decision to come back to Jos is good. If you know what you're doing, this city will work for you. And you look like you know what you're doing."

Murmula smiled, but she felt her stomach turn. She had never had to put much effort into lying, but with him she realised she would have to work harder. His gullibility, his sheer goodness, would confront her each time. It didn't help that he was practically her father in the flesh.

"Do you still need the generator? I want to switch it off."

"I don't. But Mustapha just came back. I can ask him if he needs it."

Baba Karami hissed impatiently and went outside. The droning of the generator ceased moments later, and the house sank into a heavy darkness. But it had been only one droning among many. The neighbourhood generators—in the hundreds, perhaps—droned into the night. At first, Murmula felt they were a hindrance to sleep. She turned every few minutes on the bed while Ishat dozed peacefully beside her. Mallam Aliyu next door kept his generator in front of his house, which wasn't far from the bedroom window. Its distinctive, shrill racket was more of an endless, rumbling scream. It became her object of focus, drilling into her skull, into her thoughts. It seemed to loosen the emotions she had crammed away, easing them out of their corners. A deep anguish she thought she had mastered, but her body said no. She started to tremble, and her tears slowly watered her pillow. She had walked on her father's land for the first time, had seen the house that should have been his, had entered the bedroom that could easily have been hers. Now that she had seen the face of her enemy and had set things in motion, she finally understood the scale of this undertaking, and she worried that all the might and will she had stockpiled over the years would prove insufficient. She wept silently, wary of rousing her cousin. But this was nothing new, entrusting her tears to a pillow until sleep came. In the morning she would be as good as new, and her path forward would become that much clearer.

3

Pamson felt his hands gathering sweat while he sat in the congregation, waiting to be called up. His cap was in his lap, the burgundy of his caftan and of Rahila's gown almost garish against the dark wood of the pew. She had insisted they wear anko. She had picked the fabric herself. Knowing he didn't like wearing caftans, she had arranged for the tailor to come to the house and get his measurements. The caftan, starched to a flaky crispness, ballooned and crackled like cardboard around him. Though his name hadn't yet been mentioned, he felt like every eye was on him. They had been asked to sit as close to the front as possible to save time when walking up. So here they were, in the very second row, his bald pate visible to the entire congregation.

Reverend Dogo, the current speaker, had left the podium and walked to the edge of the stage, where he leaned forward dramatically and asked, "Who among you can claim to be good?" He scanned the congregation, as if waiting for a member to raise their hand. They hadn't yet gotten to the sermon, and already he had ramped up the intensity. Pamson was dismayed at the thought that he was the preacher for the day. He found the reverend long-winded, overbearing, and shrill, though Pamson, like many other members of the congregation, derived a small pleasure from the irony that existed between the man's diminutive stature and his surname. Dogo indeed. God did have a sense of humour after all.

When Pamson and Rahila were summoned, the band started playing and Rahila began to move effortlessly to the rhythm. Pamson tried to move his arms to simulate some version of a dance, the whole time in agony over the sight he must cut. The progress to the front was slow. He felt like a giant red peacock flapping its wings. When at last they stood on the level, the stage behind them and the congregation before them, one of the ushers handed the microphone to Pamson. A few people had come up with them. Beside Paul were Paul's eldest sister, Eunice; her husband; and two of her children. There was also Alhaji Attahiru, his Muslim neighbour, who had insisted on coming when he heard that Pamson was going to have a thanksgiving in church.

"Praise the Lord," Pamson said into the microphone.

"Hallelujah!" the congregation answered.

"We are here because God is good." He realised he sounded a bit too subdued. "I said, God is good!"

"All the time!"

"And all the time!"

"God is good!"

"The Bible says that when God does something for you, you should return to give Him praise. My wife and I have come back here to give glory to God and to thank Him for His goodness in our lives. We have been married for eighteen years. Those that know us know that we struggled to have children. We tried everything. Everything you can think of. From science to medicine to technology, you name it. But nothing was forthcoming. We were also praying too. Don't misunderstand me. Prayer was the first thing. But even the Bible tells us that faith without works is dead. The years kept going, we kept getting older. I turned forty-eight this year; my wife will be forty-five. We already accepted that maybe God didn't intend for us to have children of our own. But one day six months ago, out of nowhere, she comes and tells me, 'I'm pregnant.' I looked at her. I said, 'How?'" The church rumbled with laughter. "She said, 'How do you think?'" More laughter. "I thought she was joking, so I waited. She started vomiting, complaining of headaches. But how I knew it was serious was when she woke me up in the middle of the night—as a true Ngas woman—and said I should go and buy dogmeat for her."

The laughter this time roared up and rolled on for almost a minute. Pamson waited for the voices to quieten, buoyed by the crowd's glee. The pleasure of the moment surprised him. Church had never really been his preferred crowd, despite the changes he had implemented in his life over the years. He had given up alcohol, something the church leadership had banned, but that had been a choice he'd made independently. God was a fact that existed remotely, like the laws of motion. He acknowledged and respected their existence, but he only referred to them when encountering a particularly challenging problem in his work. He got by for the most part by not getting tangled up in the details. He hadn't expected to enjoy standing in front of the congregation with a microphone and spouting about God.

When the auditorium was silent again, he said, "At the age of forty-four, when we thought all hope was lost, God decided that we should have a baby. Praise the Lord!"

The applause was rapturous. While it went on, he leaned toward Rahila and asked if she wished to say anything. He hadn't dared stand so close to her over the past six months since she'd discovered his affair with Mary, let alone touch her. He smelled the cocoa lotion she used and realised how much he missed her scent. Swept up by the crowd's delight, it took some effort for him not to wrap an arm around her and pull her even closer.

Rahila's eyes cut into him. Perhaps she hadn't appreciated the dogmeat joke, given that she was the odd Ngas person who actually despised it. But she shook her head and smiled, so broadly that her cheeks formed deep dimples. It had been some time since he had seen that smile. That her face could display both sunniness and distaste in one breath was something that still amazed him about his wife.

"We have prepared some refreshment at home," Pamson continued when all had grown quiet again. "We will greatly appreciate if you can join us. Magnify the Lord with us. Let us exalt His name together."

The band struck up another song, and the members flowed into the aisles. They danced their way to the front, shuffling their feet, swinging their elbows. They dropped their offerings into the allocated baskets and shook hands with Pamson and Rahila. Pamson clapped his hands, moving from side to side in step with the rhythm. He suddenly felt glad that they had done this, that he had worn that bright burning caftan with its gaping sleeves.

A handful of their guests accompanied them home after the service. Pamson went in and changed into a T-shirt and trousers. When he reemerged into the living room, Rahila was pressing a bag loaded with drinks and packs of rice and chicken into Alhaji Attahiru's hands.

"This one is just for you and Hajiya," Rahila said. "Tell the children to come and collect their own themselves. There's special ice cream I bought just for them."

Pamson gripped Alhaji's hand in a firm handshake after Rahila walked away.

"This woman is always trying to kill us with food," the neighbour said.

"Now you can see where I'm coming from," Pamson said, patting his belly.

People came and went. Pamson sat with two of his friends, Mark Miner and Solomon Haruna, who had just arrived under the guava tree in the garden. They asked specifically for cold kunu.

"None of that bottled rubbish," Mark said. His broad shoulders filled the short-sleeved jacket he wore, as though he'd been inflated into it. His brash voice was as imposing as his stature. He had a way of tipping the scale of attention in his favour that grated on Pamson a little. "Give me good old traditional kunu, any day, any time. Pure and natural."

"But you know the kunu of nowadays has its own additives," Solomon said. A dark-skinned man whose head reached just to Mark's shoulder, he was the quiet, pensive one among the pair. The two were inseparable and ran a law firm in Rayfield together.

"Additives?" Mark said.

"Is sugar not an additive?"

Mark indicated his companion with a mocking hand and looked at Pamson. "Can you hear him? He's speaking English here. My friend, this isn't a court of law."

While the banter went on, the kunu arrived. But what got Pamson's attention was the person carrying it. It was the girl. She had on a red-and-yellow-patterned wrapper with a matching blouse and headgear. Her decorated eyes were like two bold inscriptions on her face. When she pointed them at him, he felt somehow marked. In the full glare of the day, her skin glowed like a ripe lemon. A blue veil was thrown tastefully over one shoulder. She looked dressed for the occasion. She hadn't come today just by chance. Someone had invited her.

"Remind me again what your name is?" Pamson said when she bent to put down the tray with the drinks.

"Murmula, sir."

"How are you?"

"I'm fine, thank you."

Mark and Solomon watched her walk away. Pamson looked at them and snapped his fingers.

"Who's that?" Mark asked.

"Just someone we met recently," Pamson said, handing each of them a cold, sweaty bottle of kunu.

"She's very pretty," Solomon said, and looked at Pamson with a taunting smirk.

Mark's abrasive laughter filled the air. He leaned in and whispered, "I thought you said no more after Mary."

"There is nothing happening here," Pamson said, but his friends only laughed harder. He kept a straight face and refused to respond further.

By late afternoon almost everyone had left. Rahila was with Eunice at the dining table while Eunice's children played outside in the compound, probably trying to reach the unripe guavas. From the living room, Pamson could hear Murmula and Paul in the kitchen. There was some song playing from Paul's portable speaker. They were discussing it, arguing about the merits of the singer. Pamson went and stood in the kitchen doorway.

"Paul."

Murmula had her hands in the sink, washing the dishes and handing them to Paul, who wiped them with a dish towel. He draped the towel over his shoulder and followed Pamson into the living room.

"What is she doing here?"

Paul bit his lip before saying, "I invited her."

"Why?"

"I don't know. Because she's my friend."

Pamson stared at him for a moment. "Friend?"

Paul glanced over his shoulder in the direction of the kitchen. He lowered his voice and said, "We're friends, Uncle. I thought it would be nice."

"You're friends."

"We're friends."

"Just friends?"

"Just friends."

Pamson searched the boy's face a moment longer, but there was nothing in it to suggest he wasn't telling the truth. He turned away to go into the bedroom.

"Uncle?" When Pamson turned around again, Paul asked, "Have you thought about whether you're going to give her the job?"

"You already know my answer, Paul."

"It would mean a lot to her. Please help her."

"I said no. And don't invite her here again."

Pamson walked away and went into the bedroom and lay down. He needed a nap. He still didn't know the best way to dissuade Murmula from coming over again. Who knew what Rahila was already thinking, seeing the girl around the house? But Murmula seemed so passionate, so determined. Would he be guilty of heartlessness, of killing a dream that seemed priceless? Some part of him wanted to yield and give her a chance. Rahila didn't know much about his past and had made it clear she had no interest in the man he had been before they met, but she accused him sometimes of being politically incorrect. This happened despite his clear attempts at being cordial and generous with their neighbour, Alhaji Attahiru; it happened even though some of the boys who worked at his garage were Muslims. Maybe this was an opportunity to do things differently, convince himself and others, especially Rahila, of his open-mindedness. But there was more at stake than he was prepared to risk. He had to win back Rahila's trust, show her that she had no reason to ever worry about him being unfaithful again. Until then, he couldn't afford having someone like Murmula around him. Not at home, not at work.

When he woke up, the room was dim. Rain was heavy outside, on the ground, on the roof. He felt enclosed inside a soft wall of sound that muffled the whole world. Rahila was beside him, reading with a flashlight. She had started using reading glasses a few weeks earlier, and it still gave him a tiny jolt each time he saw them perched at the end of her nose. She was getting older—but then, so was he.

"What time is it?" he said, and raised himself into a seated position.

"Six thirty," Rahila said without looking up.

He raised the curtain of the window behind the bed and peered out. Daylight was all but gone.

"Is there light?" he said.

"Yes."

"Why are you sitting in the dark?"

"You were sleeping."

"You know light doesn't disturb me," Pamson said. He felt almost wounded. Despite all their years of marriage, she still seemed oblivious to how much of a heavy sleeper he was. She had stubbed her big toe once and snapped her nail in half because she was walking around in the darkness of the room. He found out about it the next day only because her toe was unmistakably bandaged. He ought to be grateful she was being so sensitive, but he felt ignored, un-known, like a part of him existed that had somehow failed to register to her across the years. He didn't know if she was doing it on purpose. Maybe it was her quiet, patient way of punishing him for Mary.

He stood up and turned the light on and sat on the bed facing her. She had already changed into her nightgown.

"Reverend Dogo came when you were sleeping," she said, putting the book down. It was another Danielle Steel novel. This one had a blue jacket. "He didn't stay for long."

"Thank you."

"For what?"

"For making sure we did this," Pamson said. Her hand was resting on the bed, right in front of him. Without thinking, he placed his hand over hers and left it there. There was so much he wanted to put out in the open between them, especially the thing with Mary. He was tired of pretending like nothing had happened. He watched her to see how she would respond. She didn't move, letting him hold it for a few seconds before pulling away and scratching her neck. Then she removed her glasses and levelled her stare at him, cutting off the words that had begun to form on his lips.

"I saw Murmula here today."

Pamson nodded. "I didn't invite her. It was Paul."

"Have you decided whether you'll give her a job?"

"I can't give her a job."

"Why not?"

Pamson searched his wife's face for a sign that she was toying with him. "I didn't know you wanted me to do it."

"I didn't say I wanted you to do anything."

"Then what are you saying?"

"Answer my question first. Why don't you want to give her the job?"

"Because she won't be able to do it." He realised a second after he'd said it that it was a trap, and he'd stepped right into it.

"Because she's a woman," Rahila said with that coolness that unnerved him.

"No, that's not what I meant." He closed his eyes to gather his thoughts. "I just meant that she won't fit in. And she'll distract the boys."

"All of that is tied to her sex."

"Rahila, have you looked at her hands? They're soft hands. She's soft. If I asked her to untie even a tyre bolt, would she be able to do it?"

"She said you could test her. But you're not even ready to give her a chance. Or is it because she's a Muslim?"

"I really don't understand you," Pamson said. "You make me feel guilty because she's around, now you're asking why I haven't given her the job. Do you want me to give her a job or not?"

"I'm not doing anything to make you feel guilty. If you feel guilty, you should check yourself. These are two separate things. If you aren't going to give her work, I just want to understand that it's for the right reason. Refusing to help her because she's a woman or because she practises a different religion isn't an acceptable reason."

Pamson opened his mouth, then closed it and remained silent. He felt drained of the will to argue or prove a point. He had felt this way for some time. Rahila had worked at that non-governmental organisation for nearly ten years now, but it hadn't taken her that long to sound like this. Within a year of her employment, she had come home with ideas that sounded strange on her lips, using words like *parity* and acronyms like *GBV*. They would get into arguments in which she would reel out statistics like weapons, even though he barely knew what they meant. But they were effective in silencing him. Eventually, he had learned to sidestep such arguments, like the characters walking around a landmine he had seen in a film years ago. He didn't have the brains to engage in deep, intellectual discussions; he was just a humble mechanic. There were moments, like this one, when he suspected that she wanted him to be more than that. But he didn't know how to be anything other than what he was, what he had always been.

"Do you want me to give her the job or not?" he repeated, closing his eyes.

"No," Rahila said. "But I still want to see if she can be helped. There is an opportunity at InterWomen that she could benefit from."

"Why?"

"She's very smart. Very driven, especially for a Hausa girl. That she can come here and ask a man like you for work shows that she's open-minded. We're interested in helping people from her community."

"What is the opportunity?"

"It's a training program in various skills. Cooking, tailoring, baking, shoemaking, arts and crafts. Participants can choose what they want to learn and then have the opportunity to apprentice. We're working with some good businesses in town as partners in the initiative."

"Don't you want to work with mechanics?" Pamson said. A smile spread slowly across his face.

Rahila shook her head.

"You mean to say your organisation won't pay me with some of those international dollars to do apprenticeships?" He hated himself as soon as the words had come out. The joke had failed.

Rahila just looked at him as though he was losing his mind. "Even if we wanted mechanics, you know I couldn't hire you. It would be a conflict of interest."

She stood up and started to walk to the bathroom.

"So you now believe there's nothing between us?" Pamson asked.

"We will see," Rahila said in Hausa without stopping.

"Rahila, please," he said suddenly. She stopped and looked at him. "Please, let's talk about what happened. About Mary. Let me explain."

But all she did was turn away, drift slowly into the bathroom, and close the door. Pamson sat there, staring at her glasses on the bedside cabinet. They were half-moon with plastic arms that shimmered with rainbow colours when the light hit them. He didn't move until he heard the toilet flushing. Then he got up and left the room.

4

When Murmula left the house that morning, she'd felt somehow transparent. Gogo Hauwawu was stretched out on the couch, enjoying the quiet while she had the house all to herself. When she looked up at Murmula and told her to be careful out there, Murmula felt like she could see right into the place where she kept her heart in her chest and the thing that was in it. As she walked to the junction, she kept looking back to see if she was being followed. By the time she was seated in the back of a keke napep that was bound for Terminus, she'd told herself multiple times that nobody could read another person's mind. Not Gogo Hauwawu, not Mrs. Pamson.

There was one other passenger with her in the keke, an old man who had a lobe of kolanut in his gnarled hands. Every now and then, he would raise it to his mouth and take a small bite. He wore a long, grey caftan and a matching hat, all threadbare. His goatee was a tuft of white hair on his chin that moved in circles with his chewing. She paid the fare for both of them when the driver pulled over at Secretariat Junction. She moved to come down from the keke, but the man stopped her.

"What for?" he said in Hausa.

"For the Prophet."

"I'm not a Muslim, but alhamdulillaahi."

She stood for a moment on the side of the road after the keke had jerked away, smiling to herself. Compared to Ilorin, here it was much more difficult to tell Muslims and non-Muslims apart. Jos had changed so much in her lifetime, and the news cycles had done little to rehabilitate its image as a place of peaceful coexistence. Encounters like the one she'd just had said otherwise, that mutual respect was indeed possible and did happen. Though it hadn't been her intention, she was glad the man had turned out to not be a Muslim. It reminded her to not make assumptions based on appearance.

Murmula wasn't prepared for how much Secretariat Junction had changed. It was now a roundabout, like almost every other major intersection in the city. There was an overpass too. The wall of the overpass was covered in a colourful mural of abstract shapes redolent of the bucolic aspects of Jos. She had missed that, the sense that the land was ever-giving and bountiful and that whatever she required by way of fresh produce was within reach. Farin Gada Market and Building Material Market, with their weekly hauls of newly harvested vegetables and herbs. There was also the option of borrowing a patch of field and tithing a portion of the harvest to the landowner and to one's neighbours.

Mrs. Pamson's office was located on the road that led to the Secretariat. It was a cool, cloudy day, and her appointment was scheduled for 10:00 a.m. She would walk down the boulevard instead of finding another keke. She had time. She took note of how the buildings around her had changed. Storefronts had given way to closed-off frontages with mysterious purposes. She was moved by how much she remembered, by how well she remembered. The place that had once housed a bakery was now a paint depot, white buckets stacked from floor to ceiling, all the way to the back. She remembered the smell of the bakery, the perpetually fresh aroma of baked pastries that never went away. Her father had ordered her tenth-birthday cake from there, and it must have cost a lot, because her mother had yelled about it that evening after the party guests had left. But what Murmula remembered most was accompanying Baba to pick up the cake and seeing it for the first time through its moulded plastic cover: the three figures from *The Powerpuff Girls*, with arms raised, about to blast off from the ground.

In her excitement she had leapt onto Baba, and the cake had wobbled dangerously in his hands. How could a man so alive and present simply vanish from their lives as though he'd never existed, leaving nothing behind, not even a body to bury? As Murmula's thoughts started to darken, swirling downward into gloomy depths, she took out her earphones and hit "Play" on "Pocketful of Sunshine." She left the song on repeat all the way to InterWomen.

She was asked to wait in the reception because she was early. Mrs. Pamson swept through toward another room and saw her. She was dressed in a big flowing buba that did a fair job of concealing her baby bump.

"Murmula, how are you?"

"Fine, ma."

"You came early fa," Mrs. Pamson said in Hausa, looking at her watch. The wall clock said it was some twenty minutes to ten.

"No problem, I can wait."

"Ask them to show you to my office when it is time."

"Okay, ma."

Murmula sat back down and watched the door as seemingly random people trickled in and sat around the lobby. At five past ten, they were still coming in, and the lobby was growing full. That was when it dawned on Murmula that they might be participants for a training or workshop of some kind.

At ten thirty, the receptionist showed Murmula into Mrs. Pamson's office. It was a small room with a single desk, white walls, a whiteboard, and an uncarpeted concrete floor. Voices echoed around the room like invisible balls bouncing off the bare surfaces. The smell of fresh paint clung to Murmula's nostrils. Mrs. Pamson showed her to one of the chairs in front of her desk and asked if she wanted tea. There was a tray balanced on the small fridge beside the window. It had mugs, sachets of Nescafé and Milo, and an electric kettle.

"No, thank you, ma. I already had breakfast."

"Thank you for agreeing to come and see me. I was afraid you would refuse."

"I'm very happy you asked me to come, ma." When Paul had told her of Mrs. Pamson's invitation, he had laughed from the look on her face, which he'd described as "haunted." This had been right after he'd revealed that his uncle would not be letting Murmula work for him. Paul didn't explain why his aunt—or cousin, whatever she was—wanted to see her; all he'd said was that it couldn't hurt. This made Murmula suspect that perhaps there was some kind of initiative in motion that Mrs. Pamson thought she could benefit from—she saw her as a charity case. It hurt her pride, but she had pushed her ego aside because any sustained exposure to any member of Mr. Pamson's family improved her chances of gaining the necessary access to him. So she had let her guard down and come here, which perhaps was the reason she hadn't anticipated Mrs. Pamson's first question.

"I want you to be very frank with me, Murmula," Mrs. Pamson said slowly, quietly. She had switched to Hausa. "Tell me what is between you and my husband?"

Murmula swallowed and said, "Ba komai, ma." She had foolishly wandered into a trap.

"Nothing?"

"Yes."

"You're sure?"

Murmula didn't speak for some time. It took Mrs. Pamson reaching for the tissue box and handing her a piece for her to understand that she had started crying. She dabbed gently at her eyes, careful not to blotch her makeup. She had been stupid to think she could show up at a married man's house without setting off alarm bells in his wife's head. She remembered then the way Mrs. Pamson had sat beside her husband and taken his hand on that first day. She hadn't made much of the gesture then.

"This isn't a crying matter," Mrs. Pamson said softly. "I asked you to come because I like you. I want to help you. I just want to be sure first. You can't blame me. You know the kind of world we live in."

Murmula continued to cry as she said, "I understand, ma. Truly, wallahi tallahi, I'm not that kind of girl." Her voice bounced against the walls and into her ears gratingly. Its earnestness surprised her, but she was telling the truth, after all. It might be better if Mrs. Pamson suspected her of being involved with her husband rather than of having much darker intentions, yet even that would only hurt her chances in the greater scheme of things. She needed to permanently dispel any fears this woman might harbour because of her. She had to appear immaculate, perfect in her eyes.

"Then that's the end of it. We won't talk about that anymore. This organisation will be running some trainings in different skills for young women like you. After that, you're able to do an apprenticeship with a business owner in town so you can practise while you work and get paid. I know you want to learn about cars, but we don't have anything for that, unfortunately. We're focusing on more common skills that women can easily use to support themselves and their families. Does this sound like something you'd be interested in?"

Murmula took her time wiping her tears so she could think. If she said no to Mrs. Pamson's face after she had so generously offered assistance, it might affect whatever slim chance she had of getting closer to Mr. Pamson, of embedding herself into his life. She already had an ally in Paul, but one more wouldn't hurt, especially someone with so much influence. She raised her head and nodded.

Mrs. Pamson led her to the hall, where the participants were seated in white plastic chairs arranged in a double grid. An aisle ran through the centre. Murmula sat at the end of the back row that was farthest from the door. The MC was a woman dressed smartly in a skirt suit with well-heeled red shoes that shimmered on the white tiles. Her footsteps resounded throughout the hall. The executive director of InterWomen, a middle-aged woman in a lemon-green veil that was wound around her head, introduced the initiative with a crisp Hausa accent. Other speakers came up and spoke about a variety of issues, including the importance of skills development to nation-building.

The participants were of all ages—from teens, by Murmula's estimation, to a couple of women who appeared to be at least in their sixties. Forms were distributed so that participants could select their preferred area of training. The organisers explained that not everyone would necessarily get assigned to the class they wanted; it was important to ensure an equal distribution across the different classes. The list of skills included tailoring and carpentry, as well as pottery.

Lunch was served in a buffet at the back of the room. Murmula was joined at her table by the woman she had sat next to in the back row. Her name was Beatrice. She was light-skinned and wore jeans and a pink blouse. Her artificial nails were painted the deep colour of blood and matched her lipstick.

"May I join you?" she said, then sat without waiting for a response. She spat out the bubble gum she had been chewing for the past two hours and placed it carefully at the edge of her plate, then dug into her amala and egusi with a spoon.

Murmula was only able to eat half of her fried rice before giving up. The server had dumped a giant heap onto her plate before she could protest.

"Are you going to finish that?" Beatrice said, pointing at Murmula's barely touched chicken.

Murmula pushed the plate toward her and watched as Beatrice plucked it up and tore into it. She held the drumstick between her thumb and forefinger as though it had been foisted on her.

"Which one did you choose?" Beatrice said between bites.

"Tailoring."

"Do you want to guess my own?"

Murmula looked at her for a moment, sizing her up: her satisfied smile; her loudly smacking red lips; her broad nose, which was scrunched up with pleasure, either from the chicken or the certainty that Murmula could never guess correctly. Her black wig was shiny, the fringes of her hair visible underneath the edges if one looked close enough. She had large eyes that seemed to see everything at once. Her beauty was a real thing, Murmula realised, only it was squashed under all that makeup.

"Carpentry," Murmula said.

Beatrice's eyes grew even bigger. She threw her head back and laughed. "How did you know?"

"You wouldn't have asked me to guess if it was obvious."

Beatrice pointed an oily finger at Murmula. "You're one of those hypersmart girls, aren't you?"

Murmula smiled. "How are you going to do carpentry with those nails?"

"You see me like this? I'm like a chameleon. Tomorrow you will see me and not recognise me. By the time I come to the workshop with my overalls and goggles, they will be calling me sir instead of ma."

They returned to their seats, and for the rest of the event, Beatrice kept up a steady commentary of quips and complaints.

"You can never trust a Nigerian person in this world," she said when it was announced that the allocation of participants to their respective classes would be finalised and communicated in a few days. Murmula tried to suppress her laughter. "They will never do anything in daylight. Always it must be at night, like a bunch of bloodsucking vampires."

Beatrice lived in Apata. They walked together to the roundabout in front of the State Secretariat and exchanged numbers standing beside the fleet of keke napeps awaiting passengers. Back home, Baba Karami's 406 wasn't parked in front, which meant he was still at the shop. Ishat was watching a cartoon in the living room.

"Welcome back," she called from the sofa.

Murmula beamed at her younger cousin. Ishat had been ecstatic about her presence since her arrival, and it had rubbed off on Murmula. Murmula was the closest thing Ishat would ever have to an older sister. She had stayed up the first few nights asking Murmula questions about

Ilorin and sharing how she looked forward to leaving Jos for university because it was all she had ever known. It was this pure eagerness from Ishat that made Murmula hesitate each time she wanted to speak a word of correction or urge her to help more around the house. She didn't want Ishat treating her like the other adults in her life.

"Gogo Hauwawu fa?" Murmula asked.

"She's napping," Ishat said without taking her eyes off the screen.

Murmula went to the kitchen and decided to get dinner going. Gogo Hauwawu walked in as she was peeling the first potato.

"You're back," her aunt said.

"I wanted to ask what we should make, but you were asleep."

"What have you decided to make for us, toh?"

"Potato pottage."

"Oh. I thought it was chips."

"Would you prefer that?"

"It's been long since we had it. I can send Ishat to buy eggs. When she gets back, she can help you with the peeling. That will keep her busy for the evening."

Ishat was glad to help. She chatted about her day in school while she peeled and Murmula fried the potato fingers. She was preparing to write her WAEC exams. There were rumours in the school that certain male teachers were giving answers to students who could pay, and to female students who agreed to sleep with them. Murmula watched her from the corner of her eye. The nonchalant matter-of-factness with which Ishat spoke filled her with a deep and quiet despair.

There was still power by the time they had eaten and washed up. Ishat and her parents started a movie, and Murmula sat with them at first. Musty had also started spending more time in the house during the evenings. When he walked in and took the seat next to her, Murmula got up and said good night and went into the bedroom. She woke up in the middle of the night, gasping and then struggling not to. Her own breathing was like breaking glass in her ears. She turned her head and looked at Ishat, but she was sound asleep.

Murmula had been dreaming about swimming at the bottom of a pool, scanning the floor for something that seemed important, though she didn't know what it was. Not in the dream and not now, as she sat up in the bed. She only had a vague impression that it had to do with some part of her essence. In the dream, she had tried to go up to the surface for air but had been unable to move her legs, as though something with trailing fingers had wrapped her ankles and was dragging her into the pool's floor.

After staring at the dark for minutes, she lit a candle and pulled out her old diary from her suitcase. Its purple cover was faded and worn, its corners sawn down by time. Almost ten years since she'd picked it off a shelf in a bookstore in Ilorin, and there were still miles of pages left in it. She put words in it nearly every day, though she occasionally went for weeks or even months without opening it. Now she wrote about the InterWomen event, about Beatrice Okafor and her stupendous appetite, about not waiting for Mrs. Pamson after the event because she didn't want Beatrice to think she was the kind of person who cut corners. She wasn't sure why it was important for her not to seem so. It wasn't that she cared what Beatrice thought; she barely knew her. Almost immediately, she understood what it was: if Beatrice knew about her connection to Mrs. Pamson, she would badger Murmula brazenly until she made an introduction. That was it.

Murmula was barely halfway down the page when Ishat moved. She got up without a word and went to the bathroom. When she returned, she pulled herself closer to Murmula and looked at the diary. The white page was jaundiced by the candle's flame.

"Can't you sleep?" Ishat said.

"No."

"What are you writing about?"

"My day."

"You do this every day?"

"Yes."

"Don't you get tired?"

"Tiredness doesn't stop a person from doing what they should do."

In the candlelight, Ishat looked even more elfin than usual, like an actual imaginary creature of exceeding daintiness. The shadows exaggerated her features, making her nose even sharper, her lips even narrower. Her eyes flitted up at Murmula and searched her face for a moment, then returned to the diary. Murmula steeled herself from reflexively shutting the book. She didn't want Ishat to think that she was penning down secrets, and thankfully, there was nothing on the open page she wasn't willing to talk about if asked.

"Why do you do it?"

"For the future. I usually look back and see who I used to be, how I've changed."

"Do you write just happy things?"

"I put in everything," Murmula said in English. "The good, the bad, the ugly."

"I think I'd rather forget the past. I'd rather forget things that happen once they've happened. Except if it's a really exciting thing, or something that makes me happy. And for that, I have my camera."

"Until you have something happen to you, a powerful experience, only then will you appreciate the value of recording events," Murmula said with a smile.

"What kind of experience? Like an extremely happy thing?"

"An extremely happy thing. An extremely bad thing. Usually bad things are more powerful because they stay with you longer."

"Bad things like death?"

"Yes, death."

"Are you writing because you lost your parents?"

Murmula turned and looked at Ishat. She could see in her small brown eyes that it was a real question. "I started writing before my mother died. But yes. The short answer is yes."

"I've never lost anyone close to me. It sounds terrible."

Murmula dragged her eyes up to the ceiling. Perhaps she wasn't as comfortable having this conversation as she had thought. "You get used to it."

Ishat sat up and wrapped her arms around Murmula. It was an embrace so tight that it made her wonder if she'd ever been hugged this deeply, this affectionately.

"I'm sorry," Ishat whispered. "May Allah grant them Jannatul Firdaus."

"Āmīn," Murmula said.

Ishat released her and wished her a good night.

"Good night," Murmula echoed.

She wrote to the bottom of the next page. Reflecting on whether this program with InterWomen might help her in achieving her aims. Wondering about the interest Mrs. Pamson seemed to have taken in her. Surmising about Paul and his shy smile around her and whether he probably liked her. She tried to write about the normal parts of her day but had to stop at a point because the conversation with Ishat was still whirling in her head. Sometimes when people said her father had died, she resisted the urge to correct them and say that he had only disappeared. As if death and disappearance weren't effectively the same thing. But she knew that they weren't. The fact that she still mourned her father in a way she didn't when she thought of her mother was proof. She had been with her mother through her sickness—nursing her, bathing her, feeding her, and witnessing the moment when the breath had left her ravaged and shrunken body. She had wept over her body and had been among the women who had washed it and wrapped it in the burial shroud. She squatted beside the grave and wept silently, grounded only by the knowledge that her mother's body was finally in the place where all bodies went, where they ultimately belonged.

With her father, there had been only air. It was unfinished. Someone had taken it away from her. For the longest time—leaving Jos, settling in Ilorin, growing up—she had only been allowed to carry his loss like a photograph that fit into her purse: light and thin and clear to look at, but not quite real. On her deathbed, her mother had finally taken away the photograph and replaced it with the real thing. How heavy, how ugly. The scene often came unbidden to her, as it did now in the glow of the candle. Murmula dropped the pen because this stuff . . . this stuff she never wrote down.

The waif that her mother has become speaks from the depths of the covers. She's practically lost in them, and Murmula has to lean in from her place on the edge of the bed in order to see her eyes. Her mother's voice is the only thing she can wield of her own volition, but it's a thin, rattly counterfeit. Still, she uses it because she knows, as all the dying invariably seem to know, that in a matter of days she'll be gone.

"The day your father left . . ."

Murmula does her best to help her because she knows the words are heavy. "Yes, Mama. I know about the day. He left and never came back home. His car was never found."

"But you don't know what happened . . ."

"He disappeared during the crisis. Many people disappeared."

"You don't know who killed him."

Murmula decides then to stop helping, to let the words come in their own time.

"He was building a house . . . but no money . . . no pay from work . . . You know he was working at . . . at Hill Station . . ."

Murmula nodded vigorously, willing her on. Her father had been working at Hill Station Hotel and had gone months on end without pay.

"He had built to lintel level . . . but he decided to sell the land . . . two plots in Federal Lowcost . . . The day he disappeared he left the house to meet . . . the man who was buying it. Four months later . . . I decided to go and see the land . . . I had memorised the address: Number 27, Fourteenth Avenue, Federal Lowcost. I went there . . . but the land had already been fenced, with a gate . . . and a padlock on the gate . . . I couldn't even go inside. Between the fence and the gate, I could see . . . building had continued . . . The house now had a roof . . . No one around to ask, so I knocked on the next house and asked them . . . if they knew my husband . . . They said they only knew the man who just bought the land . . . They gave me his name . . ."

"What was the name?"

"Nobody called me . . . We never got the money for the land . . . I didn't know what to do . . . We couldn't pay rent anymore . . . I wasn't working . . . so I left . . . but I want you to get justice . . . for us . . . for your father . . ."

Murmula remembered well the morning her mother had pulled her out of an ongoing integrated science lesson at school and stuffed her into a taxi that took them to the bus station. She didn't know she would be in a different city by evening, her life reimagined.

"What was the name, Mama?" Murmula was holding her voice down, restraining it to keep from filling the room.

When her mother said the name, she wrote it on a piece of paper and raised it for her mother to see.

"Yes . . . that's the name. That's the name of the man . . . killed your father . . . stole our land."

5

Pamson threw the door to his office open and went in, Luka right on his heels. He sat down behind his desk and faced the young man.

"Close the door," he said in Hausa.

Luka did and crossed the room and leaned on the wall beside the desk. There was no other chair in the room. He was strong-looking, in a wiry way. The second-in-command at Pamson's garage, he was the first apprentice Pamson had taken on when he opened shop some eight years ago. He had been nothing more than a scrawny adolescent then. Each time Pamson looked at him, he saw all the ways in which he had sprouted, matured, in body and otherwise. He'd grown into his limp and used it now as an indispensable part of his swagger. As a man, he had a quiet, restrained charm about him that appealed to the ladies. Now a pregnant girl had identified him as the father of her unborn child.

"Look at me again and tell me you're not the father," Pamson said.

Luka turned his face in his direction. "I'm not the father."

"So what would make the girl lie about it?"

Luka folded his arms and continued to pout. "I'm not going to let myself become anybody's fool."

"Did you fuck her or not?"

"So did every other boy in Tudun Wada. But I'm the one she wants to tie down."

"You know something like this can now be solved with a simple paternity test."

Luka shook his head. "I've heard those things are expensive, Oga. I'm not going to spend money on something when I know it's not me."

"So it's going to be your word against hers."

Luka watched him.

"If you don't know, you'd better know it now," Pamson said. "If there is no proof like a paternity test, the girl is always right. Except if you can disappear and not be found. But unfortunately for you, she knows where you live, because she also lives there. I've been telling you boys about not shitting where you eat, and you thought I was just speaking in parables. Luka, how do you know you're not the one?"

"It can't be me, Oga."

In lieu of Luka's biological father, who himself had disappeared when the boy was still very young, the pregnant girl's mother had come to Pamson. He was well regarded in the area. He didn't need his reputation soiled by boys who impregnated young women and refused to take responsibility. Certainly not in a place like Tudun Wada.

"I'm going to give you three days to go and think. Search inside your heart. Then come back and give me your final answer. Becoming a father can be scary, but believe me when I tell you that if this child is yours and you refuse it now, you know what the Hausa man calls tsautsayi? The tempting of fate? Toh, I'm telling you, don't tempt fate. Don't do it. You can go. And tell Maman Ivie to bring me a plate of rice with two pieces of fish herself. I want to ask her something. Close the door."

After Luka had left, Pamson looked around with disgust at the office he still hadn't fully broken in, two years into his occupation of the property. The oversize room exaggerated the blandness of the beige walls, their nakedness. Apart from his desk, there was nothing but floor and walls. He didn't even have a curtain for that giant window that gaped out over the front yard where they worked on the cars. He shouldn't have listened to that quack architect who had designed the blueprint and overseen the building project. Mark and Solomon had recommended him as someone who came cheaply; only with hindsight did he understand why cheap wasn't always better. He should have used up less space on the two plots and left more room for parking his clients' cars.

There was a knock on the door, and a matronly woman entered. She was wearing an old wrapper, a dirty blue T-shirt, and a headscarf. She deposited the plate of food she was carrying on the desk.

"That you wanted to ask me something?" Maman Ivie said.

"Yes. There was a girl that came around here last week. A Hausa girl. Did you tell her where my house is?"

"Hausa girl?" Maman Ivie looked confused.

"Yes."

She shook her head. "You know I see many people; customers are always stopping by."

"So you don't remember anything? Last week, Friday? That day it rained all afternoon and evening?"

"Oh," Maman Ivie said, and slapped her forehead. "I remember. Yes, she said she was looking for you."

"Did she just stop and give you my name? How did she know who I was?"

"She asked me who the owner of this garage is. She said she had an important message to give him. So I told her your name and said she should come back when you're around, usually in the mornings. She asked where you live, and I only said that you live in Federal Lowcost."

"Please don't give random people descriptions of my house, Maman Ivie."

"But I didn't describe your house. I just said you live in Federal Lowcost."

"You still gave her my name. Don't be giving people my private information. You know the kind of town we live in." He didn't bother to elaborate.

Maman Ivie flattened her hands on her chest. "Ah, please forgive me. The way she sounded, I thought maybe you knew her from somewhere."

"Knew her from where? Do I look like I hang around people like that?" Pamson said. He realised a moment later that he had raised his voice, and that Rahila would have readily misconstrued his words. He could just imagine what she would say had she been there, the shape of her mouth as it curved around the words *politically* and *incorrect.* "You can go now. Thank you for the rice. How much?"

He paid with an additional tip. At the door, Maman Ivie asked if he wanted some kunu as well, but he shook his head. The stew was spicy and made with palm oil. Rings of onion swam in the steaming redness like eels. The fish had been fried to a wonderful near-crispness. Rahila had long stopped packing any lunch for him. He couldn't ask Paul because he was out before seven and on his way to school. Maman Ivie had been selling her food right by the side of the road. She had enjoyed the steady stream of customers, but the dust and fumes had begun to affect her. When she was diagnosed with bronchitis and announced that she was shutting down, Pamson offered her a spot at the gate of his property. It had worked out well for her because she serviced the boys who worked at the garage as well as Pamson's clients. Her old customers from her days on the roadside were only too happy to walk the two hundred metres down the dirt road to her new spot. For a moment all he could think about was whether Maman Ivie also thought he might have been romantically involved with Murmula. Was that why she had given her answers so easily? It didn't make any sense to him. Perhaps he was reading too much into it, looking for reasons where there were none.

After his meal he went outside and resumed work on the engine of a Ford Explorer that belonged to a House of Assembly member, an old friend. These politicians. Once they got into some money, they would buy the first big car that came their way. He had advised the man to go for a Land Cruiser or a Sequoia, or even an Xterra—but no, he had wanted an American car with original leather seats. Well, his pristine leather seats came with a faulty engine. All cars had their issues, but American cars had issues that were distinctly bad for a regular Nigerian's budget. They also drank too much petrol and were expensive to maintain. Pamson shouldn't complain, because it was good business. Over twenty years at this job and he was still telling himself he needed to care less about his clients and their pockets.

Pamson's other boys who apprenticed at the garage were all younger than Luka. Two of them, James and Al'amis, were about the same age, around seventeen or eighteen. The skinny James had started working with him shortly after Luka and was nearing the end of his apprenticeship. He was quiet and dignified in a way that Pamson appreciated because it seemed to allow him a subtle influence with the younger boys. Al'amis, on the other hand, had a toned body and was vain in all the ways it was possible for a man to be. Thankgod was ten and Bala eight—they were more trouble than they were worth. Pamson had never worked with boys this young, and there wasn't a day that he didn't toy with the idea of ending their apprenticeships and sending them back home. The only thing that stopped him was the knowledge that their mothers wouldn't know what else to do with them.

He sent Al'amis to Farin Gada to buy cylinder head bolts for the combustion chamber, then proceeded to hoist the engine block up on the swing frame he kept in the work yard. The engine dangled from chains while he poked about underneath it. When he was done, he had Thankgod buy petrol so they could wash it. At two o'clock, he dropped his tools and packed up for the day.

"Oga, what about the engine?" Luka said from the door to the office.

Pamson swung his bag over his shoulder. "When Thankgod brings the petrol, wash it. But nobody should touch it again. John will bring the screws for the chambers. I'm going to look at it myself tomorrow."

"But you know I can do it, Oga," Luka said quietly.

Pamson paused and regarded him for a moment. "I'll do it myself, Luka. Focus on Mama Galadima's car."

"But Mama's car can wait. She doesn't even go anywhere. Let me focus on Honourable's car for today, please."

"I said no."

"Where are you going, Oga?"

"I'm going out. See you tomorrow."

Luka stood in front of the office building and watched Pamson back out of the yard. Pamson had heard the wounded edge in Luka's voice. He had sensed a growing hunger in the young man for more responsibility. Luka wanted to prove himself in a grand way. Pamson had no reason to doubt his capabilities; he had shown good judgement and talent, after all. But the Honourable's car wasn't one Pamson was comfortable letting anyone work on, especially with something as sensitive as the engine. It wasn't a risk he was prepared to take. At the main road, he turned left and pointed the car north toward Millionaire's Quarters.

Jonah's Baked Delight had a shop just inside the gate and built into the fence, where the baked goods were sold. The rest of the compound was dedicated to the bakery. The main building was a large bungalow that had once been the residence of a retired general, now deceased. There was a rumour around town that the late general's brothers had sold off his properties and squandered the money, to the detriment of his young wife and her children. This property now ostensibly belonged to a hotshot lawyer who was a Senior Advocate of Nigeria. The buildings and grounds were impeccably maintained year-round.

Pamson parked his car in the lot. A few of his classmates had arrived early. Jonah was in his office with one of them, Mrs. Ibrahim, a newly married young woman who wanted to learn how to bake because her husband loved cakes. She and Pamson had started the six-week training together two weeks ago. Jonah and Mrs. Ibrahim looked up at Pamson in the doorway and waved in greeting.

The classroom had a large island where Pamson and other students practised their lessons. Mrs. Adeoluwa and Mrs. Abdulrahman were already in their aprons and caps, ready to go. He went into the men's room and washed his hands as thoroughly as he could. Jonah had complained about his grease-stained nails, about the faint scent of motor oil and petrol that followed him around. But no matter how hard he scrubbed his hands, no matter how deeply he lathered soap into his skin, he couldn't remove the evidence of what he did for a living.

There were eight of them in the class. Jonah was a patient teacher. Soft-spoken and calm, he used words like *spectacular* and *powerful* to describe the baked items they produced. Pamson had little trouble with kneading the dough and getting the correct texture for regular bread. But the delicacy and patience required for pastries had eluded him so far. Today Jonah instructed them to mix their dough to a specific recipe and leave it to rise. When the required time had passed, Jonah inspected the results.

"Too many lumps," he said about Mrs. Ibrahim's dough.

"Very powerful," he said to Mrs. Abdulrahman.

"Didn't rise properly; not enough yeast."

When he reached Pamson, he leaned close, bringing his nose to within an inch of the pale, amorphous blob. He raised himself and gave a silent thumbs-up, but at the same time he dropped his eyes to look at Pamson's hands before moving on. Pamson glanced at his nails, at the faint blackness that outlined them, and wondered what would happen if he soaked them in bleach.

They made chinchin. With their hands, they beat the dough into submission. Oomphs and grunts rose around the room as they went at it. Flour puffed into the air as they scooped it and dusted their boards to keep the dough from sticking.

"Manage your flour," Jonah called out. "Don't overuse it. You just need a little."

They flattened the dough with rolling pins, cut it into thin strips, chopped those further down into pebble-size nuggets. They took turns at the stove deep-frying the pieces of dough. At the end of the class, bowls with chinchin of varying shades of brown stood on the island. Jonah went around, tasting.

Afterwards, Jonah walked Pamson to his car. "Your chinchin soaked up too much oil. That's why it was crumbling like that. The thing you should know about baking is that everything you do is like the foundation of the next thing. If you get it wrong, it will affect everything after."

For a moment Pamson stared at him, wondering if he was referring to more than just baking. They were standing beside Pamson's BMW. "So what made it soak up oil?"

"Too much margarine," Jonah said with a smile.

They shook hands and said good night.

Pamson's decision to register for the baking class advertised by Jonah's Baked Delight a few weeks earlier had not been on a whim. The idea had taken shape slowly over the preceding months, even before he'd seen the advert, before he knew such a thing existed. The seed of it had been planted on the day he found out Rahila was pregnant—the day so much had come to light in their marriage. That October evening that remained both blessed and cursed in his memories. Everything had come tumbling out in a single moment, though it had felt like an entire age passing before his very eyes as it happened, slow and grand and terrible. Often when he was alone, this was one of the many scenes that would unfold in his head like one of those moving pictures he sometimes received on WhatsApp, playing to the end and then repeating all over again, over and over, a visual roll call of his sins, unspooling across a dark stage inside his head until some manifestation of mercy interrupted. Some memories had blood in them, sticky and stubborn, holding fast to everything like tar. In others he saw only a tangle of dark human limbs with no indication where one ended and the next began. Such memories were like raucous uninvited guests who had barged into his head and refused to leave. But this memory, the one that accounted for his presence at Jonah's Baked Delight three times a week, this memory he surrendered to, letting it have its way with him.

It unfolded something like this:

He takes a bath, feeling unburdened and pleased in a general way. Part of it is because of the afternoon tryst he had with Mary at Hill Station

Hotel and the dirty-worded WhatsApp messages they have been trading all evening.

Nxt tyme I'll show u hw dp I cn be.

Next time I want you on top.
I want to be looking at your duwawu when you cum.

I'll evn let u pt it in my duwawu

I will do wonders to that your duwawu

He comes out of the bathroom wrapped in a towel. The bedroom light is off, and the light from the bathroom spills across the bed in the shape of the doorway, framing Rahila. She's wearing her nightgown, frozen, her face lowered from him. She raises it, and it's apparent she has been crying. Her tears and his phone in her hand—it hadn't been there when he went into the bathroom—with its glowing screen can only mean one thing. He steps forward and swallows whatever it is that has begun to gather in his throat. It is a useless action because it gathers again.

"What is it?" he asks.

She doesn't speak for a while, and he realises that the water on his body has almost dried. He's beginning to feel cold. He's about to get his pyjamas when she speaks.

"You're going to be a father."

Pamson doesn't dare move a muscle. He has stopped breathing altogether. Why would Mary inform him of a pregnancy by WhatsApp, after all the rubbish messages they have been sending each other for the past four hours? He has been careful, using a condom with every round. Was there a breakage? Or did she deliberately make a puncture? On several occasions he has allowed her to unroll the plastic coating over his turgid member, marvelling at how deft she is despite her long nails. What if she used a nail to pierce the condom? It would be quick, undetectable.

Rahila is watching him. Her eyes are two raw, red spots. He takes a step forward.

"Rahila, let me explain." But he hasn't the slightest clue how to explain an infidelity that has now resulted in a pregnancy. A pregnancy that's essentially a slap in her face, no less, since she is the one who has been unable to conceive, the one who has failed to give him a child. How can he make her see that he would never put her in such a position on purpose?

"I didn't want that to happen," he says.

"What?" Rahila says quietly, still watching him.

"I didn't mean to get her pregnant."

Rahila closes her eyes, then opens them again. "I'm *pregnant."*

His relief is instant, but the moment morphs again, altering its form before his eyes. A new meaning emerges. She's pregnant, which should be a jubilant thought. But the fact of the other woman hasn't disappeared. It's still there, in the shape of his phone in Rahila's hand. And he has just admitted to being unfaithful.

"Won't you say something?" Rahila whispers in Hausa.

"What do you want me to say?"

"Anything."

"When did you start checking my phone?" he says before he can stop himself. It isn't anger speaking but what the Hausa man calls borin kunya, the madness of shame.

"I was going to message your cousin Musa to tell him so that when he calls to congratulate, you would be confused and insult him. I thought it would be funny."

Pamson believes her. She has never shown any interest in the content of his phone, in who calls him regardless of the hour. Consequently, he has never felt any need to fortify it against her. He feels relief again, but of a different kind. He would never have had the courage to confess to her, so he's glad it's all out in the open now. This is an opportunity to get them back to what they once were. But before he can sink to his knees and beg,

Rahila gets up and leaves the room. He hears her car start, but he doesn't go after her. She isn't given to theatrics. If she's leaving the house at eleven at night, it's because she wants to leave, not because she wants to be pursued. He picks up his phone and sees the most recent message from Mary: I can't find my lipstick. *It is all the more annoying for its guileless prosaicness. Of all the things that gave him away, it had to be a stupid, flippant message about fucking lipstick.*

Rahila returns the following morning, gets ready for work, and leaves. He doesn't ask her where she spent the night, and she never brings up the other woman again. She's distant for weeks on end, but she eventually begins to respond to his greetings. They settle into a brittle civility that he learns to live with. But she refuses to give him any information about the child. She keeps him completely locked out of the pregnancy. No updates on antenatal visits. No discussions around names. There are days when she lets Paul feel the baby kicking in his presence, the two of them laughing in wonder, and all he can do is leave the room because he never gets used to the way it hurts.

But he still hopes for a way back. He sees the training advert from Jonah's Baked Delight on Facebook. Rahila's cravings have been powerful and consistent by this time. She has a liking for baked foods: bread, rolls, cakes. But puff pastries are her favourite. The connection between a man's heart and his stomach has been pointed out too often, but perhaps it is also true for women. Perhaps it is true for all people. He decides to enrol with a single aim: to win her back by going through her stomach. On certain days when she seems to be in a good mood, he thinks he stands a chance. But most of the time, her silence around his infidelity and her distant cordiality remind him that he has been relegated to living his days under a judgement deferred. It is its own torture.

This was what he was thinking of when he drove into his compound and turned off the car and sat in the dark, thinking.

6

Paul was in the driver's seat of Mrs. Pamson's car when Murmula and Mrs. Pamson walked out of InterWomen. Murmula didn't know he would be there. Mrs. Pamson told her to get in the back seat. Her sudden self-consciousness surprised her. She chided herself for fretting over how well her veil complemented her purse and whether her exposed toes appeared clean enough. She hadn't painted them and was badly in need of a pedicure. Thankfully, he wasn't in a position to look at her feet. She watched the back of his head and caught glimpses of his eyes in the rearview mirror as he glanced this way or that. They came to a red light, and once or twice she caught his eyes resting on her through the mirror.

After he had parked the car in front of Ostrich Bakery, Mrs. Pamson asked him what he would like. He said he wanted a yoghurt and a meatpie. Mrs. Pamson told Murmula to come with her. She loaded her tray with a variety of large loaves and a sponge cake. They filled three plastic bags when the cashier bagged them.

"Is that all you're having?" Mrs. Pamson said, looking at the bottle of Fanta in Murmula's hand. When Murmula nodded, Mrs. Pamson turned and grabbed another meatpie and put it in front of the cashier.

Back at InterWomen, the training continued. Beatrice had ended up being assigned to tailoring because carpentry hadn't had enough interested participants. She spent that first day grumbling to Murmula.

"Why would they include it in the first place if they knew they may not offer it? I would have just minded my own business."

There were fourteen of them in the tailoring class, the largest group of students. They were given use of the main auditorium. The instructor was a tailor at one of the shops where they would have their apprenticeship. He had slim, dark fingers; smelled of tobacco; and was exceedingly amiable with the ladies.

"It's like you're his favourite o," Beatrice said.

"Why do you say that?"

"Because the material he gave you is the biggest."

Murmula looked down at the purple yard of cotton she was supposed to cut into equal squares, then stitch onto shoulder-pad foam. She didn't see any difference between it and the one Beatrice was folding just as the instructor had shown them. Murmula waited for her turn to use the scissors she was sharing with Beatrice. As she worked, she consoled herself yet again with the thought that tailoring was the best training she could have picked. It meant she would no longer be lying when she told Baba Karami and Gogo Hauwawu that she had gotten a job as an apprentice with a professional tailor. It wasn't what she'd had in mind when she approached Mr. Pamson for work, and it didn't bring her deeper into his circle, as she'd hoped. She tried to believe that this was still progress, but the way her fingers held the scissors and disregarded the pencil line she had marked out on the fabric as they cut told her it wasn't working. She hated having to sit here and pretend to be interested in something that bored her to an inch of the grave while that murderer continued to thrive on stolen property and live out his days without consequence.

The sun had taken on a warm blush by the time she got back home. All she wanted was to kick off her shoes and crash into her bed, but she still put down her purse and went to see how she could help Gogo Hauwawu.

"Murmula, you look tired," her aunt said as she walked in. She was at the stove, vigorously stirring a pot of something that had the woody aroma of dried-okra soup. "Go and rest. Your sister will make the tuwo for us."

"Where is she?" Murmula said. She hadn't seen her in the living room or the bedroom.

"She's at the back, sifting the maize. We're eating tuwon masara tonight."

Gogo Hauwawu had a triumphant twinkle in her eye. Murmula had a feeling her aunt had specifically picked tuwon masara to keep Ishat busy now that she was a bit more amenable to the idea of house chores. Murmula opened the door and watched her cousin toss the maize grains into the air with a large matankaɗi. After that she would have to take the maize to the neighbourhood grinder up the street before bringing back the maize flour and making the tuwo.

"Sannu da aiki," Murmula said.

Ishat looked up and smiled. "You're back?"

"Do you need help?"

Ishat shook her head and continued working. When Murmula returned to the room and picked up her charging phone, a text from Paul was waiting for her: Can I take you out?

She sat down, delighted by this confirmation that Paul had indeed fallen for her and wanted to do something about it. A moment later she realised she was wearing a sad smirk. What had stayed her impulse to seize the reins and deepen their connection was less inhibition or feminine restraint and something closer to pity. She had been holding herself back because she felt a bit burdened by the idea of using someone so clearly good-hearted as a tool in her plans. But this was exactly the kind of opening she needed, and she would be foolish not to act on it.

She typed:

R u asking me out?

Her phone dinged immediately:

Lol. Not OUT out. Just out on a date.

Oh. U want 2 test market 1st abi?

The phone dinged again: a laughing emoji.

Ding:

I can't with you.

Can I take you on a date to a nice place?

Murmula typed her answer, but her thumb hovered over the "Send" button. In pressing it, she would be opening another door. There would be devastation behind it, and it would be her doing. But she would have to go about her task responsibly, without hurting the innocent, without dragging people like Paul and Mrs. Pamson into the path of her retribution. Although she didn't yet know how she might achieve this, she still went ahead and pressed "Send":

Owk.

She put the phone down and went to heat some bathing water. After her bath, she got her dinner and sat in the living room with Musty, Ishat, and Baba Karami. They ate in silence, watching *Ratatouille*. Musty seated there with the rest of his family, slashed like a lazily drawn squiggle into the armchair, was a presence that continued to take nips at her. Murmula kept glancing at him, and more than once she caught him staring at her. He would never stop, she realised. Baba Karami laughed so loud at the antics of the rat that he almost choked and had to take a swig of water.

"God forbid for a rat to cook food for me?" Musty said in English. "These cartoons don't make sense at all."

"It's an animation," Ishat said, "not a cartoon."

Musty ignored her.

Murmula tasted the silence before speaking: "It's not supposed to make sense. It's about your imagination."

Musty looked at her. After a moment of staring back, she tore her eyes away. She didn't want to encourage him. Who knew what thoughts he might begin to get in his clouded head.

He switched back to Hausa. "Are you still looking for work?"

"I'm going to be doing an apprenticeship."

"Where?"

"A tailoring shop."

"A tailor's apprentice? Will they pay you?"

"Shhhh," Ishat said loudly.

Musty glared at his sister and turned his attention back to the TV. The rat was hidden underneath someone's hat, controlling his movements like a marionette by pulling his hair. Murmula remembered playing this movie with her father once, but she didn't remember much else. Not the place or whether it had been a pirated copy with bad quality or if they'd watched it while eating a snack. Her memories of him were disappearing, just like he had disappeared. Had he ever held her hand and walked the dusty streets with her to the neighbourhood store to buy sweets? Had he joined the boys next door once to play football in their front yard, bunching his caftan together while he stole off with the ball? Had he once balanced her sobbing frame on his knees after she'd called her mother a name and said to her that he loved her but still had to discipline her? Had any of these things truly happened, or were they just hallucinations of her grief?

"Tailor's apprentice when you have a degree in engineering," Musty said. It came out in a rumble, and it seemed to be directed at the TV because that was what he was looking at.

"If it pains you so much, you can go and get your own degree and use it to get a job," Baba Karami said.

"Degree? You'll have to pay for it, then."

"I already paid for it. You just didn't bring it home."

Their exchange was quiet, a decibel or two below the TV. They never took their eyes off the screen.

Gogo Hauwawu came out to join them while Murmula cleared up the dishes. When she was done washing, she returned to her seat just as the skinny, evil-looking character was eating a special dish the rat had prepared. His eyes widened in his head like portals opening into his childhood. Murmula stole a glance around the living room. The whole family was here, bound together by the TV's spell. Except for Gogo Hauwawu, who had fallen asleep with her head in her husband's lap. Murmula had taught herself through excruciating rigour to stop imagining what her life might have been had her father never gone missing. Finally seeing the house that he had built—partially, at the very least—and stepping into it had unravelled some of that work because she now had a real place she could populate with imaginary versions of herself and her parents and the faceless siblings she'd never had. As she beheld her uncle and his family strewn about the living room in careless bliss, she was also witnessing her own family, all that they could have been.

The rest of the week continued without incident, and the training at InterWomen wound to a close. Murmula was glad for it to be over. On Saturday afternoon she walked into the Net Café ten minutes before the agreed-upon time. Paul was already seated. He had on earphones and was nodding his head rhythmically. He stood up when he saw her and pulled out a chair.

"You're such a gentleman fa," she said in Hausa, smiling. "Na gode." She tried to look at his phone screen, but he put his hand over it.

"Guess," he said.

"Wizkid."

Paul shook his head. "I'm giving you two more guesses."

"Davido?"

"Nope."

"Ice Prince!" Murmula said desperately.

Paul shook his head and started humming the tune.

"'Mad Over You,' Runtown!" she said, laughing.

They ordered a large pizza and drinks. Afterward, Paul asked if she wanted ice cream, but she was already so full.

"I see you're a Fantastic girl."

Murmula rolled her eyes and took another sip of her Fanta.

"I'm sorry," he said. "I couldn't help myself."

"You're forgiven."

"But you should be warned: I'm the king of bad jokes."

"Is that so?"

"It's a specialty of mine. It takes exceptional skill to make them."

Her laughter spilled out of her with disarming ease. An hour and a half later, they were still there. When she noticed the time, she chided herself for getting distracted by smooth-flowing conversation and tasty food. She needed to get back on track.

"My training ended this week," she said abruptly.

Paul seemed thrown off-balance for a moment and gave her a look of confusion. They had been talking about Ilorin and Jos, the hilly landscapes they had in common and the colonial vestiges that ran like scars through both towns—dilapidated old buildings and, in Jos's case, abandoned mining ponds. He recovered and said, "How was it?"

"I'm so grateful to your aunt—sorry, cousin . . ."

"You can call her my aunt, it's fine. She's basically old enough to be my mother."

"I enjoyed some of it," Murmula said, "and I tried to keep an open mind, especially out of respect to Mrs. Pamson. But my mind wasn't really there. I ended up pricking my fingers so many times." She showed him her hands, lowered them again immediately, suddenly self-conscious.

"I feel you, but you know your hands would look much worse if you had actually gone to work for Uncle Dareng. The grime never washes out."

"But I'd have been happy. Passion cures the pain."

"Can I be honest with you?" Paul said, lowering his eyes briefly before looking at her again.

Murmula nodded.

"I don't understand your love for cars. It's very strange, a little random."

"Because I'm a girl?"

"I've seen girls who like cars; they know all the latest models and so on. But you actually want to fix them. It's weird."

"I guess I'm a weird girl," Murmula said with a smirk and sipped her drink.

"I guess you are," Paul said. He picked up his own drink. He seemed embarrassed, but his beaming face told her he liked that she had weird taste.

"Isn't there something I can do to convince your uncle?" she asked.

"When Uncle Dareng makes up his mind, it's hard to change it. He can be very set in his ways. I went through Aunty Rahila once to try and convince him to upgrade his business, treat it like a proper company. He refused. He prefers to run it like every other mechanic in this city. Aunty complains sometimes how contented he is with very little."

"How long ago was that?"

"I'm not sure, maybe two or three years. Around the time I entered hundred level."

"Maybe it's time to try again."

Paul put his Coke back on the table and looked at her.

"I'm serious, Paul. You clearly have a good head for business and numbers. You should make a proposal and present it to him. Let him make you his business manager, while he can continue to focus on the technical parts. You've said it yourself, how most of these tech companies have two cofounders or more. One person focusing on business, the other focusing on the technical aspects. Why can't you do the same with your uncle's business?"

Paul's eyes had gone wide in his head, and he was staring at her.

"That's a brilliant idea," he said.

Murmula leaned back smugly and said, "And now you owe me."

Paul laughed. "You really do deserve a treat. Plus, I'm beginning to feel like that waiter has been eyeing us since."

She finally let him buy her ice cream—a flavour she'd never had before, with an Italian-sounding name she couldn't spell.

"These white people won't kill us," she said in Hausa. "Isn't this just vanilla with chocolate inside?" After a few more spoonfuls, she added, "Don't think you're going to pay me with ice cream for this consultation o."

Paul chuckled softly.

Rather than driving up Ahmadu Bello Way and passing through the banking sector, Paul took the long way around. But Murmula didn't remember the names of the areas they passed. She simply watched the city flit by while Asa's "360°" thumped through the speakers. Paul pointed out landmarks to her. The junction that led all the way to the city of Bauchi. The University of Jos Permanent Site. Tomato Market. The National Metallurgical Development Centre. She remembered driving through the city with her father, back when they had lived in this older part of town, in Nasarawa. He had complained about the density of the population and the state of the buildings and briefly mentioned his plans to move them out to a neighbourhood with more space, where the sky felt boundless; she remembered her heart swelling with anticipation. She leaned her weight against the door and let Paul drive in silence.

He finally turned into Daɗin Kowa and said, "Can I walk you home?"

She smiled but said nothing.

When she entered the house several minutes later, she went straight to the bedroom and closed the door. Ishat wasn't back, thankfully. She spread herself out on the bed and let the thumping of her heart subside into its regular tattoo. She went out to the kitchen afterward to help with dinner. They made ƙosai and kamu. Because Ishat wasn't around, Murmula had to take the beans to be blended. She stood in line with her plastic bucket, watching the boy who operated the grinding machine. He was younger than Ishat, but he conducted his business with the coolness of someone who had seen enough of life to know you didn't rush anything; you took your time. He raised the bucket of the teenage girl wearing a burka in front of Murmula and tipped its contents into the mouth of the machine. Tomatoes, peppers, and onions all tumbled through the air. The shrill rumbling of the grinder softened momentarily as it digested the ingredients. It spat them out into the bucket at the other end in the form of a reddish mass. The boy poured a cup of water down the throat of the grinder to expel the dregs, received the payment, and turned to take Murmula's bucket.

Ishat still hadn't returned by the time the ƙosai was frying. As Murmula was boiling water for the kamu, the portable stove ran out of kerosene. Musty walked with her to buy more, despite her assurances that she was fine going alone. He tried to make small talk, but she only gave him curt responses. He carried the refilled gallon on the way back and walked beside her in silence. It was already twilight, and the call to Maghrib prayers was loud. They passed by the mosque and the ablution stations where mostly men were purifying themselves for their salat. When they came to a stretch of darkness out of reach of the mosque's floodlights, Musty grabbed her arm and pulled her against the nearest wall. He scrunched his lips against hers, and she felt his flicking tongue, wet, insistent, searching. She pushed him away, then raised her hand instinctively and smacked him on the cheek. He became still. She couldn't make out his eyes in the dark. She thought he would strike her back, but he only walked away. When she looked on the ground, she saw the gallon of kerosene tipped over. The squeezed plastic bag that had been used as a stopper had fallen out. When she raised the container, it was only half-full.

Back home she met Gogo Hauwawu in the kitchen. She turned to her and started to rant.

"Can you imagine the time your sister is coming back from school?" she shouted.

"Where is she?"

"She's gone to change her uniform. I told her to come straight back here. She must do this housework she's been avoiding."

Murmula didn't know how to respond. Ishat had been helping a bit more, but Murmula had sensed a growing frustration with the amount of work her mother assigned her. She had never been this late coming home from school before, and Murmula had already suspected the possibility that she was trying to dodge. After what happened with Musty, Murmula didn't want to have to placate her aunt and defuse the tension. She just wanted to be alone. But Gogo Hauwawu continued to raise her voice, and she couldn't just walk away. Ishat came in moments later wearing her black abaya, and her mother rounded on her.

"Where have you been?"

"Mama, I already told you," Ishat said, trying to keep her voice down, "the extra lessons went longer than we expected."

"You're a liar!" Gogo Hauwawu shouted. She pointed a finger in Ishat's face. "Don't you dare lie to me."

"Mama, I'm not lying—"

"Just because you did some work for two days, you think you're off the hook, ko? You think you deserve a break, ko? Look at your sister!" Gogo Hauwawu raised a hand, indicating Murmula. "Just look at her! Do you know how hard she works in this house? What would I do if I didn't have her? She will come back from work and still come into the kitchen to help me. But you, all you can do is complain and sit in that parlour, watching films with your father. Why can't you be like her? Why?"

When Ishat looked at Murmula, Murmula understood that something had snapped between them. Her cousin's eyes brimmed with tears. She turned and walked out of the kitchen.

"Come back here!" Gogo Hauwawu shouted. "I said, come back here!"

Ishat didn't return. They heard the front door banging. They stood there for several seconds, neither saying anything. Baba Karami appeared at the door.

"Why do you have to shout about everything, Maman Mustapha?"

Gogo Hauwawu's response was to make herself busy with frying more ƙosai.

Baba Karami looked at Murmula. "Let me go and bring her back. I don't think she will go far."

Murmula nodded, then returned to making the kamu. Everyone ate alone that evening, and Murmula had her dinner standing in the kitchen, too tired and tense to process what had happened with Musty. His was the second attempt at a kiss she had fielded that day. The first had been from Paul, just before he dropped her off. Only when she was bathed and lying in bed did she go over it again, what had happened in the car.

By the time Paul pulls over at her junction, they're holding hands. She doesn't know when this happened, and she doesn't want to unclasp her hand from his. She doesn't want to explain to him why he can't walk her home either. He should know better. She herself has spent less than two weeks in Jos, yet she understands this. She knows that a kiss is coming even before he leans toward her, before he moves. Her heart is a frantic, pulsing light in her chest. She lets him brush his lips against hers, briefly and lightly. He doesn't linger, and for that she is grateful. She squeezes his hand, then wrenches herself out of the car and into the waning day, where she can wrestle privately with her confusion and what it all means.

7

Pamson rolled out from under the Ford and found himself gazing into Paul's face. He got to his feet and wiped his hands.

"Good afternoon, Uncle," Paul said.

"Paul, lafiya?" He had no memory of Paul ever coming to visit him at the workshop. "Where's your aunty's car?"

"I left it for her at the office. I came to see you."

Pamson looked at the boy again. He was wearing a navy-blue polo shirt and had a fresh haircut. Paul was usually neat in appearance, but today he seemed even more dapper.

"Are you going to a party?"

"No."

"A wedding?"

"No, sir," Paul said, giving him a worried look.

"Is everything all right?" Pamson asked again.

"Everything is fine. Can we talk in private?"

Pamson led him inside. "You haven't been here since I built this, have you?" he said in Hausa. They passed through the empty reception and into Pamson's office.

"It's very big. A lot of space."

"There's only one chair," Pamson said, grabbing the new plastic chair he had bought that morning on the way to work. He was tired of having to apologise for having no seats. "I don't usually have visitors."

"I heard it was big," Paul said, looked at the walls, the ceiling. "When are you going to paint it?"

He stood in the middle of the room with his hands in his pocket. The window was open, letting in a cool breeze and arguing voices—Bala and Thankgod, most likely. Luka shouted for someone to bring him water. Pamson often wondered about his wife's young cousin, why he seemed so aloof, so oblivious to much that went on around him. Paul had lived with him for over five years, yet he couldn't tell apart a gasket from a tyre. One time, Rahila's car had refused to start and she had called Pamson home from the workshop to look at it. One of the battery terminals had been dislodged. This was after Paul had checked every part of the car without discovering the problem, according to Rahila. Pamson sometimes wondered if the boy was challenged in some way that was yet to be determined.

"I don't know yet," Pamson said. "When I have money. It's not important for now."

Luka's livid voice pierced the air, unleashing a number of expletives in Hausa: none of the boys had brought him the water he'd asked for. An awkward silence lingered in the office.

"How is the business?" Paul said.

Pamson chuckled. "Business is good. Do you want to invest? Maybe you have some millions none of us know about."

Paul smiled. "I don't have money, Uncle. But I have ideas."

"Ideas?"

"Yes, sir. You know I'm studying business admin."

"Yes, I know. I pay your school fees."

Paul swallowed. His discomfort was plain—his pocketed hands, the way his eyes kept falling to the floor. "We've talked about this before, you may not remember. It was a long time ago. But I'm very serious this time. I want to make you a business proposition. But first I wanted to ask you some questions."

Pamson leaned back in his chair. "Okay."

Paul produced a small notebook and a pen. He read from the notebook: "Do you have an accounting system?"

"No."

Paul wrote it down, then asked, "Does the business have a bank account?"

"Why should I need another bank account when I can use my own?"

"No bank account," Paul whispered as he wrote. "Can you give an estimate of the size of your business?"

"Size?"

"How much your business makes in a year."

Pamson stared hard at the boy, trying to determine what he was driving at. Was he spending his money educating someone who had the audacity to come to his place of work and make him look clueless? He had been reluctant to take the boy on, but Paul had grown up without a father, and his mother had flayed herself to put him through one of the best secondary schools in town. After his graduation, Rahila had pleaded with Pamson to let them become the boy's primary guardians. Against his better judgement, he'd accepted. Now the ingrate was sitting in his office, asking him questions about his business, jotting down notes. Like a fucking doctor.

"Paul, what do you want?"

"Sir?"

"Put the notebook away."

"But, Uncle—"

"Put it away. I don't want to see it."

Paul obliged and returned his hands to his pockets.

"You can see I have work to do," Pamson said. "Just tell me what you want."

"I want to become your business manager."

"Business manager? What makes you think I need a business manager?" Pamson realised what a stupid question it was the moment he'd said it.

Paul pulled a rolled-up document from his back pocket that Pamson hadn't noticed. "I won't waste any more of your time, Uncle. Here's my proposal. We can talk when you've read it." Paul placed the document on the table. It had even been spiral-bound and had a transparent cover the colour of a deep sky.

"Don't you have classes today?"

"The professor is sick."

Pamson nodded and stood up. He extended his hand. "Thank you for coming. I'll see you at home."

Paul shook his hand and left. Pamson looked down at the document, at the large-lettered words on the front page: BUSINESS PROPOSAL FOR PAMSON MOTOR CARE. He picked up the document and dropped it into the otherwise-empty desk drawer.

For the rest of the day, as he hammered crankshafts and tinkered with timing belts, as he pummelled dough and whisked egg whites, he couldn't get the words out of his head: Pamson Motor Care. He stayed back in the kitchen until Jonah had finished speaking to Mrs. Abdulrahman. She was such a reserved woman that Pamson wondered what it was she and Jonah discussed after every class. Their conversations went on and on. After she left, Jonah came over to where Pamson was seated on a bench by the wall.

"Sorry," Jonah said in Hausa. "You know that as a teacher, I must give every student the time and attention he or she needs from me."

Pamson recognised the twinkle in Jonah's eye and shook his head. "Are you being serious? That woman?"

Jonah took out a pack of cigarettes and asked for them to go outside. It was already dark. Pamson's car was the only one left in the visitors' parking lot. Across the compound, customers streamed in through the gate to buy baked goods from the store. Jonah lit his cigarette, pulled deeply on it, and closed his eyes. He opened them again as he exhaled.

"Isn't she married?"

"Her oldest child is a medical doctor in England," Jonah said, tipping ash into the air.

Pamson shook his head again. "Anyway, I didn't come for advice on women. I came for advice on business."

Jonah chuckled good-naturedly. "I'm all ears," he said in English.

"How many years did it take you to get to this point?"

"You mean, from when I started baking? Or when I started the business?"

"Both."

"I'm thirty-nine. So twenty years from when I started baking. Seven years from when I started the business."

"You built this in seven years?"

Jonah nodded and went on smoking for a while.

"You must work very hard."

"There's hard work. There's luck. There's working smart." Jonah exhaled. "You can be the hardest-working person in this world and still remain in the same place."

Pamson looked at his black work boots. They were the sturdiest shoes he'd ever owned. He had picked them out by sheer luck at the secondhand shoe market that had sprung up on Sundays on Ahmadu Bello Way, and had paid good money for them. Six years later the soles were lopsided, the seams beginning to yawn in small ways. But the steel toes remained solid and unyielding as ever. He looked at his BMW, an '89 model 3 Series, with its cracked windshield and the dent in the rear door on the passenger's side and the paint job that had been scrubbed thin by ten years of the elements.

"What's the size of your business?" Pamson heard himself ask.

"You mean, turnover?"

"Yes."

"About four to five million."

"A year?"

"A month."

Pamson said nothing.

"You're a mechanic."

It sounded like an accusation. Pamson waited to hear more.

"How many mechanics in this town provide their customers with a quiet, clean place to sit and wait while their cars are fixed?" Jonah let the question hang for a moment. "That's just basic packaging. Imagine if you provide a waiting area that has AC. And cold water." He took another drag of his cigarette, then said, "Do you know why I can charge five hundred naira for my bread when others are charging two hundred or two-fifty? Because I've made the customer believe my bread is worth five hundred."

"Don't you lose customers?" Pamson said.

"I just told you how much I make. Does it look like I'm losing customers?" Jonah pointed across the lot at the store. The people coming and going hadn't ceased. "The problem with mechanics in this country is that they behave like labourers instead of service providers. Even bakers are the same way. People will treat you the way you ask to be treated. I just saw an opportunity and took it."

Pamson stopped at the workshop on his way home. He left the car running with the headlights on. There was no electricity on the premises. He unlocked the front gate and walked across the yard. The ten or twelve cars waiting to be resurrected were stark in the beams of his car, with their dusty bodies and opaque windshields. The smoky stench of motor oil was thick in the air. It had taken a night like this for him to become aware of it. He unlocked the building and entered his office and opened the drawer. Paul's proposal lay at the bottom. He took it and left. As he drove up to the main road, he passed a group of about five young men who recognised his vehicle and waved. Vigilantes paid by the community to patrol the area.

He parked the car outside his compound and sat in it, letting his mind rove over the day's conversations. He'd been stuck in a room breathing foul air for years, and it had taken a young man half his age, whom he'd considered inept, walking in and pointing it out. For the first time since he'd begun this work, he realised that his body was tired.

He acknowledged his perpetually hunched shoulders and that persistent tightness in the small of his back for what they were—a language his body had been using to gain his attention. Somehow he had failed to register. It was like going still and hearing the singing of crickets for the first time and understanding that they had always been singing. There had been a time when all he had known was the violence of the streets, when even the idea of a basic life outside of thuggery had seemed like a blessing beyond his reach. In recent years he would pause and gape in awe at the shape his life had taken on, at how far he had come. Now here he was, daring to want more. And why the fuck not?

Next morning he sat up in bed and started reading Paul's proposal with a clear, rested mind. Rahila came out of the bathroom. He'd opened the curtains to let in the young daylight, but she still clicked on the light.

"It's past seven and you're still in bed," she said. "Are you not well?"

"I'm fine."

"What's that?" she said.

"Paul came to see me at the garage yesterday."

"Yes, he told me." She turned her back to him and started to dress. "You came home late."

It was a question disguised as a statement. "I was doing some thinking at the garage," he said, trying to be truthful. Not that she would believe him anyway.

Since the incident, she had stopped going naked in front of him, opting to dress or undress in stages so that most of her body remained covered. He had never even seen her unclothed with the baby bump.

She turned around, fully dressed. "You should listen to that boy. He has good business sense."

"He wrote a proposal for the workshop." Pamson raised the document.

Rahila stood by the door with her handbag. "If you'd listened to me from the beginning, you would be having a different conversation today."

Pamson said nothing.

"You're looking at me like you don't understand what I'm saying."

"I don't," he said, and meant it.

She checked her watch, then came and sat on the edge of the bed. "You don't remember me telling you when you started the workshop, 'Don't let your personal finances mix with it, treat it like a business'?"

Pamson shook his head.

"I told you to open a business account and to hire someone to do basic bookkeeping for you. It didn't even have to be an accountant. You don't remember?"

"You'll think I'm lying, but wallahi I don't remember."

"I believe you," Rahila said with a rueful smile. "It just shows that when we women give you good advice, you don't ever listen. You go ahead and do what is on your mind because you're men."

Her hand was lying on the bed between them. He placed his over it. "I want to talk about Mary. Please."

Rahila let her gaze stretch over him like a net, then said, "You may have your reasons for why you slept with another woman, but they are only excuses. Not reasons. If you want to talk, we can talk. But I am the one who will talk, and I will tell you why you cheated."

Pamson released a huge gust of breath and nodded. "Okay."

"You cheated because you're insecure."

"What?"

"Yes. You're insecure. Your wife is more successful than you are, and like a typical Plateau man, it made you feel small. So you found someone to do your bidding, to call you sir."

Pamson chuckled. "Have you met Mary?"

"You think I'm joking," Rahila said, her eyes suddenly growing distant, barbed. "But this is very serious. You're not taking it seriously."

She stood up and left the room before he could finish his protest. Pamson stared at the door after she had closed it. He remembered a time when the question of who the breadwinner of the house was had never been in dispute. Before she started her work with InterWomen, back when she sold kitchenwares from the boot of her car. His work at the garage had built this house and paid for most of their upkeep. The cash flow was inconsistent, scant for months at a time and then suddenly robust. It made him think of the seven years of famine and the seven years of plenty in Joseph's story from the Bible; though, unlike that case, there was no predictability to the pattern. There had been periods of intense needs, close calls, missed opportunities. There had been windfalls, lavish expenses such as her car (the previous one, not the one she currently drove) and the building on the garage lot that was his office. They weren't wealthy, but they'd made it through the year, sometimes with excess cash to spare.

Everything changed when Rahila got the InterWomen job. The transformation was a wonder to behold at first. They replaced the furniture they'd been using since their wedding and redid the decor. They could suddenly afford to paint the exterior walls of the house. They swapped the old rusted corrugated-iron roof for painted aluminium, maroon. They got cable TV and an internet modem that was perpetually left on. As their lifestyle changed, so did the tenor of their lives. Rahila began to speak about savings and trips abroad, things that sounded strange to him—and put on.

As far as he knew, they had enjoyed their lives before InterWomen. But he'd sensed a growing hunger in Rahila, and he'd been unable to share in that hunger. Before long they had started keeping separate finances. He'd insisted on continuing to pay for groceries and utilities, but several times a year she'd come home with a loaded car and stock the pantry with food that would last them the better part of a year. She had wanted to pay for Paul's upkeep and school fees since it was her idea to adopt him, but he'd resisted. They settled finally for an uneasy truce: he would handle Paul's school fees and she would take care of everything else.

Once, by accident, he had glimpsed at the balance of her savings account on her phone. The amount, deep into seven figures, had left him stunned, and he'd had to sit alone for several minutes to steady himself. It was true that the pressure on his wallet had lessened considerably; he had come to find himself with more disposable income than he'd ever had. He had once thought of himself as a modern man, letting his wife work, helping with the housework when he could, even cooking for her. But this was more than he could swallow—the fact that when it came to this silent battle for cash supremacy that had snuck in and planted itself between them, he had lost. He ought to know better, that it shouldn't matter. But it did. Now each time she spent money felt like some slight against him. It seemed important for him to continue to appear oblivious, to not give her the satisfaction of knowing that he knew. It made her victory incomplete. So perhaps she was correct to call him insecure. Perhaps she had given him the answer to the riddle of what he needed to do to win her back. Rather than be rankled by what she had said to him, he felt motivated, egged on because he was already on the right track.

He spent the next half hour going over the proposal. Then he went to the living room and found Paul puttering around in the kitchen, making breakfast. Paul regarded him in his sleeping clothes with concern and asked if he was well, then whether he wanted chips. After breakfast, Pamson called the boy to the living room and told him to sit down and tell him what exactly he had in mind for Pamson Motor Care.

8

The tailoring shop where Murmula and Beatrice were to have their apprenticeship was in a compound on Beach Road, just across the street from the UBA Building. A man dressed in suspenders, a white shirt, and a flat cap sold music CDs from a wheelbarrow parked on the sidewalk, just by the entrance to the compound. He played songs all day long from large speakers. It wasn't yet clear to Murmula how he'd managed to fit the speakers as well as all his wares on the wheelbarrow. How did he power his electronic devices? Where did he store the wheelbarrow at night? How far did he have to push it to get here?

"You're the one wasting your time on him," Beatrice said to Murmula. "Talatu said he has been coming every day except Sunday for more than five years, morning to evening."

Talatu was the attendant who managed the store when the madam, Mrs. Manuel, wasn't around. She had no clue how to make a single stitch, but anyone who walked in off the street would think she had been making clothes all her life. She talked down at the tailors and disparaged them in front of clients. Whenever a clearly wealthy client walked in, Talatu would put on a phoney accent and begin to present the range of apparel and fabrics on display.

For their part, Beatrice and Murmula restricted themselves to the tailors' room, where they were supposed to watch and learn. The windowless room was separated from the rest of the store by a sliding glass door and had air-conditioning that kept it at unbearable temperatures.

Murmula had learned after her first day to always bring along a shawl with her, no matter how hot it was outside.

She was restless by the end of the first week. The days felt longer than they needed to be, and her mind kept reverting to Paul and whether he had made any progress in convincing Pamson to hire her. They texted often, sharing small commentaries on how their day was going, but Murmula was reluctant to broach the matter repeatedly. She didn't want to seem desperate. She decided to subtly apply pressure in other ways.

"How is the apprenticeship going?" Mrs. Pamson asked Murmula when she stopped by the office to give her a gift she had gotten for her with part of her first payment. It was a print wrapper of a deep-oceanic colour, with gold and red tones appearing in scattered patterns. Murmula had selected it from the display in Mrs. Manuel's shop and transferred the payment into Mrs. Manuel's account.

"You didn't have to do such a thing, Murmula," Mrs. Pamson said, wiping away a tear. "Look at how beautiful it is."

Murmula smiled but said little. She hadn't expected such an emotional reaction from Mrs. Pamson. Mrs. Pamson stood in the middle of the office and placed the unrolled fabric against her dark skin. She gave a tiny twirl, then returned to her desk. "I'm very touched by this, Murmula. Very touched. But don't buy me any more presents, before my colleagues hear and accuse me of collecting bribes," she said, laughing. "Please come to me with any concerns you have during the apprenticeship. If you run into problems, my door is always open."

"Thank you, ma," Murmula said, and started to leave. She stopped at the door, then turned around. A thought had just dropped into her head. Rather than weigh it privately first, she decided to act on it immediately. Sentiment would win if she gave it room to thrive, and this mission required a calculating ruthlessness if she was to succeed at all. "Please, ma."

Mrs. Pamson looked up. "Yes?"

"Please, ma, you know I'm very grateful for this opportunity. I'm going to stay and learn in Mrs. Manuel's shop for as long as I can, but you know my passion. Please, if you know of any other mechanic that is willing to take someone like me, I'm still interested."

Mrs. Pamson took this in for a moment. Her face was hard to read. "Okay, I'll see what I can do."

Back at home, after she'd said maghrib prayers, Murmula remain seated on the prayer mat in the corner of the room and wondered if she had overstepped. She couldn't tell if Mrs. Pamson believed her or if she was only humouring her and could see that Murmula was trying to use her. How much of her husband's sin was Mrs. Pamson privy to? Did she know she was living in a stolen house, on stolen land? What if she did and had made her peace with it? That made her nearly, if not fully, as culpable as Mr. Pamson. If that was the case, it made Murmula's desire to limit the collateral damage that might result from her actions less of a concern. But only time would show everything for what it truly was.

Paul had made arrangements for them to go hiking the next day, a Saturday. Murmula didn't enjoy being out in nature much, but it presented an opportunity to see Paul and hear more about his progress with Mr. Pamson. She told them at the house that she sometimes had to work on Saturdays. Gogo Hauwawu complained about it only being her first week and already she was doing overtime. Murmula walked to the junction, where Paul was waiting with Mrs. Pamson's Honda. He went down and stood outside the vehicle while Murmula changed in the back seat. She swapped her gown and hijab for the T-shirt, jeans, and sneakers she had stuffed into her backpack. She topped it off with a hijab and a face-cap. The Honda's windows were all tinted, so she could change without worrying about passersby.

Paul had on a playlist exclusively of M.I. Abaga songs as they drove.

"He's my best rapper," Paul said, nodding his head to a song that was displayed on the music console as "Area." Murmula was only peripherally familiar with the rapper's music. That he hailed from Jos was a fact that had piqued her interest in a couple of his songs years ago, but the affective connections she had to the city and anything associated with it had become severely eroded by then, dwarfed by her grief and the frantic memories of them having to leave Jos abruptly, as though they'd been chased out. She had come to be familiar with a few M.I. hits across the years, but she identified them only by sound, not by title. A song called "Blaze" came up, and she listened in silence as exaggerated huffing and puffing issued from the speakers.

"Do you know what they're singing about here?" Paul asked.

"Well, it sounds like they're smoking and singing about weed. But I guess the weed is a metaphor for music."

Paul nodded. "You're right, and that's the conventional interpretation. They even say it in the song. But I have another interpretation."

Murmula looked at him. He was wearing his characteristic knowing grin, which was both smug and coy at the same time.

"The weed is a metaphor for the Holy Spirit. My theory is that this song is the most profane gospel song of all time. You know about the Holy Spirit, right?"

Murmula nodded. "We had Christian neighbours when we were growing up. They used to pray in front of us when we went to their house."

"There's even that line in the song about a sermon of the holy word."

Murmula chuckled. "I'm not an expert on the Holy Spirit, but I don't know how you came to that conclusion."

Paul shook his head stubbornly. "You just need to listen to the song a thousand more times. Then you'll get where I'm coming from."

"Isn't that the problem?" Murmula said in Hausa. "No song was meant to be listened to a thousand times. You start to see and hear things."

"Your English is so good," Paul said. He kept his eyes fixed on the road.

The smirk remained on Murmula's face, but she felt the joy skip inside her like a CD. "You forgot to add 'for a Hausa girl.'" She tried to keep the bite out of her voice, but she wasn't sure she succeeded.

Paul tore his eyes from the road and looked at her. "I didn't mean it that way. I'm sorry."

"I'm sorry too," Murmula said. "I get told that a lot. It's a little tiring, and boring. It's like for people, if you're Hausa and you're not rich, then you can't be educated and you can't speak English properly. If you're not Dangote's child, then you must be the child of a pauper."

"Or if you're from the north, then you must be Hausa, nothing else," Paul said quietly, gently nodding his head.

"That too."

In the gap of silence between songs, Paul said, "I envy the way you're able to switch languages. Your English is good, but so is your Hausa. You're equally comfortable in both. I wish I could be like that."

"But you speak Hausa."

"Have you ever noticed that I don't speak it much in front of you?" Paul's shoulders shook as he laughed. "I can't have you judging me. At least, not this early."

He seemed suddenly uncomfortable, as though the words got stuck in his throat. His Adam's apple bobbed up and down. He leaned forward and turned up the volume.

"This song is about Jos. Do you know it?" he said.

Murmula shook her head. The song had a heavy bass that made the car shudder. The seat shook under her in a steady, marching rhythm. A thin, whining blast persisted throughout, like a nonhuman background vocal. She stared out the window at the passing scenery. Densely populated neighbourhoods were falling away in favour of greenery and stony outcroppings. The rap lyrics passed through her head in a steady stream, depositing vaporous images on the banks of her mind. A posse of men in cowboy hats marched in tandem to the beat across a wasted landscape that looked nothing like the one before her. The image of a pistol merged with a vest, and then a rosary string that was also her tasbih beads, each bead a raindrop falling—again, along with the rhythm—drop by drop, each drop a supplication rising like bomb smoke that was also the souls of the dead. Where would her father's soul be among them? The city had swallowed her father whole like he'd never existed, but it had been the fate of countless others too—all the many nameless and faceless thousands dragged and slaughtered in the streets, in unseen corners in front of unseeing witnesses. Perhaps this was what this city was: a gaping mouth that devoured loved ones and spat out eternal questions.

"I don't like the song," she heard herself say when it ended.

"Why not?"

"It's just complaining. It isn't giving any solutions."

"Is he supposed to give solutions?"

"It's like he's cursing the land."

"I think he's describing what people are thinking, not what he wishes it would be."

"But people already know what they're thinking." She didn't like the way she was beginning to sound—short, rude, entitled. "Can we change the music?"

Paul switched up the playlist, and they continued without speaking. When she finally stepped out of the car, it was next to an overbearingly tall hill. She could smell freshly upturned earth from a nearby field that had just been planted. The black, loamy ridges were rich and stark against the surrounding vegetation.

"Where are we?"

"This is close to Jos East. Around Lamingo Dam. It looks like we're the first here."

A tall man with a greying goatee and dreadlocks approached them. He wore a straw hat with a wide brim and had a long staff and sturdy, brown boots. There was a vibrant intelligence in his eyes that countered the air of weariness that seemed to follow him. His dark-blue T-shirt had a slacked neck, the printed text on the front all but faded.

"This is our guide," Paul said. "Dr. Gbenga."

Dr. Gbenga extended a hand to Murmula. She hesitated before taking it. Paul had explained that Dr. Gbenga was a veterinarian who lived in the area and conducted ecotours. This would be Paul's second time going on one of his hikes. He refused to tell her how much he had paid for both of them.

"If the others don't come in ten minutes, we will go," Dr. Gbenga said. "They know the policy about coming late."

Five minutes later a muddy-brown Toyota appeared. When it parked next to the Honda, two young men and two young women climbed out. They all appeared to be around the same age as Paul and Murmula. It was plain they were two sets of couples by the way they immediately fell into pairs. Dr. Gbenga gave a few instructions about drinking water, the duration of the hike, and littering. He led the way, and Murmula and Paul followed right after. Dr. Gbenga kept pointing out birds and flora whose names Murmula couldn't remember.

"This region has the most diverse species of birds in West Africa," he said to the whole group when they stopped to watch a blue-breasted kingfisher with a rich turquoise cap swoop over the skin of a pond and fly off with a fish in its beak. Murmula wondered if her father had known this about Jos, what he might have made of it, given the dreamer he'd been.

They started the hike up the hill, and forty minutes later the climb didn't seem close to ending. Murmula stepped on a loose rock and lost her footing. She screamed as she tumbled backward. But Paul caught her in his arms, bracing himself against the impact. For a moment, she thought they would both topple back into the others. Paul was laughing, but all she could think to herself was that she should have stayed at home.

It was past noon when they reached the top. A large, flat rock emerged out of the ground like a crown on the hill. They found comfortable spots and ate their lunches. Jos was spread out before them like a banquet, a course of its own. The sun was gentle on their necks, and a nice breeze had prevailed so far. Dr. Gbenga warned them to be careful because there were steel inch-long nails and pegs lying around, discarded by the campers who frequented the area during the dry season.

They lay about like strange metal twigs intent on becoming one with nature. Many of them had the amber tint of rust.

"How does he know when it will rain?" Murmula said.

"He chose today because he was sure it wouldn't rain. I don't know how he knew." Paul stood up. "I'm going to ask him."

Murmula stared at the landscape before her that had what must have been every geographical formation known to man: rocks, hills, woods, ponds, plains. The built-up parts of Jos seemed almost like an afterthought.

"My name is Abdulmajid," a voice said in Hausa. "What about you?"

Murmula cranked her neck to see one of the young men in the group. He was light-skinned and portly, but had still managed to fit into a pair of tight black jeans and a white T-shirt that accentuated his flab. He was the one accompanying the brash girl who had brought fake nails to a hike and complained loudly about everything.

"My name is Murmula."

Abdulmajid remained standing at a distance and didn't sit. He faced the same direction, gazing down at the city. He started pointing. "There's Secretariat. There's Main Market and Terminus. There's Murtala House. There's J. D. Gomwalk House."

Murmula followed his arm, barely making out the landmarks.

"Are you new here?" he asked.

"Yes and no. I was born here but left when I was a teenager. I just came back. What about you?"

"Born, raised. This is all I know." He squatted and picked up a nail and threw it over the precipice. "Is he your boyfriend?"

"Yes," Murmula said, and kept her eyes on his face. She knew what had prompted the question, and she'd answered it more out of defiance than a desire to speak the truth. "Is something wrong?"

"No," Abdulmajid said with a smile. "Nothing's wrong." He raised his face-cap and wiped off sweat with the back of his hand. The dark prayer spot on his forehead was like a scar on his skin. "You're a sister in the ummah. And I believe we're the only two here."

Murmula said nothing.

"I just want to remind you, as a brother, to be careful. Sometimes you can get drawn into strange situations before you realise it. He doesn't look like someone that offers salat. Men like this can sometimes have bad intentions toward our women. And before our women know it, they are trapped."

"So it's possible to know a person that offers salat by just looking. I never knew that," Murmula said with half a smile. She chose not to dwell on the words *our women*—matan mu—the way he spoke them, the malignant sense of entitlement they carried. She looked around at his companion several paces away. She and the other girl were swigging their soft drinks and talking and throwing glances in Murmula and Abdulmajid's direction. The other girl wore a short purple gown over her jeans and had her braids tied in a bun. Both girls had on cowboy hats that reminded her of the M.I. song that had played in the car, "Wild Wild West." The girl with the purple gown said something, and Abdulmajid's companion threw her head back. Her chortling reached them. She had a rich, husky voice.

"Is she your girlfriend?" Murmula said.

Abdulmajid smiled and shook his head.

"I was mistaken, then. You seemed quite close. As your sister in the ummah, I should also warn you to be careful. Sometimes these women have bad intentions toward our men. Before you know it, you can become trapped in a strange situation."

Abdulmajid was still wearing his smile, but Murmula could tell it was now only skin deep.

"I know your type. You're one of those Muslim girls who likes to compare themselves to men. You think that everything a man can have, you should also have."

Murmula shrugged and said, "Why not?"

"Toh, let me tell you, a man is a man. Allah knows how he has made him. A man can sleep with and impregnate many women at the same time. But a woman can only have one man at a time."

"So it all comes down to fucking," Murmula said before she could stop herself.

"No, let me finish. Let us keep fucking aside and look at religion. The Prophet, Peace Be Upon Him, has allowed for a man to marry up to four wives. But nowhere does he say a woman can have more than one husband. So how can you compare the two when our religion doesn't compare them?"

Murmula stood up and dusted her hands. She could feel the words rising in her, all tipped with venom. She folded her arms around her body, as though to contain her indignation. But before she could speak, Paul appeared beside her.

"What's going on?" he said.

"This is Abdulmajid. We were just talking about Jos."

Paul reached out his hand. "Hi. We haven't met. I'm Paul."

"Abdulmajid," Abdulmajid said and shook his hand, then walked away. Murmula wished then that she had said something to embarrass him.

When Dr. Gbenga asked them to get ready to move on, Murmula walked a little distance from where Paul stood, scanning the ground.

"What is it?" Paul asked.

"My house key," Murmula said as she spotted a nice long nail with very little rust. When she was certain Paul couldn't see what she was doing from his position, she bent and picked it up and slipped it into her pocket. "Found it."

Later, on the way back home, Murmula was quiet in the car. Her body ached, yet she felt alive in a way she didn't remember ever feeling. Like some slumbering part of her had been roused awake. Paul was also quiet, but only when he asked about Abdulmajid did she realise what had been on his mind.

"Did you know him before?"

"I've never met him."

"You looked angry when I came back."

"You noticed." She smiled and took his right hand.

"Did he say something?"

"Look at me," Murmula said.

Paul turned his face toward her, and she held his gaze. He kept glancing at the road, waiting for her to speak. They both burst out laughing.

"If you want us both to get home safely, you'd better say what's on your mind. Before I stop looking at the road and focus my attention on you."

Murmula forced herself to stop laughing and said, "We were just arguing about stupid things. It's a Muslim thing." After a moment she added, "He was warning me about dating a non-Muslim."

Paul became serious again. She held on to his hand.

"I'm with you because I want to be with you," she said, but didn't know why she needed to say it. They weren't officially dating, and she needed to be careful about the entanglements she was creating. Moreover, Abdulmajid had inadvertently exposed a nagging worry that she'd refused to acknowledge until now: dating a non-Muslim came with a set of complications she didn't even want to have to think about. She wasn't a bigot; it was just the truth. The simpler she kept things, the more she remained focused on her mission, the better it would be for all involved. "I actually lied," she said suddenly.

"Lied? When?"

"When I told you I was looking for my key up on the hill. I was actually looking for a nail."

"To do what?"

"To use it on Abdulmajid's car."

Paul broke into laughter. "What exactly did you do?"

"Before we got in the car, while they were talking to Dr. Gbenga, I punctured his tyre."

"Wow, that's crazy. Remind me never to get on your bad side."

"It was just so annoying. I would have kept beating myself up if I hadn't found a way to get back at him. He was so disrespectful."

"What exactly did he say?"

"I'd rather not dwell on it."

Paul smiled, then said, "Whatever it is, I'm sure he deserved it."

"Trust me, he did."

"So, I have some good news for you."

Murmula looked at him, smiled, tore her eyes away and stared at the road, waiting to hear more.

"Uncle Dareng has agreed to hire you as a receptionist at the garage. It'll be a paid position."

Murmula's mouth dropped open. "How did you do that?"

Paul shrugged the question away. "Aunty helped a bit. But the important thing is that you'll get to be around the workshop and learn about cars, how to fix them."

She forced herself to be cheery the rest of the way, gushing with gratitude and excitement about what this meant for her. But once she got out of the car, the apprehension that had been waiting in the shadows finally came over her. She walked home from the junction slowly, partly from exhaustion and partly from stupefaction. The house was within view when she decided she was going to lie that she had a headache, take a bath, perform her prayers for the day—including the ones she'd missed—and go to bed. A knotted worry had settled in her chest. She needed solitude to parse it and arrive at some kind of clarity.

There was no one in the living room, no one in the kitchen. But when she opened the door that led from the kitchen to the backyard, Musty was seated on an upturned bucket, smoking a cigarette. She froze all over and wished she had just gone to the bedroom instead of coming here. He'd never have known she was in the house.

"Ina wuni?" she greeted.

"You're back?" Musty said. He was unbearably still. The end of his cigarette glowed in the deep shadow cast by the roof. The only part of him that moved was his hand as it ferried the butt to his lips.

"What about Gogo Hauwawu and Ishat?"

"They went out with Baba. Where have you been?"

"I was working today. My madam wanted us to come because one of her clients has a wedding next week."

Musty remained silent for some time. Finally, he said, "Is that so?" He stood up and went to the verandah in front of his room in the annex. He pushed his door open and turned to look at her. "Come inside."

Murmula stared at the dirty, pale curtain that hung in the doorway for a moment before shaking her head. "No."

Musty kept his gaze on her. "Do you normally go to work in a Honda CRV with Kanke plate number . . ." He blurted out the license number. She didn't know if it was correct or not. She'd never bothered. All she could confirm was that it was indeed a Kanke license plate. "Do you normally change clothes in the back of the car before you go?"

Murmula finally understood what was happening. He knew she had a secret, and he was going to blackmail her.

"If you don't come inside this room, I'm going to tell Baba and Mama that you've been lying to them since you came to this house."

Murmula took a deep breath, shut her eyes, and steeled herself momentarily, then walked across the courtyard and into her cousin's room. He closed the door behind her.

9

When he was with Paul, Pamson would sometimes pause midaction and look at his wife's cousin again, to be sure it was still the same person he had always known. The boy's appearance remained unchanged, but Pamson sensed a confidence in the way he explained the financial projections he'd set to paper, in the way he said that he expected the business to begin to turn a profit in about six months. Who knew he had it in him? In those moments when he stole glances at the boy, he would ask himself if he had actually lost his mind in employing Paul as his business manager. *Business manager.* He still wasn't sure what it meant, just as he wasn't sure about the meaning of half the things Paul had written down. But Rahila had gone over it, and she seemed resolute in her opinion that hiring Paul was the best thing Pamson had ever done for Pamson Motor Care.

He enjoyed hearing the name. The whole affair seemed like a reasonable wager since Paul had forfeited any salary. Instead, he expected to be paid when the profits started coming in. It was proof of his belief in the business's potential as a viable, long-standing venture. Furthermore, and contrary to Pamson's expectations, Paul had so far demonstrated an impressive frugality. He rejected Pamson's notion that the office building needed to be painted. The budget he proposed made allowance only for a sign with the business name; seats for the reception, where customers could wait; and a desk, a chair, and a computer with internet access for the receptionist.

The receptionist. That perhaps was the most surprising part of all this. Murmula's name had somehow resurfaced. Between Rahila's nudging and Paul's badgering, he'd been unable to argue against their assertions that she was a good fit. She was computer literate (Paul claimed to have personally tested her skills). She had a good command of both spoken and written English. By the time he had gone through her CV, he worried that with a degree in mechanical engineering, she might be overqualified.

He had interviewed her in his office with Paul standing by the window and smiling the whole time. She seemed certain in her convictions that this was the right place for her. When he brought up his concerns, she reiterated the bottom line: she was determined to learn about cars, and money was the least of her priorities. He stood in the yard and watched Paul and Murmula walk to Rahila's car and drive away. That was when he began to perceive that a triumvirate of some kind had formed between his wife, her cousin, and this strange girl.

On Murmula's first day, he showed her around and introduced her to the boys. Luka pulled him aside to ask if he was joking. Pamson watched with some amusement as the younger boys offered to run errands for Murmula. It occurred to him that this might be a good thing, that they may cultivate some discipline and actually do the work they'd been assigned on time. After he'd seen her to her station, he went into his office and closed the door and sat behind his desk. He was supposed to start dividing his time between his office and the yard while Paul developed a plan for hiring an extra hand or two so that Pamson could transition to more of a supervisory role. "It's time to start MD-ing, Uncle," Paul had said. *MD-ing*, Pamson thought with a chuckle. Where did the boy get these words from? He had even gotten him some office stationery and arranged it on his desk. There was now an in tray and an out tray. The in tray already had a document in it. He picked it up. It was a draft of the formal letter Paul had written, addressed to the managing director of the largest bakery in the city. The letter was pitching a promotional offer to service the company's vehicles at a 50 percent discount for a three-month trial period. Pamson signed it and looked at his name and title below the signature: *Dareng Pamson, CEO/MD*. He slid the letter into the out tray. It had been a small action, picking up the pen and signing the letter and putting it in the tray, but he felt like he had accomplished more with it than with three hours bent over the engine of a car. The way Paul had explained it, Pamson was now going from being self-employed to being an employer.

He was still in a reflective mood when someone knocked at the door. "Come in."

Murmula entered. She was wearing smart indigo trousers, a matching suit jacket over a white shirt, and a matching head covering. He still wasn't used to seeing such extravagant colour around the garage, but he appreciated the effort she put into dressing formally.

"Sir, Honourable Bot is here to see you," she said.

"Bring him in," Pamson said, barely recognising his own voice.

Murmula stepped out of the room and left her perfume hanging in her wake.

Philip Bot was short in a way that reminded Pamson of Reverend Dogo. Success had made him corpulent, further highlighting his limited stature. He cut a very different image from the dashing and agile young man he had been back when he and Pamson used to run together. That had been a long time ago—a different time, when Pamson had been a different person.

Pamson stood up to shake his old friend's hand and showed him into the guest chair. The House of Assembly member looked around.

"Dareng Pamson kenan," he said gleefully, "you've become an important oga fa. This is very nice. You even have a receptionist."

"I still have to paint and install curtains, if I can convince my business manager. The time has reached for us to start doing things more professionally."

Philip nodded, his face split into a wide grin. "I like that. I like that very much."

"I didn't expect you to come to collect the car by yourself."

"When I heard your receptionist's voice say she was calling from Pamson Motor Care, I said I had to come and see what is happening, so the driver dropped me. This is nice, Pamson. I'm impressed." Philip switched to English. "Why don't you write a proposal, and I will table it before the Speaker? Maybe the House can retain you as our go-to mechanic."

"Seriously, Honourable?" Pamson asked with a deep cackle. He and Philip slapped their palms together in a high five.

"Look at you, suddenly calling me Honourable because you heard money," Philip scolded, still laughing. "Can you bring it to my house by the end of the week? Come, let us have dinner. Or even better, let's meet somewhere. There's a new place in Rayfield, near Jos Business School. Their food is better than anybody's mother's food. We can discuss, catch up on old times."

They stopped in the reception, where Philip paid his bill in a large bundle of thousand-naira notes. Murmula collected the money and wrote out a receipt. Philip held it up and looked at the business monogram on it as though the piece of paper had become its own currency. He kept saying, "Very impressive, Pamson. Very impressive."

Luka was waiting for them by the Ford Explorer. He handed the key to Philip with a deferential bow, saying, "Honourable."

"What's your name again?" Philip said.

"Luka, sir."

"Take," Philip said, handing Luka a thousand-naira note.

"Nagode, Honourable," Luka said. He bowed again and received it with both hands.

Philip turned to Pamson. "Your wife's birthday. It's like it's this month ko?"

"You have a good memory," Pamson said. "It's next week."

"You know that Rahila is my person. I will send her a little something so she can spoil herself. You can give me her bank details when we meet. Call me when the proposal is ready, and we'll arrange the time."

"Honourable kenan!" Pamson said, and did a mock salute. He kept waving as the Ford backed out of the gate. He felt so light, so filled with possibility.

He went back to his office and called Paul.

"Good afternoon, Uncle."

"Hello, Paul. We need to write a proposal and address it to the Speaker of the House of Assembly. I have a contact who may be able to help us so that Pamson Motor Care becomes the official mechanic to the House."

"That's incredible, Uncle. Okay, I'll start putting it together immediately."

Pamson could feel the boy's excitement. "How long will it take you?"

"I need to do a light feasibility study to be sure about market rates, but I can have the draft ready by tomorrow evening."

After he hung up, Pamson made a list of the ingredients he would need for Rahila's birthday cake. If he bought everything this week, he could ask to store them at Jonah's. That way he wouldn't scramble at the last minute, knowing his tendency to forget things. Maybe he could even bake the cake in Jonah's kitchen.

When Pamson climbed into his car, Luka leaned over the passenger window.

"Oga, I need to talk to you," he said gruffly. Luka hadn't concealed his disappointment at not being able to drive the vehicle back to Philip's house himself. Pamson knew the boys who worked for him liked to ingratiate themselves to wealthy clients, and as long as they didn't cross certain boundaries, he didn't mind it. But Luka's petulance had begun to grate on him lately.

"Get in." Pamson started backing out as soon as Luka shut the door. "I'm in a hurry, so we can talk until we reach the main road."

"Bringing a woman to work with us isn't a good idea, Oga. A Muslim woman, at that."

"And what about Yunusa? He's a Muslim. We've been working together for years."

"It's not the same thing. His work is not on this site."

"But he's part of the business. I'm planning to buy the adjoining land soon, and he can come and be together with us, in the same place."

"Oga, I don't understand all these changes. Nothing was wrong with how we used to do things."

"You're complaining about working with Muslims. What about Al'amis, even Bala? They're all Muslims." Pamson realised he was beginning to sound like Rahila.

"They're just small boys, Oga. It's not the same thing."

"You just don't want me to hire a woman ko? It's not about being a Muslim."

"Oga, you didn't just hire a Muslim woman. You hired a fine Muslim woman. I know how these things can be."

Pamson chuckled out loud. "Are you afraid of being tempted? You didn't even come back to let me know what you decided about the pregnant girl."

"Sorry, Oga. But it's not mine. What else is there to say?"

"That girl is here to help us grow our business. She's one of us now. Make sure she feels welcome, and treat her with respect. Do you hear me?"

Luka remained stone-faced. Pamson stopped the car at the junction, and Luka opened the door and put one leg out. He remained like that for a moment, pensive and still.

"Oga," he said finally, "I don't like the way that boy looks at us. He thinks he's better than us just because he went to school."

"Which boy?"

"Your wife's nephew."

"Paul?" Pamson said, surprised. "Isn't he your tribesman? I thought the two of you would get along."

"And so?"

"Did he ever disrespect you?"

"He just likes to look down on us, asking us stupid questions, as if we don't know what we're doing."

"This is a good thing for everyone, Luka. Change isn't comfortable. But it's a good thing. The business will grow, there'll be more money. You'll even begin to get a salary. Just accept it."

"Whatever you say, Oga. Until tomorrow."

As Pamson drove to Jonah's Baked Delight, he thought about Luka's hesitation. Two weeks ago, he had felt the same way. The idea of a woman in the garage had seemed almost sacrilegious. Having Murmula work as a receptionist rather than in the yard was a fair compromise. Rahila could no longer accuse him of being prejudiced and sexist and anti-progressive—all words she had used in the past—even though he never understood what progress had to do with it. Garage work was tough, dirty, and humbling. Men were accustomed to such conditions because, well, men were brutes, and he would be the first to admit it. He could never imagine his wife going to work as a mechanic, let alone allow it. She could choose any other profession—she could even be one of those civil engineers who worked in the field wearing a helmet, safety jacket, and work boots—but not a workshop mechanic. A woman didn't deserve to be in such a place. And who could blame Luka for his feelings, given all that had happened over the years between Christians and Muslims in the city? Pamson disagreed with the sentiment, but he understood where it sprang from. He himself had once thought that way, and aggressively so; the violence he had meted out against presumed Muslims remained fresh in his mind, two decades on. He had now come a long way. Being exceedingly accommodating to his Muslim neighbour. Letting a Muslim stranger work for him in such a sensitive area of his business. Maybe it was penance to ease his guilt, maybe it was out of genuine conviction, but no one could accuse him of being prejudiced.

The evening's lesson was a continuation of how to make the perfect crust for pies. They had mixed the dough and left it in the fridge during the previous class. Tonight they rolled it out into thin sheets that were filled with meat and vegetables.

"Your rolling technique has improved," Jonah said, placing the meatpies Pamson had made into small cellophane bags. The kitchen smelled pleasantly of the minced beef they had fried with cabbage, onions, and carrots, and of baked dough, but this was only part of the reason for Pamson's buoyant spirits. Praise from Jonah was hard-earned, and he found that it was the thing he looked forward to most on the days he came here. His hands, permanently stained as they were with the marks of his trade, excelling at a task of such delicacy, such refinement, and Jonah deeming it all worthy of commendation. Jonah gave his permission for Pamson to store the ingredients for the cake in his pantry once he had them, and to use the kitchen on Rahila's birthday. When he got home and handed Rahila the meatpie, she asked him where he bought it.

"Jonah's Baked Delight," he said.

"I didn't know their meatpie was so delicious," she said, and stood up from the couch to make herself a cup of tea that would go with the meatpie.

"Don't worry," Pamson said quickly. "I'll make it for you."

He smiled all the way into the kitchen and all while making the tea. He left Rahila in the living room, watching a movie on DStv, and went to bed, falling asleep to a profound sense he rarely had of the day having been well spent across its disparate parts. It had been a good day.

He had barely been in his office twenty minutes the next morning when Murmula knocked to say that a woman named Mary wanted to see him. The girl looked a little confused, and who wouldn't be after meeting Mary for the first time?

"Did you tell her I'm in?"

"Before I could even respond to her question, she said she saw your car, sir." There was a soft edge of protest in Murmula's voice.

Pamson looked out the window. It was barely eight thirty, and his boys were still trickling into the yard, late as ever. Even Luka, who was responsible for keeping them in line, was habitually late. He had expected the new changes to make them more compliant.

"When you go back, wait for five minutes, then bring her in."

Murmula nodded and closed the door.

Pamson tried to gather his thoughts. He hadn't seen her in almost eight months. He'd been avoiding her, ignoring her calls and messages. How did she know to come here today of all days? A day he had resumed early for the first time in a long while. What language could he use to explain to her that he was a different man? That the things that had mattered to him half a year ago no longer did? Maybe Murmula had already begun to suspect something. He stood up and took a turn around the desk, trying to think of a way to handle this. How dare she come here?

The door opened abruptly before the five minutes were up. Mary was a tall woman in her thirties, with a shape that made her seem sculpted. It had been that figure that had snagged him, those hips. She stood in the doorway for a moment, regarding him like a lost-but-found object. As she turned to close the door and sashayed into the room, he understood her intent, that she meant to deploy everything he had once loved about her during this encounter. The jeans that hugged her thighs and backside; the tucked-in yellow shirt with the top three buttons left undone, exposing her fleshy bosom. She had him cornered, and she clearly wasn't going to be taking no for an answer.

Even though he had braced himself, the first thing out of her mouth still threw him off guard.

"How come you never brought me here to fuck?" she said in Hausa, looking around. "All those times we were looking for a private place."

Pamson opened his mouth and closed it like a goldfish.

"You look like you've lost weight. Have you been eating kuwa?"

"Mary," he finally said, "what can I do for you?"

Mary took the seat he had failed to offer her and crossed her legs.

"I need money."

"How much?"

"Fifty-K or more."

"You think I'm just packing money from the ground, don't you?"

"There are things I know about you that even your wife doesn't, Dareng. There are things I've done for you that she can't even imagine, things you wouldn't dare ask her to do. And when I did those things, there was no amount of money I would call that you wouldn't give me. As long as you had it, you gave it to me. Fifty-K is nothing to you. In fact, I've changed my mind. I want hundred-K."

Pamson leaned back in his seat, half-amused. "I'm not giving you any money, Mary. Those days are over. How many times do I have to keep saying it?"

"Dareng, if I hadn't played with your balls myself, I would have said you didn't have any. You sent me a text to tell me it was finished. You kept rejecting my calls. You didn't have the guts to tell me to my face. And you're lucky my mother raised me well. I would have come to your house to show you real madness."

Pamson glanced out the window and saw Luka speaking with Murmula.

"You will look me in the eye today and tell me why it is over," Mary said. "Look at me, Dareng."

Pamson had forgotten the power she held over him. Her ability to seduce him by merely being in the same room, within easy reach, was the reason he had refused to see her. "I'm going to be a father. My wife is pregnant."

Mary held his gaze for a moment, then started laughing. When she managed to compose herself, she said, "I thought you said she was barren."

"I never said that. I just said we couldn't have children."

"So what happened?"

Pamson looked at her, confused. "I just told you, she got pregnant."

"Is it a virgin pregnancy? Did she impregnate herself? Did the Holy Spirit come down and do it?"

Pamson felt a dark rage being slowly born at his centre, spreading out, radiating.

"So your wife told you she was pregnant, and you just accepted it. I didn't know you were also fucking her; I thought it was just me. Now I don't know if I should be angry. But, truthfully, were you sleeping with her at all? Because I think the reason you came to me is because she was refusing to give you pussy."

"Mary, that's enough."

"I will say what I came here to say. Did you ever stop to ask yourself how your wife became pregnant? Suddenly, she's pregnant. Maybe you're the one who was impotent. Did you ever think about that?" Mary chuckled again to herself. "That your wife. She's smarter than I gave her credit for. Maybe she found out that you were sleeping with another woman, and her revenge was to go and get pregnant for another—"

Pamson lunged and was suddenly on the other side of the desk. He grabbed her, had her pinned to the wall in two seconds. His hand was on her throat. The racket of the last three seconds echoed around them. She tried in vain to loosen his grip. That was when he realised she couldn't speak—he was strangling her. He let her go and looked around. Her chair had tipped over. He picked it up and returned to his seat. She coughed briefly, cleared her throat, and sat down again, as though the last ninety seconds had been part of the plan.

"You don't know me," he said quietly. "You don't know who I am. You don't know the things I've done, the things I'm capable of. I'll transfer fifty thousand to you. After that, I never want to hear from you again. If I see you anywhere near me or my family, you won't like what I'll do."

Mary levelled a defiant stare at him but said nothing. He picked up his phone.

"Which account do you want it in?"

"FirstBank," she said, and cleared her throat again.

After he made the transfer, he deleted both her FirstBank and Diamond Bank account numbers from his banking app. He had blocked her number months ago, but now he erased her name from his contact list.

There was a loud ping, and she took out her phone from her handbag.

"Did you receive it?" Pamson asked.

Mary nodded and put the phone away.

He raised his phone with the screen pointed at her.

"I no longer have any of your information. No phone numbers, no banking details. We will continue with our lives as if we never met. You can go now."

But she didn't move. There was a sad, knowing smile on her lips.

"I always knew you were a coward," she said quietly. "But now you have shown me exactly the type of coward you are." She stood up and slung her bag over her arm. "Erasing a number from your phone isn't the same thing as erasing a deed that you want to forget. At your age, you should be smart enough to know that."

She closed the door gently behind her. Outside, Pamson could hear one of the boys laughing. It sounded like Al'amis. That was when it occurred to him for the first time, the possibility that he'd rather be out there lying under a car with greasy hands instead of in here, behind this stupid desk.

10

Mary, the strange woman who had come to see Mr. Pamson, came out of his office and stopped at Murmula's desk.

"So Madam is going to have a baby!" she said in a surprised tone. "He just told me. Congratulations fa."

Murmula smiled, unsure of how to respond. She was a little out of breath because she had been standing at the door, listening through the wood, and had needed to hurry back to her seat when she heard the chair scraping the floor. It had sounded like a commotion at some point, as though Mr. Pamson had attacked the woman. But it could easily have been the other way around. Mary didn't seem like the kind of woman who could be cowed by a man.

"How many months is she now?" Mary said.

Murmula studied the woman's face, unbelieving of her own luck. Knowing now what this woman represented in Mr. Pamson's life, she felt like she had been handed the keys to a well-guarded secret. What if this was a better way? She made a snap decision then.

"Almost nine months," she said. "Is everything all right? I thought I heard something fall in there."

Mary flitted her eyes over her, sizing her up, then said, "You heard it all the way from here?"

"It was very loud."

"Who are you?"

"Mr. Pamson's receptionist."

Mary tossed the trailing ends of her weave over her shoulder. "Is that so?" When Murmula nodded, she said, "You're very pretty. I really hope that is all you are to him," and walked out.

Murmula sat with this for a moment, staring at the swinging hips retreating in a blur of yellow. She had anticipated such insinuations. They were inevitable. But she hadn't expected them to be raised by a woman. It rankled, but she realised the biggest tool she so far had at her disposal was slipping away. She pushed back her chair and stood. She caught up with Mary outside the gate, a few yards past Maman Ivie's spot. Mary turned and stared at her through large sunglasses that hid most of her face.

"What do you want?" Mary said in Hausa.

"Please don't take offence, but I didn't like what you said to me back there."

"What?"

"You insinuated that I was sleeping with Mr. Pamson. I don't do that type of thing."

"You're a woman, my dear. Nobody has ever called you a prostitute before?"

Murmula opened her mouth to say she had never behaved like one, then realised it was the worst thing she could say. "They have."

"Then you should be used to it by now. It's our lot in life as women. Whether it's true or not."

"But it doesn't mean we should call each other that. Besides, Mr. Pamson isn't even that kind of man."

Mary made a sound that seemed to come from nowhere in particular, low and guttural. "What is that thing they say about men? That thing they call them? Men are . . . something?"

Murmula shook her head.

"Whatever it is," Mary said, "that man back there is it."

"Scum?" Murmula said suddenly as the word dropped in her head. "He's the original scum."

Murmula stifled a smile, wondering if Mary would be offended if she laughed. But the other woman only took off her glasses and aimed her eyes at Murmula. She had impossibly long eyelashes.

"What's your name?"

"Murmula."

"When did you start working here?"

"A few days ago."

Mary nodded and started to turn.

Panicking, Murmula said the first thing that came to her mind. "Are you friends with Mr. Pamson?"

"Friends?" Mary squinted at Murmula through her lashes. "Are you well at all? Do I look like I want to be friends with a man like that?"

Murmula stared at her without answering.

"I'm servicing him behind his wife's back. Are you satisfied, or do you want to know if I also give him blow jobs?"

"I'm sorry. I just . . . Please, can I collect your number? Maybe you can be giving me advice. I'm just not sure if I'm doing things wrong, and you're the first person to come that isn't a client since I started working. I'm nervous because I don't want to do anything that'll make me lose my job."

Mary had an amused look on her face. "Are you sure you don't want to fuck him?"

Murmula blushed and averted her gaze.

"You Hausa girls—I know your type. Pretending to be shy until you enter the bedroom."

"I don't want to do anything with him," Murmula said, regretting that she had ever started this conversation.

Mary belted out the number so fast that Murmula almost missed it. She put the sunglasses back on. "You can text me so I will have your number."

"Okay. Thank you."

Mary walked away without another word.

Murmula returned to her desk, simmering quietly while typing a sweet text saying how nice it was to meet Mary. It hurt to send it. She'd had to stand there and take one insult after another—from a shamelessly loose and cheap woman, no less, who called other women prostitutes when she was practically one herself. She turned her mind to the task at hand. Paul had instructed her to transfer all the transactions from the old receipt booklet into the new accounting software they were using. It was fairly quick work because the booklet had been infrequently used. The amounts recorded were large sums that she imagined had been requested for special contracts or the like. She had seen the same thing in Ilorin, when she had worked briefly at a petrol station. The odd customer might ask for a receipt, but the receipt booklet had mainly been retrieved when money from some lucrative deal was coming in. Most of Mr. Pamson's receipts had been properly filled out, but there were two of them with significant sums that had no payer's information and one that had no date. She decided to get some fresh air before going to ask Mr. Pamson about them.

She stood on the verandah and looked at the yard. Work was ongoing but in a disinterested, languid manner. Luka had gone out to return a client's car. There were no customers to stand over the mechanics and demand that their vehicles be fixed there and then, or that the work continue. All the cars in the yard, as far as she knew, had spent the night there. No new ones had been driven in—yet. Al'amis was leaning against the fence, combing his thick Afro in a mirror he kept in his back pocket. Murmula didn't understand how the mirror remained intact in that position. She could hear Bala and Thankgod squeaking with laughing voices, perhaps hidden in the corner beside the metal storage room. The boys liked to sit there and have their meals with a helping of gossip.

She went to the gate and watched Maman Ivie between the bars. The woman was seated under an umbrella with a child strapped to her back. She'd barely left her seat all day. Murmula was yet to taste her cooking, but it seemed everyone at the garage, including Mr. Pamson, had been won over by it. She had noticed the food warmer that Mr.

Pamson kept on his desk, and that he made frequent use of it because it had been unwashed when she had arrived on Monday. It was kept in his office because of Maman Ivie's food, no doubt. Mr. Pamson's kindness toward people in general had been an interesting complication, and she was almost moved by the affection and loyalty people like Maman Ivie had for him. But Murmula saw his altruism for what it was, a superficial attempt to distract onlookers from his true nature. What if she and her family weren't his only victims? What if this was also stolen land? Murmula was certain he had targeted her father because he was a Muslim, but she didn't believe Mr. Pamson's cruelty to be restrained along religious lines. Self-interest was the only creed that guided thieves and murderers like him.

Back inside, she picked up the receipt booklet, placing her fingers on the problematic pages to keep them open. She bent and lifted her purse from the floor, placing it on her seat. She plunged her hand in and dug through her effects until her fingers closed around the cold metal object at the bottom. She brought it out by only a fraction and stared at it, as if to make sure that her sight and her touch were in agreement. A long silver penknife with a curved handle that looked like the arms of a soft *k*. It was sharper than a razor blade—Musty had demonstrated it on his mattress before folding it and putting it in her hand. She was meant to use it, but she hadn't made up her mind when or if at all she even wanted to. She had simply taken it and left the room. Now that she had discovered a potential avenue in Mary, she started to question this approach proposed by Musty. Yes, it would be quick, decisive, but she might get into trouble.

Murmula returned the knife and took heavy steps toward the office. She hesitated at the door. When she raised her hand to knock, it trembled. When she entered and stood before him, she felt a weight pressing on her chest. She wasn't breathing.

"What is it, Murmula?" he said in English without looking at her. He was reading a letter.

Then she understood that she had never been alone with this man, this murderer, this thief. All her interactions with him had been in the presence of others until now, when she stood, not by the door to poke her head in and announce a visitor but right in front of him, mere inches away.

Mr. Pamson snapped up his head suddenly and slammed the desk with his fist. Murmula flinched. "You're wasting my time, just standing there! What is it?" he shouted. His brow was scrunched, his nose looked like an overpronounced, ugly feature that hadn't been there before. She saw it then, the true face of the man who had undone her life. He had been wearing a masquerade the entire time, causing her to wonder if perhaps she was mistaken or had the wrong person. But here it was.

When she bent over the table and showed him the pages, the thought that his fingers may brush against hers made the skin of her neck move like a worm. Her hand still shook, and she noticed him noticing it. She took a couple of steps back and waited as he filed through his remembrances. He looked tired and small behind his ridiculous desk. He shook his head and pushed the booklet toward her. "The one point five million was from Dogara Secondary School, if my memory serves me right. They gave me the money to supply a station wagon for them. But the rest I can't remember."

Murmula thanked him and hurried out. She sat at her desk and slowly let her chest rise and fall again. She stared blankly at the laptop screen, keeping still. Everything that had happened in that office had felt like an assault, and she had just stood there and taken it in. Slowly, she tilted her head upward so that her tears would flow back into her eyes. Any sudden movement may cause some part of her to break. She looked at the time at the bottom of the screen. Just past ten—the day had barely begun. She couldn't spend a minute more in this place. She powered down the laptop and packed it up, then stood by her desk, torn between announcing her departure and leaving quietly. She chose to leave.

She was halfway across the yard when Luka walked through the gate.

"They just called me that my little cousin was rushed to the hospital," she said without being asked. "I have to go and see if she's okay. Please help me tell oga. I just got up and walked out."

"You have a mouth. Tell him yourself," Luka said. His expression told her she could be the one in the hospital and he wouldn't care.

As she passed through the gate, she heard Maman Ivie calling to her, but she didn't turn. Her steps were sharp against the ground. At the main road, she flagged down an unoccupied keke napep.

"Where to?" the driver said in Hausa.

"Daɗin Kowa."

"I'm stopping in State—"

"Charter. I'm chartering," she said impatiently.

"Get in."

The keke was a steady rumbling beneath her, around her. Her fingers punched out a text to Paul. Going home. Emergency. Will talk later. Sorry. Send. She switched off the phone and banished it into the chasm of her handbag. The city was a faint shimmer, flying past. She spoke very little, meting out directions to the driver like morsels. She handed him a five-hundred naira note and didn't stop for his reaction. Thankfully, the front door was locked, which meant there was no one at home. She let herself in, locked the door behind her. Somehow made it to her bed. The glue holding her together melted away, and she felt herself break apart as her head touched the pillow.

When she woke up, it was still bright outside. She could hear movements in the house, but the room itself was quiet. She lay in the dark, exhausted. She felt like she had crawled out from underneath a boulder-size blanket muffling her existence. Like she hadn't been able to breathe for hours. She didn't understand what had happened back there at the garage, but a flood of images had washed through her head that she thought she had forgotten. Clearly she had underestimated what it would take to be in proximity to the enemy. She wasn't as tough as she had believed. She sat with her diary on the bed, found the page marked *December 8, 2010*:

> *Two years today. It's hard. So hard. Why is it so hard? Why does everything have to be so hard. It's like the more time passes, the harder it becomes.*

She had been barely seventeen when she wrote that. She had attained a clarity that day that had been unavailable to her before. It had come to her like a revelation out of Al-Jannah that the world didn't treat weak people kindly, and certainly not helpless women. She didn't have to look past her mother for it to be any clearer. She would need a new kind of strength. The effort she had put into toughening herself up over the years, building a protective scab over her heart—it had all been a waste. She had buckled at the first sign of pressure. The enemy had yelled at her, and she had quailed like a frightened little girl.

She knew what she had to do.

After she had put on some makeup, she stepped out into the living room clutching her purse and found Gogo Hauwawu watching an Indian film she didn't know. Her aunt jerked up at the sight of her, then grabbed her chest.

"You scared me," she blurted out.

"Sorry, Aunty. I came back early today. I was feeling tired."

"Are you going out again?"

"Not far. Just to get something."

She walked to the main road, then turned in the direction of the market. Fifteen minutes later she was bent in front of a display box with a mesh screen, pointing at a large black rooster. The legs were tied, and she carried it back home by its wings, marvelling at how heavy it was. She went around the house to the backyard and put the bird on the ground. She watched it for a few minutes as it clucked gently, too hobbled to go anywhere. It flapped its wings as it tried in vain to move. Murmula reached into her purse and pulled out the penknife. When she opened it, she felt like she was seeing it for the first time. Its shiny curve was an exclamation point of chrome and leather. Under the red light of Musty's room, it hadn't looked so long and so deadly, despite his demonstration.

This was after the short, whispered exchange in which he looks her in the eye and asks her where she has been. After she tells him, because she would rather go in that direction than the one he had in mind the night he pulled her into the dark and kissed her. After he doesn't blackmail her, as she expects him to, but instead says with an air of gravity that she is wasting her time.

"When you've finished destroying his life, then what?" he says.

She looks at him, lost to his meaning, trying not to cough from the stale smoky air.

"You can try to break his marriage, destroy his business, damage his relationships. But as long as he's alive, he will rebuild and heal."

The room's pathetic lighting casts his eyes in shadows, but she can sense something in his voice, a hushed earnestness that sounds to her like respect.

"He killed your father, my uncle. The only thing that can give us satisfaction is blood. Because if it was reversed, their people wouldn't waste any time. You weren't around, but what they did in Rukuba Road, in Tudun Wada, in Vom . . . it's unforgiveable. Can you kill his wife?"

Murmula shakes her head.

"His nephew?"

She shakes her head.

Musty smiles. "Are you in love with him?"

Murmula shakes her head again.

"Good, because as long as you're dealing with an infidel, you can't be certain. You may think he likes you, but the moment he has a chance, when it's life or death, he'll sell you out to save his neck."

Murmula lets her eyes fall.

"If you can't kill the nephew, it's going to have to be the murderer's blood. Blood for blood."

Then he produces the knife from a pocket between his mattress and its frame. Whips it out like the surprise it is. Presents it to her like a gift. She doesn't touch it. He opens it and flashes it around. Murmula thinks about her mother. When she had told her to get justice for the family, what had she meant? Murmula has never been able to answer the question. Did her mother know she would be faced with a choice like this? Did justice include taking a man's life as well?

"It'll save you time," Musty says. "Quick and easy." He does a horizontal slashing motion. "You can do it like this, cut his throat." He pushes the blade through the mattress; the knife sinks into it as though it were butter. Pulls it out. "You can push it into his heart. In and out. Then you disappear."

"Have you done it before?" Murmula asks quietly. "This type of thing?"

"Killing?" Musty chuckles and shakes his head with an if-only-you-knew smirk. "Let me just say that every infidel I met during the last crisis got what he deserved."

He places the knife in her hand and closes her fingers around it and tells her she can go. As she leaves, she knows she will have nothing more to fear from him.

Now Murmula swished the blade through the air like she had seen her cousin do that night. She picked the bird up by its neck in one hand. It was rubbery, bendy in her grip. She had seen her male cousins in Ilorin kill chickens multiple times. She had never done it herself, but she knew the proper way to lay out the bird and hold it down under your feet while you drew the blade over its neck. This needed to be different, like nothing she had seen before. She raised the rooster until it was in front of her, then pushed the blade into its chest. Its wings exploded in her face, and for a moment all she saw was a black blur. When the red appeared, it came with warmth that she might have found soothing under different circumstances. The rooster quivered like a gust in her grip, and it was difficult to keep it still. But she was stronger. She stabbed it again and again and again, hoping that the next one would whisk the life out of it once and for all. The bird beat its wings, but she held on; even when it seemed to her like she was holding an undead bird that would walk the earth, haunting her all its days, following her wherever she went, she held on. With a desperate, final slash of the blade, she took the rooster's head clean off. Its body dropped to the ground, where its legs jumped into action, propelling it around the yard like a wind-up toy that had lost its bearing. The neck and the head remained in her hand, anointing the ground with a stream of blood.

When she finally looked up, there was someone in the yard with her. It was Baba Karami, standing by the rear entrance from the street, staring at her. His eyes and lips were parted in horror, but it might have been awe. Her heart seemed to stop, then it seemed to start beating again as she realised it wasn't her uncle but her cousin: How had she, in all her years, been blind to the haunting resemblance Musty shared with his father, and by extension, with her?

11

Pamson hadn't been aware of the new location of the Jos Business School. After turning off Rayfield Road and driving up the access road, his headlights fell on the sign a hundred yards away to the left. On his right was an open gateway. He swung the car through it and arrived at an unpaved parking lot full of cars. A small bungalow stood against a fence, fronted by a pair of gazebos with bamboo poles and potted plants and creepers. The lawn beside the building was lined with walkways and dotted with outdoor lanterns and paved slabs that carried square tables. In the cool evening, the place had a magical glow and enchanting atmosphere. He found Philip alone at one of the tables, chugging down a bottle of Gulder.

"I never knew a place like this existed," Pamson said as he sat down. There was a large pond right next to the property, separated by a fence. The white light from the outdoor lanterns glinted off the surface of the water.

"It's some young boys who are running it. Once I arrange the money, I'm going to buy the place."

Pamson brought his full attention to his old friend. Philip was dressed casually in a grey T-shirt and jeans, wearing a face-cap that hid the top of his face. Pamson was struck anew each time they met how time and success could transform someone into a different person entirely.

"I'm sure it's not going to be a small amount of money," Pamson said.

"Rayfield, of all places, it won't kam. We can start discussing while we wait for our order," Philip said, waving a waitress over. He recommended the mashed potatoes and grilled fish, then ordered it for both of them when Pamson nodded. Pamson asked for a glass of fresh pineapple juice.

"You were really serious when you stopped drinking alcohol," Philip said, surprised.

Pamson shrugged. "You thought I was joking?"

"I don't take anyone serious who says he will stop drinking."

Pamson smiled and turned his head again to look around. Pamson didn't like how small he felt beside this man, who, twenty years ago, had shared a room and mattress with him. As if some invisible part of him had been inflated so that even if Pamson couldn't see it, he still felt it. He found himself questioning everything before he said it. True, they had grown apart after Pamson had decided to learn a real skill and pursue an honourable path while Philip had taken the deep dive into politics. But Philip's enthusiasm each time they met reassured Pamson that nothing substantial had changed between them. So why did he feel somehow straitjacketed in Philip's presence?

Pamson lifted the document sitting in his lap and placed it on the table. "This is the proposal."

Philip spun it around and started to flip through it, scanning the pages quickly, nodding. Paul had produced it even more quickly than he had promised, and it hadn't taken long to get Philip's attention. He was supposed to have left that day for an official tour around the state with some of his colleagues, but he'd put off his departure to have this meeting.

"I will table it before the Speaker," Philip said, and shoved the document to the side. "But that isn't really why I wanted to see you."

Pamson frowned, then relaxed his face. "Okay."

"I'll be honest with you, Pamson. Sometimes I feel like you're not happy with me."

Pamson raised a hand and placed it on his chest. "Me?"

"Yes. Ever since that time you changed your name officially from Pam to Pamson. Around the time I became a councillor. By the way, you have to tell me why you changed it. But I wanted you to be coming around. Other people were coming, some of them I never even knew. But you, it's like the more progress I made, the more you ran away from me. Sometimes I wonder if maybe you're jealous of all that I've achieved."

"Me?" Pamson said again. "Why would I be jealous of you? I'm very happy for you. I never wanted to be a politician."

"But you had the opportunity. You and I had the same opportunity. Late Senator Garba was even prepared to be our mentor. I stayed with him. You left."

"I didn't like how he was doing things."

"What things?"

"Things mana. Things he was making us do?"

"He was training us to be politicians."

"We were thugs!" Pamson realised he had raised his voice. Philip stared at him as though trying to decide if he was losing his mind. He leaned back into his chair and softly said, "When he wanted someone to start trouble, he didn't ask his sons. They were all abroad. He sent us."

Philip let a few seconds pass, then said, "Pamson, look at me now. Tell me: Do I look like a thug to you?"

Pamson took in the expensive phone on the table's glass surface, the manicured hands and groomed beard, the black watch with a leather strap he was sure had been picked out from a store in London or someplace like that. Philip had made his point, and Pamson resented him for it.

"So you never wish you had stayed with him?" Philip said at length.

"Senator? No." Pamson kept his head steady, trying not to look away or blink. There was some truth to it in that, while his mind often returned to moments in his life that had been major crossroads, he never regretted the choice he'd made at that juncture. The understanding had settled over him one night as he supervised the shallow grave being dug by some of the boys he and Philip controlled.

Philip stands on the far side of the grave, ablaze with a coating of moonlight. Everything is alive with the silver sheen. The figures hunched over and tearing pieces out of the earth. The six dead bodies piled like great pieces of detritus, leftovers from the street clash earlier. His black sneakers being pelted by black soil. His eyes meet Philip's, and he decides in a matter of milliseconds—it's barely a decision, it's a simple knowing, like a tiny current of electricity coursing through him. This will be the last time he buries a body.

"You didn't even come to the funeral," Philip said. "His second wife asked about you."

"That was six years ago. She remembered."

"So why did you change your name?" A smile crept over Philip's face.

"Everyone had already been calling me Pamson. I liked the way it sounded. There were too many people with Pam."

"Where did that name even come from?"

"Wallahi I don't remember. Maybe Rufus or Audu, somebody with a big mouth."

They both chuckled, shaking their heads, caught for a moment in the web of remembrance.

Switching to English, Philip said, "You know I'm now the House committee chairman on Works and Transport?"

Pamson shook his head. "I don't always watch the news nowadays. Congratulations."

"It means there will be opportunities to interface with industry." Philip fell silent for a moment, then asked, "Do you understand what I'm driving at?"

Pamson shook his head slowly.

"I'm the House committee chairman for Works and Transport. You're a seasoned mechanic. You don't understand what I'm saying?"

"Do you want to give me an appointment?" Pamson said, chuckling to hide his discomfort from being so clueless.

"You've become a complete blockhead fa," Philip said in Hausa, then continued in English: "There will be contract opportunities, opportunities for all kinds of business. I can't go and create a company that anybody can tie back to me. That will be a conflict of interest. But if I can recommend an already existing company, it will be easier."

As the understanding settled on Pamson, he felt torn between thrill and concern.

"Is your business registered?"

"We're registering with CAC now."

"Business name or limited liability?"

"Business name."

Philip made a frustrated gesture, as if he wanted to dissolve Pamson into thin air with the wave of his hand. "You know my main problem with you since before is that your thinking is so small. You need to start thinking big, Pamson."

Pamson took a deep breath, resisting the urge to lash out with his own words. Paul had suggested they register the company as a limited liability, but Pamson had shot it down, saying it wasn't needed. He'd sensed Paul's frustration and that the boy had held back from pushing further only out of respect for him. Now Pamson felt like a fool, sitting here in front of his friend and being chided for being small-minded.

"You need to change it," Philip said suddenly. "Change it to a limited liability. Go with the highest share capital. If you need money, I can pay for it."

"I have money," Pamson said automatically.

Philip nodded and said, "I know. I know you have money, my man. Just let me know if I can help in any way. Once you've completed registration, we can look at things. Normally I would bring someone I trust to add to the board of directors, but I already have you. So, no need."

Pamson nodded but said nothing. Should he thank his friend or make an intelligent comment or express some measure of enthusiasm?

"All of this is assuming you're interested," Philip said. "Are you interested? Do you want to think about it?"

"I'm interested," Pamson said. "I want to do it."

Philip grinned this time, flashing his teeth broadly. He picked up his bottle. "Let's toast."

Pamson raised his juice and they clinked the glasses.

"To thinking big," Philip said.

"Cheers," Pamson said, and flashed his own teeth.

Back at home he lay awake into the night while Rahila dozed peacefully beside him. He was still adrenalised from his dinner with Philip. His thoughts were awash with images of a kind of success that he had never even entertained as a daydream, let alone as something concrete within reach. The shininess of the pictures in his head helped to quieten the nagging sense that he was somehow being dragged back into a world he had managed to escape. But the vision Philip had dangled before him during their meal seemed nothing like that former existence that was shrouded in smoke and tear gas, as his old friend had pointed out. There was nothing violent about it. No street clashes, no bodies to get rid of, no covert meetings in secret locations at odd hours with political godfathers who would rather remain anonymous. Instead, Pamson would be able to attain a level of wealth that had so far eluded him, without giving up the work that had become his true passion. With all the changes Paul had been helping him implement in the business, it seemed he was already on the right path. All he needed was to just expand his imagination a little.

The next morning, he waited in his office for eleven o'clock, when the meeting he had scheduled with Paul, Solomon, and Mark would take place. They would be discussing incorporating the company with the Corporate Affairs Commission. Paul had been so excited when Pamson told him of his decision that morning that he offered to skip his class, but Pamson had insisted he attend, which was why the meeting was not first thing. He could go out and do some work on Mama Galadima's car, but he would be distracted. Besides, he had already given Luka permission to take full responsibility of those repairs. It would be unfair to go back on his word.

A knock sounded and the door opened. It was Murmula. She stood in the doorway, looked back at something in the reception behind her, then finally entered. She had been acting strangely the last couple of days. She seemed jittery, ill at ease. He wondered if yelling at her yesterday had contributed to it and considered apologising. But that would make him look weak and perhaps give her reason to become lax. She was carrying a booklet and came and stood at the desk, right beside him. She opened to a specific page and pointed at a figure. He waited to hear what she had in mind, but she was silent. Her perfume was stronger than ever. He turned his head and looked up at her, resisting the urge to yell again.

"What is it?" he said in Hausa, trying to make his voice gentle.

The door opened before she could respond, and Solomon and Mark entered.

"Peace be upon this house," Mark said loudly.

Pamson stood up and welcomed them. When he turned back to Murmula, she was already at the door.

"Murmula."

"Sir?" she said, turning around.

"Please, can we borrow your chair briefly for this meeting?"

"Yes, sir."

"Kai Pamson, you need to stop this rubbish," Mark said. "How can you have only one chair in your office?"

"The matter has our full attention," Pamson said in jest as Murmula brought in the extra chair. She turned to leave, and she and Paul passed each other in the doorway.

Paul leaned against the wall while the others sat around the desk. They took out a number of forms and spread them out.

"The first step is to give us three names, in order of preference," Solomon said. "They will have to run searches at CAC and go with the one that's available. I'm sure your preferred name will be, it's just a formality."

"Paul, you can write down the names for them," Pamson said.

Paul grabbed a pen and tore a page from the notebook he was carrying.

"We're also going to need the names, signatures, and passport photos of all the members of the board of directors," Solomon continued. "How many will you be?"

"Myself, Paul, my wife. That's all."

"You're also going to have to decide what your share capital is and how it's distributed," Mark said. "You can start with one hundred thousand."

"We want the highest. Paul will have twenty percent, Rahila ten percent, and myself the rest."

Paul raised his head. "Uncle, maybe we can start with a lower share capital—"

"Don't worry, Paul."

"Your boy is right," Solomon said. "The higher the share capital, the more expensive your registration fee will be."

"Not to mention our own fee," Mark said with a grin.

"You're going to give me a big discount after all the business I've brought for you two," Pamson said. "How long will it take?"

"As soon you fill out the forms and give us the money, we will carry on. All in all, we can finish it in a week, if there are no issues with the portal in Abuja."

"We'll fill out the forms now," Pamson said. "I have my passport photo and Rahila's."

Everybody looked at him.

"What about her signature?" Solomon said.

"I can forge it," Pamson said with a straight face. "She has the simplest signature. She won't mind. I'm sure even Paul could do it."

Paul smiled and nodded sheepishly.

"This is the kind of talk I like to hear," Mark said. "No wasting time when there is money to be made." He slapped Pamson a high five.

12

Murmula stood over the desk, thinking about what had just happened in Mr. Pamson's office. If she had used the knife then, the lawyers and Paul would have walked in on her. It was reckless to have even considered that. What if they had discovered the knife on her by mistake? Killing the chicken had injected boldness into her blood, but it was not like killing a man. If measured against each other, the two couldn't even be tested on the same scale. A spasm seized her body and didn't let go until she hurried outside and around the back of the building. She steadied herself with a hand against the wall, bent over, and tried to get her breathing under control. Her head felt like it was about to float away into the atmosphere. She closed her eyes and remained still for several minutes. When she opened them again, feeling anchored to the earth once more, she noticed she stood next to a clump of wild nettles and tall grass that had commandeered this portion of the compound. Stolen land, all of this, she was sure of it.

Unable to work without a chair, she went out to Maman Ivie's stand and apologised for walking by yesterday without saying goodbye. Maman Ivie offered her some leftover ƙosai that was still warm and refused to take payment. She took it back to her desk and ate slowly with a toothpick.

Realising she couldn't finish the ƙosai, she stood on the verandah and called over Thankgod, who was sitting under a shed playing a game with some bottle caps.

"Will you eat?" she said when he was standing in front of her.

He took it immediately and said, "Nagode."

Before he could turn away, Murmula said, "What about Bala?"

"He's sick. His mother sent to say he has chickenpox."

"What about you?"

"Me?"

"Aren't you afraid you might have it?"

"I already had my own. Didn't they say if you have it once, you can't have it again?"

"That's true."

He had started eating the ƙosai with his dusty hands right there.

"Do you live far from here?"

"In Tudun Wada." Thankgod pointed vaguely.

"Can you walk, or do you have to enter keke?"

"I don't have any money to spend on keke. So I walk."

"How long does it take you?"

"Like two hours."

"Two hours? Isn't Tudun Wada nearby?"

"It is. But sometimes my leg pains me so badly I have to go slowly." He tapped the leg but didn't say more. He had finished the ƙosai and was standing there rubbing his oily hands over his skin as though putting on a lotion.

Murmula could tell he was lying, preying on her sympathy. "Are you full?"

He shook his head.

She went to her purse on the desk, fished out a hundred-naira note, and brought it back to him. "Buy ƙosai of fifty naira, bring the change back, and keep it on my—"

"Thankgod!" It was Luka, who had raised his head from under the hood of the car he had been working on. He looked peeved. "What are you doing there? Stop fooling around; I want you to go and buy me fuel."

"Please don't be angry, Luka," Murmula shouted across the yard. "I was just sending him to get me some kosai. Can he go after he brings it?"

Luka glared at her, then lowered his head back under the hood again. She could hear him grumbling to himself.

"Kosai of fifty only. Leave the change on my desk. I'm going to use the ladies' room."

She fished out a key from the drawer and made her way toward the back of the property where the toilets were. It had been one of the first things she had asked for: a private toilet she could use since she was the only female. She had been surprised at the speed with which it had been raised, the soakaway pit dug, the water closet system installed. On her way back, she decided to stop by the light-gold Mitsubishi, where Luka was working.

"Did Oga ever tell you that I'm interested in cars?" she said.

Luka raised his head, looked pointedly at her, and returned to his task. "Is that so?"

"Yes. I want to learn about them. I want to build them one day."

Luka pulled his head from under the open hood and wiped his hands on a rag. There was that stupid look again, a smile that wasn't a smile but an impossible blend of pity and spite. "Is that so?"

"Yes, that is so."

Luka nodded. "Okay." He moved to the other side of the hood and plunged his hand back into the car's entrails. He had wound a strange-looking chain around a cylindrical object and was trying to pry it loose.

"What are you doing?"

"Trying to remove the oil filter."

"What does it do?"

"It keeps the oil in the engine clean."

"What about the brakes? Which ones are the brakes?"

Luka raised his head. "Aunty, I have serious work today, if you don't mind. I can't be doing this and answering stupid questions."

Murmula was still processing Luka's rudeness when she stepped back into the reception and saw the fifty-naira change beside her purse. Luka didn't like her. He gave off a sense that he was somehow better than this place, than all of them. From day one, she had sensed a cold, joyless inclination from him toward the boys under his care. She didn't like the relentless harsh tone he used with them, the way he seemed to always threaten violence at them and sometimes followed through on those threats. He had sent a wheel spanner whirling at Bala's head a few days earlier, and her heart had stopped. But the boy had ducked with such fluid ease, laughing as he did, which confused her all the more. With his straight posture and gentle swagger that seemed to function as a limp at the same time, Luka seemed to be communicating to anyone who cared to pay attention that this wasn't his final station in life, that he had bigger things ahead of him. Fastidious to a fault, he always had a bath behind the storage room at the end of each day. He arrived in clean clothes each morning, changed into his filthy blue overalls (he was the only person who wore overalls), and left each evening without any indication on his clothes or skin that he had spent the day around grease and motor oil. For all his arrogance, she knew that Pamson trusted him, and she wished there was a way to undo that, set him in his place for the way he had just spoken to her.

The door to Mr. Pamson's office opened, and Paul poked his head out. They hadn't spoken since he had tried reaching her yesterday. She needed to think of what to say to him before their meeting ended.

"Uncle is calling you," he said icily and went back inside.

Murmula stood at the door.

"Ehen, Murmula," Mr. Pamson said, "do you have any cash here with you?"

"Yes, sir. I haven't yet taken this week's payments to the bank."

"How much?"

"About a hundred and fifty."

"Thousand?" said the big man with the annoying, grating voice. Murmula remembered seeing him at the Pamsons' on the day they'd had their thanksgiving. "Do you have a safe?"

"No," Paul said. "We're working on getting one."

"You can't be keeping that kind of money around without a safe," the other man said.

"You either go to the bank every day or every two days, or get a safe," the big man said.

Murmula nodded uncertainly, trying to be polite. "Okay, sir."

"Murmula, please bring all the cash you have with you."

"Okay, sir."

She returned to the desk and pulled open the cash drawer. There were loose five hundreds and one thousands scattered about, but the fat bundle that Honourable Bot had given her was missing. Over one hundred thousand naira. She usually locked the drawer each night and hid the key, but left it open during the day with the key dangling from its lock, as it now did. The money had been there when she opened the office. There had been no transactions all morning, so she hadn't needed to access it again. Then she remembered why she had opened it not long ago.

She marched out of the reception. In the yard, she stood and cast her eyes about until she spotted Thankgod walking in the direction of the toilet. She followed him, making her way down the incline, wary of the loose boulders that formed the path. When she rounded a bend, she found him with his back to her, urinating against the fence. She waited for him to finish.

When he turned and saw her, his eyes went wide.

"Where is it?" she said, baring her teeth, closing the distance between them.

"What?" The word trembled on his lips.

Murmula gripped the front of his shirt. "If you make me ask you one more time, I will drag you to Oga's office right now. Where is it?"

Thankgod shook as he raised his hand and pointed at the toilet building behind them.

"Go and bring it. I'm waiting."

The boy disappeared around the building. When he returned less than a minute later, he was brushing off sand from a black plastic bag. He handed it to her. The money was inside. She could tell from its appearance that the cash was all there; the seal that bound the notes together was also intact. When she raised her eyes, Thankgod had tears and snot streaming down his face.

"Because of God, Aunty. Please. Because of God. I won't do it again."

"Why did you take it, Thankgod?"

The boy remained silent while his tears fell. The consequences would be severe if she reported this. He might be let go from his apprenticeship. Then what would he do? What would his mother do? She could just keep it quiet, go and hand the cash over, pretend this had never happened. But suddenly she had an idea.

"I won't report you to Oga, but only if you agree to do what I ask."

Thankgod nodded, wiping his tears away.

"Somebody is going to have to bear responsibility for this, because I already told Oga the money was missing. It's either going to be you or someone else. Do you understand?"

Thankgod nodded.

"Are you willing to say that you saw Luka taking this money?"

Thankgod took this in, hesitated for a moment. Then he nodded again, but slowly.

"I've seen the way he treats you boys around here. It's not right. He doesn't treat me well either. If someone has to leave this garage, it's Luka. Don't you agree?"

Another nod.

"Do you know where he keeps his bag and his clothes?"

"Yes. Inside the store."

"I want you to go and put this inside his bag. Then come back and tell me when you've done it. Hide the money in your pocket. Don't run."

She stood there waiting, her mind turning frantically, searching for any gaps in her plan. She had been toeing the border of recklessness all morning, but nothing else stood to give her satisfaction. Luka had to pay for his insolence.

Thankgod returned, walking slowly down the slope toward her—too slowly, she realised.

"Have you done it?"

"Yes."

"When they ask you, say that you saw him enter the reception when I went to the toilet. And after he came out, he went straight to the store. Repeat what I just said."

He repeated it word for word.

"Go and continue with what you were doing. Don't say anything. Do you understand?"

Thankgod nodded and headed back to the front yard. She followed after him, rehearsing the words she would use once she stepped into that office. There would be no way to undo whatever damage this would cause. She paused with her hand on the door handle. What was she doing? If this backfired, it would sink her plans completely. But it was too late to back out now. She took another deep breath and went inside.

Everybody looked up at her.

"Murmula," Mr. Pamson said, "what's taking so long? We've been waiting."

"There's a problem, sir."

"What is it?"

"The money has been stolen," she said slowly.

More than one person said, "What?"

Paul, who had been against the wall, snapped into attention.

"Where was it?" Mr. Pamson said.

"In the drawer where I normally keep the cash."

"Didn't you lock it?" Paul said.

"I lock it at night. But nobody comes around my desk."

"So who could have taken it?" Mr. Pamson said.

"I was asking around before I came here; Thankgod said he saw something."

"What did he see?" Mr. Pamson said impatiently.

"I think you should hear it from him yourselves."

"Go and call him."

The boy was with Luka when she shouted his name across the yard.

"He's doing something for me here," Luka yelled back.

"Oga wants to see him."

She entered the office behind Thankgod, closed the door, and stood against the wall. Thankgod stood among the men, visibly terrified. He looked like he might change his mind and run out of the office. Mr. Pamson said in Hausa, "Thankgod, did you see something?" Thankgod turned and looked at her briefly. For a split second, she believed he would forget everything they had discussed and destroy her plan.

"Yes, Oga."

"What was it?"

"I saw Oga Luka enter the reception when Aunty went to the toilet."

There was a heavy silence.

"When was this?" Pamson said quietly.

"Not long ago," Thankgod said.

"Did you see him take the money?" the smaller, darker man said.

Thankgod shook his head. "But when he came out of the reception, he went straight to the store."

"Is that where he keeps his things?" the big man said.

"Yes," Thankgod said.

"Go and call Luka. Let us ask him," Pamson said.

Before Thankgod could move, the big man said in Hausa, "He will deny it ai. He will say he doesn't know anything."

Murmula cleared her throat. "Can I say something, sir?" She didn't know why she felt the need to speak in English. Everyone looked at her, and the many stares hit her like one giant stare. She pushed past her nervousness and said, " Maybe Thankgod made a mistake. Even if Luka went inside the reception, it's possible he didn't take anything. Luka has worked with you a long time. If you accuse him of anything without proof, it will affect the relationship."

"So what are you suggesting?" Mr. Pamson said.

"You should go to the store and search his bag. If you don't find anything, we will know he didn't take the money. He doesn't have to know that you suspected him of theft."

"I like the way your receptionist's mind works," the big man said.

"What if he has the money in his overalls?" Paul said.

"We will worry about that later," Pamson said. "Murmula is correct. Luka shouldn't know for now, just in case he's innocent." He stood up and said in Hausa, "Thankgod, take me to his bag. The rest of you should wait here so that we don't attract attention."

After they left, the big man stood up and stretched. "Theft," he said in Hausa. "Theft is a serious thing. I hate hearing about it. It's like a cancer, it'll just be eating you quietly from inside; you won't know."

Murmula stood on the verandah, holding her breath. Luka was still bent over the Mitsubishi, oblivious to all that she had set in motion around him. Paul came over and stood beside her.

"What happened to your phone?" he said quietly. She could hear the masked sound of hurt underneath.

"My battery died and there was no light. I had to go and attend to an emergency. I'm sorry."

"What was the emergency?"

"My cousin had food poisoning. She was in the hospital; there was no one to stay with her."

She kept her face pointed away from him, toward the yard. It was important that when she lied to him, she did it with shame, face averted. She could lie barefacedly to others, but not to him. It might be the only way to preserve an essential part of herself, the part that was soft and thrummed with warmth and goodness. It might be the only way back to herself once the deed was done. Then she remembered what Musty had said. Would Paul really sell her out to save his life? Under different circumstances, would he raise a weapon against her because she was a Muslim? What would he do if he could read her mind, if he could see the real colour of her heart?

"How is she?" Paul said.

Before Murmula could respond, Mr. Pamson's voice rose sharply, an explosion slicing the air. "Luka!"

Murmula and Paul stepped out into the yard. Mr. Pamson was walking up from the store, holding a wad of cash in one hand. Thankgod was coming up behind him. Luka had stopped what he was doing and begun to move toward Mr. Pamson.

Mr. Pamson raised the money when only a few feet separated them. "What is this?"

Luka stared at the money for a long time. His hands were wiping themselves on his overalls, seemingly of their own volition. "Oga, I don't understand."

"I found this in your bag."

"My bag?" Luka said.

"Murmula!" Pamson yelled.

She rushed forward and he threw the cash at her. She barely caught it.

"Count it."

Her fingers moved quickly, flipping the notes one after the other. She finished and said, "One hundred and fifty thousand."

"Does that look like the money Honourable Bot gave you?"

"It's the one, sir. I remember this mark," she said, pointing at a purple ink stain.

Mr. Pamson turned to Luka fully. "Luka! You stole from me?" The inflection in his voice told Murmula a nerve had been hit. "From me! After everything I've done for you."

"Oga, wallahi, I don't know anything about this." Luka suddenly looked small, a little more slouched.

"I found it myself, inside your bag!" Pamson said again, taking a step toward Luka.

"Oga, someone put it there. Wallahi someone put it there."

"How could you do such a thing, Luka? When you're the one who should be setting a good example for these boys?"

Luka suddenly turned and looked at the faces bearing witness. Mr. Pamson's guests had come outside and stood on the verandah beside Paul. Luka's eyes fell on her, and he raised a finger and pointed.

"Oga, she's the one! I know she's the one, that bitch!"

"Hey!" she heard a voice behind her say. Paul came into her peripheral vision suddenly, and she turned to see him properly. He looked livid, but something had stopped him in his tracks. By the time she looked back, Mr. Pamson already had Luka in a chokehold. He smacked him in the face, again and again. Luka tried to ward off the blows. The two men jostled for a moment. Luka tried to get away, but Mr. Pamson's grip was a vice. Luka slipped on the blackened, oil-slicked ground and fell, dragging Mr. Pamson down with him. They rolled around for a moment. Mr. Pamson, despite his girth, got up first. He started kicking Luka. Each time the steel-toed boot connected with Luka's flesh, he released a cry of anguish. Paul took a step forward, but Mr. Pamson's big friend put an arm out in front of him, blocking his way.

"Never pity a thief," he said with a shake of his head.

Mr. Pamson dragged Luka to his feet and levelled a punch right into his face. He grabbed the scruff of his neck and hit him again. "You think you can steal from me?" The next punch laid Luka flat on the ground. "After everything I've done for you!" Mr. Pamson's voice sounded unstoppered, a boiling vat of water overflowing, a train car that had gone off its rails. Maman Ivie had come over to stand by the gate and watch. "Do you know who I am?" Mr. Pamson stumbled around, and at first Murmula wasn't sure what he was doing. He seemed intoxicated, made unhinged by his rage. But finally he bent over the toolbox that sat open in the shed and pulled out a large adjustable spanner. Murmula realised he had been looking for something to wield. "You don't know who I am." Mr. Pamson bent over Luka, grabbed his shirt, and struck him over the head with the spanner. The ugly sound of bone on metal that followed made Murmula shut her eyes. "I'll kill you here and nothing will happen!" Mr. Pamson shouted. "Go and ask about me in Angwan Rukuba and Eto Baba." He slammed the spanner into Luka's temple. "Are you mad? Daring to steal from me?" Mr. Pamson stood up and threw the bloody spanner at Luka. The younger man was nearly lifeless on the ground. His head was a red, bloody mass.

Mr. Pamson spun around and pointed his finger at the watching boys. "Let this be a lesson to all of you. Anybody who tries to steal from me, I'll kill that person with these hands." He used the back of one of said hands to wipe the spittle that had accumulated in the corners of his lips. He was breathing hard. He raised his finger and pointed again at Luka. "If you insult that girl in front of me again, I'll break your teeth. Go and pack your things and get out of my garage. I never want to see your face here again."

The sight of tears on Luka's bashed-in face stilled something in her. He brushed off the mud stains on his clothes as he limped in the direction of the store. Mr. Pamson stood there, breathless, the contortion of rage on his face slowly relaxing.

Later, after Mr. Pamson's friends had left, Paul walked up to her in the reception and wrapped his arms around her. She buried her face in his chest and started to sob, wondering as she did if it was part of the act or if she was just trying to shed off a burden that had become too much. Paul had been prepared to fight Luka because of her. She felt a little bit dirtier.

"I'm sorry you had to hear that," Paul said. "I'll call you later."

The rest of the day unfolded without event. She tried to continue with her work, but she couldn't get the image of what Mr. Pamson had done to Luka out of her head. What would he do to her if he knew who she really was? He spent the afternoon working in the yard. A few customers came and went. She wrote them receipts and registered their payments in the accounting software. She would offer them cold water from the cooler while they waited in the lobby, accepting compliments from them about how special this was, that they didn't have to sit outside in the sun and the dust and the noise of the yard. A few work emails from Paul, but one of them was him just checking in to see how she was doing.

Around 3:00 p.m., Mr. Pamson came inside and invited her into his office. She followed him and stood by the door while he went over to his desk. He turned back to her with his food warmer in his hands.

"Please don't be angry," he said. "I usually send one of the boys, but they've all been sent on errands. Could you wash this and tell Maman Ivie to put two pieces of meat with the rice? I'm very hungry."

Murmula was out on the verandah, on her way to the tap beside the building, when she stopped and looked at the green food container in her hands. It was orb-like, shaped like those oranges hawked in traffic or sold in the market with their tops and bottoms sliced away. The answer she had been looking for was right in front of her the whole time, but she hadn't been paying attention. When she returned the food warmer with his lunch in it, the door was still open and Mr. Pamson was behind his desk, his head lowered. He didn't seem to notice her presence immediately. He raised his head and nudged his eyes with a fist. Tears.

"Are you all right, sir?" she said quietly, despising the sound of her own voice.

"I'm fine," he said with a forced smile. "Thank you."

She performed her prayers that evening, cleaned up in the kitchen, and then walked through the darkly lit backyard and knocked on Musty's door. She hadn't been able to shake off the image of Luka's battered form on the black, greasy ground. She had seen the real Dareng Pamson today, and it terrified her.

Musty closed the door when she entered and turned to face her. The room's red light bathed him like blood on his skin. Murmula looked at her arms. She was covered in the same stuff as well.

"Is it done?" he said.

No words had passed between them after she had killed the chicken, but she knew it had impressed him. Yet over the course of the day, she had made peace with the realisation that she couldn't do to a human being what she had done to that chicken, no matter how much she tried to convince herself otherwise. Now she swallowed the lump that appeared in her throat and placed his penknife in his hand. He looked down at it, back up at her, confused.

"I think I've found the best way to do it," she said.

13

There was something stuck in Pamson's throat when he woke up. His first thought was that a piece of food had clambered back up his gullet and lodged itself right below his Adam's apple. Maybe the orange he had eaten on his way home from Jonah's Baked Delight last night. He swallowed, but it didn't go away. It could only be one thing—a lump of anxiety. It had to do with what day it was and the tangle of reasons it held: it was Rahila's birthday, which meant he was going to be baking her cake; the baby's due date had come and gone two days prior, and they were all holding their breaths, hoping it might be today; and ever since he'd fired Luka earlier that week, he'd carried around something in his chest that resembled a confused fusion of hurt and remorse. Despite this clarity, he still couldn't shake off the dread. Yes, that was the better word: *dread*, fargaba.

He went through the day slicked in it. He arrived at the garage a little after eight. Murmula was already there, but only Al'amis had arrived. He sent him to buy him ƙosai in his green food warmer. The boy brought it back filled to the brim and barely closing, more than the amount he had paid for. He didn't know when Maman Ivie was going to stop this nonsense. How would he make her understand that he didn't need the extra portions she gave him? Now that he was thinking more as a businessman, thanks to Paul, maybe he could point out to her that she was in danger of killing her trade if she continued like this. He ate only one or two pieces of ƙosai before losing his appetite. The rest of the boys had come in by then, and he gave the rest of his meal to them. He didn't know why he had let Jonah talk him into committing to ice the cake in addition to baking it. Jonah had flat-out refused Pamson's request for help with the icing, flipping it around and shoving it back at him with the words, "How much do you love your wife?"

After his ƙosai, he spent the next four hours working in the yard. With Luka gone, he had to pick up the slack. He installed a new fuel pump inside a Toyota Camry, which had taken longer than the thirty minutes he'd assured the client because the old fuel pump's rubber seal was stuck and had to be melted off with a candle. He carried out the operation holding his breath while sweat propagated on his forehead, fully aware that fewer than five inches below were several litres of petrol. When he was done, he realised that the idea of icing a cake terrified him more than the reckless procedure he had just executed. He replaced the entire support system on the front wheels of a Peugeot 206, which lasted three hours because none of his spare-parts suppliers had the correct bushings. When he went into the reception, the Peugeot's owner, a slender young man with glasses, was fast asleep in one of the guest chairs. Before going into his office, Pamson gave Murmula the details of the bill and asked her to wake up the client.

He sat behind his desk and drank Maman Ivie's cold kunu. He dropped his hand to his stomach. He was starving. He needed to eat before heading out to Jonah's. Murmula was alone in the reception when he went out again.

"Can you send one of the boys to get me rice," he said. "Two goat meat, as usual." He gave her the cash.

"What about the food warmer, sir?" Murmula said.

"Ask Al'amis or Thankgod."

He went back inside and saw that he had missed a call from Solomon. There was also a text from Philip asking if the registration had already been completed. He decided to call Solomon back before replying to Philip's text. Solomon answered on the first buzz and explained that they needed more money for the registration.

"But I gave you the money you asked for, Solo," Pamson said, trying to keep his voice steady.

"If you're going to get a share capital of up to five million, you have to pay more. They've increased the money."

"Since when? I thought this is something you do every day."

"You don't know CAC. They can be difficult to deal with."

"How much more?"

"Two hundred thousand."

"Two hundred thousand?" Pamson shouted. "Haba, Solo!"

"I know the money is much. I'm sorry to have to be doing this. But if we want to move quickly, that's the amount we're going to pay."

Pamson sat quietly for a moment, thinking. "I want to see the announcement from CAC about the price increase," he said finally.

"They don't ever announce it officially. That's just how it is."

Pamson shut his eyes, trying to contain his growing rage.

"Dareng, I'm your friend," Solomon said, sounding a little wounded. "We've been together for years. I would never cheat you."

"I need to think, Solo. Let me call you back."

"Okay, can you send one hundred, just so we don't have to stop the process?"

"I'll call you back."

Pamson hung up. He was still thinking a few minutes later when Paul called about needing to do more to standardise the business's accounting process. He said it was the only way for them to ensure profitability and a fair wage for all the workers.

"Paul, you know that I only have a diploma in mechanical engineering. All of this accounting grammar you're blowing, I don't understand."

"Our business needs to be predictable," he said. "If you collect two thousand today from someone for servicing their car and you collect five hundred from another person for doing the same thing, we can't predict the amount of money that will come in. But with a price list, we can say that if five people come on a normal daily basis to service their cars and we charge one thousand for that, we will be making five thousand naira every day from just the servicing of cars. So we can put it on the price list, but we will also put on it everything else you do. The customers that normally deal directly with you who you're shy to charge big money, if they only see Murmula or me and we show them a price list, they will understand that you mean business."

"Okay," Pamson said, his mind spinning. "But what did you say about workers' wages?"

"If we're going to make this a formal business with proper accounting and tax filings, you're going to have to stop using child labour."

"Child labour?"

"Those boys that work for you are underage. If this was America, you would be prosecuted for using child labour."

"But this is not America," Pamson said heatedly. "And I'm teaching them how to fix cars. They should be paying *me* for the experience they're getting."

"We will have to find a way of packaging it. Maybe call it an educational internship for the less privileged. You can ask Aunty for ideas; her organisation may be able to even partner with you."

"I'll think about it," Pamson said. "But listen, Paul—slow down with your changes. There are too many things happening very fast. Even I am feeling dizzy. Slow down a little."

"My job is to speed things up, Uncle. Time is money," Paul said with a laugh and hung up.

Five minutes later, his meal arrived. After Thankgod had left and closed the door, Pamson opened the food warmer. A cloud of aromatic steam ballooned into his face. He closed his eyes and took it in. He opened them again and looked at the jollof rice with peas and carrots and golden slices of fried plantain. Two large chunks of goat meat crowned the meal like prizes. His hunger had evaporated, and the dread hadn't let up. He had a suspicion that Solomon and Mark were trying to get more money out of him; perhaps they were unhappy that he had negotiated their lawyers' fees so low. Now Philip was breathing down his neck. He needed to bake this cake and get through to the end of the day. He decided it was time.

He closed the food warmer, packed up his things, and went outside. As he passed through the lobby, he told Murmula he was closing for the day. In the yard, he called over Thankgod and Al'amis and gave them the food warmer.

"Make sure you wash it properly with omo and take it back to the office," he barked before hopping into the car.

He drove with the radio turned off. He decided to take the long route through Bukuru to clear his head. He was worried about Rahila and the baby. She seemed fine and kept insisting there was nothing to worry about, as they were still within the safe-window period. He had only wished her a happy birthday that morning but hadn't yet given her the card and the gift he'd got her. He didn't want to ruin the planned surprise. Hopefully, after tonight, everything would return to normal; nothing would ever come between them again. The baby would arrive soon. The business would grow. Everything would work out in the end.

Yakubu Gowon Way was largely clear of vehicles. He let the BMW glide down the highway, keeping his foot completely off the brake. The breeze cascaded sideways through the windows and into his face. He turned off the highway at D.B. Zang Junction, drove up the road that would take him into the heart of Bukuru, and made a U-turn in front of St. Jarlath's Catholic Church. By the time he drove up to Jonah's Baked Delight, he was feeling better.

Jonah said very little and kept to his side of the kitchen, only throwing brief glances in Pamson's direction. Pamson was going to bake a three-tier cake. He placed the batter for each tier into its pan and slid them all into the oven. While they cooked, he tried to occupy himself with the poem he had been writing. It had been Jonah's idea, even though Jonah had refused to help in that regard too. He only offered to look it over when it was finished. It had been over a week, and he still wasn't sure what to make of it. He crossed out the last line he had written, then wrote it again in the same order.

The timer rang, and he removed the cakes and tipped them out of their pans. They thudded onto the counter like oranges snapping from their branches and hitting the ground. They were perfectly brown, without any hint of burning. He stood for a moment, feeling a little outside of himself. He had made these perfect things. Next, he lined up the icing tools: The butter-icing mix—a deep minty green, because that was Rahila's favourite colour. The spatula and scraper that Jonah had used to demonstrate for him last week. The rotating cake stand. Jonah came over and watched silently while he placed the largest tier on the cake stand and started to lay the icing. Pamson's hands shook, but he ignored them until they no longer existed, only the tools they wielded. The way he lathered on the green stuff reminded him of the grease they applied to the end of a crankshaft before sliding it back into the wheel. And the way he smeared it in layers reminded him of Yunusa, his panel beater, and the several coatings he applied to a vehicle before the paint job was done. But perhaps it reminded him most of those three years he spent in his early twenties after quitting Senator Garba's employ; first he'd been a mason's assistant, then a mason. The scooping and spreading of plaster on walls, the shaping of it, the soft and assuring scrapy sounds it made against the spatula. They were twin professions, plastering a wall and icing a cake, the sharp, clean finish on a process that produced an otherwise rudimentary outcome. An untreated wall and an untreated cake were the same thing. They were the failure to fully envision and maximise potential. They were the failure to imagine. He saw it in his life and in his work. The failure to imagine. In breaking away from his former life, he had settled for the first version of bliss he had ever known. He had grown comfortable, failed to imagine further, deeper into the future. Philip, on the other hand, had transfigured himself completely. What was that thing Mary had said to him, that it was impossible to alter the past? That it was undeletable? But Philip had found a way to delete his past, while he, Pamson, hadn't. He may have changed his name, but that was merely a superficial fix, like swapping labels on a shitty product. It all came down to a failure of imagination. But that was about to change.

After he had done three coatings, he flattened out the icing with his scraper, enjoying the effortless spinning of the cake stand as though it had become the wheel of a smooth, silent car that was bearing him somewhere far-off but safe. His hands shook as he inscribed the words at the base of the cake: *Happy Birthday, Rahila*.

Pamson and Jonah stood next to each other and surveyed the work. Pamson realised he was holding his breath, and that tears had filled his eyes. He blinked them away. The cake looked like something out of the many culinary magazines Jonah had in his office. And it was he, Dareng Pamson, with the bloodstained hands and the grease-stained hands, who had done it. The two lower tiers of the cake represented the two decades that Rahila had been married to him, one tier for each decade. The sweetness increased with each tier, and the top tier was his promise to his wife that their future would be sweeter than ever. Unlike with the other tiers, brandy, dates, and raisins had gone into this one. They would cut up and share the other cakes with the people in their lives, but this topmost, crowning cake was for them alone. It would last them years. They would be reminded each time they ate it of the promise he had made once when his wife had turned forty-five and had given birth to their child.

It was already past four by the time he was driving home. He kept glancing at the cake through the rearview mirror, worried a bump on the road would cause it to topple out of the back seat. He went reasonably slow, keeping his eyes on the clock, because Rahila left work at five, and it was imperative that he get the cake set up and have it waiting for her when she walked through the door.

Paul was at home. The cake required two people to carry it, and together they manoeuvred it through the front door and placed it on the living room coffee table, the curved edge of the cake board shooting out over the lip.

"Aunty's cake," Paul said to no one, staring at it. "It looks like a wedding cake."

They set out the drinks that Paul had bought; the jollof rice, peppered chicken, and salad he had made; and the gifts they had both got her.

"What did you buy for her?" Pamson asked, staring at the wrapped square several times the size of his own present.

Paul shook his head. "It'll be a surprise."

They both waited for her in the living room with the TV on. Manchester United was playing against Everton, but Pamson's mind wasn't on the game. They heard her car honking, and Paul hurried to get the gate. When Rahila tottered in and saw the things on the coffee table, she stopped in her tracks. Pamson stood up, his tongue suddenly airy and vacant.

"Welcome back," he said in Hausa. Feeling outside of himself once more, he went and embraced her.

Paul ran in a moment after, out of breath, and shouted, "Surprise!" Then he seemed to realise it wasn't the time for it as he saw them clinging to each other.

Pamson didn't know where the embrace began or ended between them; he didn't know who was holding whom. They finally pulled apart, and he led Rahila to the sofa, where she sat down. She was watching him. He could sense her deep shock, but he wanted to move past it quickly.

"How was your day?" he said.

"It was fine."

Pamson picked up the plate. "Do you want rice?" He dished rice on her plate when she nodded. She wanted chicken and salad too.

"Uncle, let me do it," Paul said.

"Sit down," Pamson said. "I'll serve you too."

They sat around the table and ate the meal, watching the football game unfold. Rahila enjoyed football, another thing he had always loved about her. Once again, Pamson felt like a spectator, watching himself, his wife, and this boy who was the closest thing they had to a child for the moment, sharing this experience. The commentary passed between them like a ball. Each time he laughed at her outburst, he marvelled at the sensation of being amused by his own wife. The pleasure stunned him. Where had he been? What had he been doing his whole marriage? Was it conceivable that such happiness could be his? After everything he had done?

"Who made this?" Rahila said after she'd taken a bite of the cake.

"Do you like it?"

"It's delicious."

"I made it."

Rahila stopped chewing and stared at him. Paul, whose eyes had been glued to the TV, also turned his head.

"Truly?"

Pamson nodded, smiling. He pushed past his embarrassment and explained how he had done it, the classes he'd been taking, hence the late nights. Afterward, he could feel the glances she stole at him, as though trying to be certain it was still her husband seated there beside her.

Paul left to get scissors so Rahila could start opening the presents. A moment later, he came back into the living room and stood over them.

"I forgot something at the garage," he said quietly. "I have to go and get it. You can open the gifts without me?"

"What is it?" Pamson said.

"It's just a document." The boy seemed subdued. "Aunty, can I use your car?"

Rahila nodded. She looked at Pamson after Paul had left.

"I can wait for him to come back before opening the present."

Pamson nodded his agreement, and she returned her attention to the TV. They sat in silence, watching the match, but Pamson sensed from her restless twitching that her mind was barely with the game. Neither was his.

Paul hadn't returned by 8:00 p.m. As though by some act of cosmic synchronisation, it started to rain right on the hour. The power went out three minutes later. Pamson called Paul's number, but he didn't answer.

"Maybe you should go and see," Rahila said.

"I don't know where he is."

"He said he was going to the garage."

"But he could be anywhere."

At seventeen minutes to nine, Pamson picked up his keys and headed to the door. His phone rang just as he pulled it open. It was Paul.

"Paul, lafiya?"

"Lafiya, Uncle. I'm on my way back."

"What is going on?"

"I'll explain when I arrive."

Pamson and Rahila were waiting in the living room when Paul entered. Rain dripped off his drenched clothes, forming a pool around his feet that reflected white light from the rechargeable lamp they had on.

"Paul, what is it?" Rahila said.

"There was an emergency," Paul said. "But it's fine now. Can I explain after I change?"

They continued to wait in the living room until he returned in dry shorts and a white T-shirt. He sat across from them and seemed to choose his words carefully as he spoke. After they had listened and said good night, they went to bed and lay listening to the rain on the roof. Pamson could tell Rahila was awake because she kept releasing a heavy sigh every few minutes.

"What a strange story," she said finally.

Pamson made a sound from the bottom of his throat. He didn't know how to respond.

"But he said everything is fine now."

"Yes," Pamson said. "I'll see for myself in the morning."

There was a pause; then Rahila said in English, "It was a nice evening."

"It was kam," Pamson said. "Apart from when Paul had to go out."

"Yes."

"Yes," he said again.

He realised a moment later what he'd just said, and they both laughed at the same time. But Rahila didn't stop laughing after a minute, and it occurred to him that it wasn't laughter. He inched closer and drew her into his arms. Her head was now leaning on his chest.

"You're crying," he said quietly.

"I'm sorry, I'm just very happy. This was such a nice evening."

"Okay," Pamson said. A warm feeling was spreading through his chest. "Good."

"You've never hugged me when I came home from work."

He fell silent.

"You really hurt me, Dareng."

"I'm sorry. I won't do it again."

"You stopped calling me baby."

"I will be doing more of that from now on."

Rahila was silent for a moment, then said, "Thank you for the cake. You must have put a lot of work into it."

"It's the hardest thing I've ever done," he said, chuckling. A few more seconds passed; then he said, "I'm worried about the baby."

"I spoke with the doctor today. He said if nothing happens at forty weeks, they will induce. Do you want to feel the baby?"

"Yes," Pamson said with a surge of joy.

"Okay. I'll tell you when she moves."

"She?"

"Yes. Ultrasound. I've known for some time. But I was angry with you."

"I'm sorry."

"I'm sorry too."

Pamson closed his eyes. The knowledge that he would be a father had introduced an illumination into his life, but one whose source he couldn't discern. Now that he knew his child would be a girl, the illumination took on a definite quality. Like a blurred image that had suddenly come into focus. He could ascertain its nature; he could discern its source. He had known before that change was essential, inevitable, but now he knew how he must go about it.

"She just moved," Rahila said.

She took his hand and placed it on her belly. At first all he could feel was the warmth of his wife's body, which startled and comforted him all at once. How he had missed it. Her hand on his; his hand against the smooth, silken grain of her nightgown. All a kind of sanctuary. Then he felt a sudden tiny jerk.

"Jesus!" he cried.

Rahila let out a laugh, and her belly shuddered with each rumble. It seemed to excite the baby, because he felt a series of kicks in quick succession. Something like pure, concentrated joy swished through him. He, Dareng Pamson, had made this. He, with the stained hands and the stained soul, had made this.

"She's so active," Rahila said.

"She must be playing football in there."

"It is in your stomach they will play football," Rahila said, reaching over and tapping his head. That gave him permission to raise her head and squash his body deeper against hers. He kissed her, then buried his face in her neck. How good it felt to hold her, the woman who was his wife and no one else's. Next thing he knew, she was hitching up her nightgown, reaching into his shorts. Her hand came out filled with all of him.

He could barely restrain himself. "Can you do it?"

A vigorous nod was all he received.

Afterward, they lay wordlessly, their bodies conjoined and peaceful. Her back was pressed to his chest, and his hand was on her belly. He felt the kicking of the child through the silky nightgown, falling asleep to the rhythm of his daughter's existence. He woke up to the endless sound of rain and tried stirring under the suffocating weight of sleep. He was vaguely aware of two things: that it wasn't yet morning and that Rahila wasn't in bed. Sleep won, and he foundered in its embrace.

14

Her heart struggled viciously against her ribs the whole time, as though it would sprout hands and rip the cage apart and escape. She waited until Mr. Pamson had walked out of the yard. She waited until she heard his car pull away. She waited until the sound had faded completely from her hearing. At last she stood up and took slow, steady steps to the misshapen monstrosity he called an office. She opened the door and walked up to the desk. The food warmer wasn't there. Had she missed something? Surely she would have seen the warmer if he had been carrying it. Unless it was hidden from view by the files he was carrying and his jacket.

Outside, the boys were nowhere in sight. She walked around the side of the building toward the tap and nearly screamed. Thankgod was huddled over the green food warmer, stuffing rice into his mouth with a filthy hand.

Murmula ran over.

"Where did you get that?"

Thankgod tried to answer, but his mouth was full. He swallowed hastily.

"Oga gave it to me," he said.

Murmula looked around frantically. James had been standing by the gate, talking on his phone. Al'amis had gone out on an errand to Farin Gada.

"Give me that." She took the warmer from Thankgod and looked inside. It still contained a few spoonfuls of rice, but most of it was gone. "Go," Murmula said. "Get out of here."

She washed out the remaining rice and rinsed the container thoroughly. The drops of water on the container vibrated like silent little drums from the shaking of her hands. She placed the warmer on Mr. Pamson's desk and sat back down behind hers. But that was all she could do—sit. Her mind was a flurry. Her phone rang, and she stared at Ishat's name on the screen, unable to move.

"Aren't you going to answer that?" asked the middle-aged client who was waiting for James to finish servicing his Mazda.

Murmula reached for the phone absently, but it stopped ringing before she could receive the call. She put the phone back down and placed her fingers on the keyboard of the laptop, trying to look busy. Her eyes flitted to the door every few seconds, looking for Thankgod. But she couldn't see him from her desk. After a few minutes, she went and stood on the verandah. Thankgod was under the shed, playing with a spinning top he had carved out of a snail shell. Nothing seemed out of the ordinary. She closed her eyes, trying to still her raging mind. But she realised only one thing was waiting for her in the darkness. When she opened her eyes, James was coming toward her.

"I've finished," he said, wiping his greasy hands on a blackened rag.

Murmula nodded. "Just servicing?"

"Yes."

She went inside and gave the client his bill. She collected his name and issued him a receipt. After he had left, she closed the door to the reception, praying no one else would come. She sat in one of the empty chairs and held her head for several minutes. Either she or the world was spinning too fast, she didn't know which. The spinning wouldn't stop. She started to pray.

"Ḥasbiya Allāhu lā ilāha illā huwa ʿalayhi tawakkaltu wa-huwa rabbu al-ʿarshi al-ʿaẓīm." *Allah is enough for me. There is no true god but Him, in Him I put my trust, and He is the Lord of the Great Throne.*

She repeated the prayer multiple times until she felt a bit steadier. She went outside and called Thankgod over.

"How are you feeling?" she said.

"Lafiya."

"You don't feel somehow?"

Thankgod shook his head.

"You ate a lot of that rice," she said, trying to dispel the concern that was showing on his face. "And two whole pieces of meat. You alone. As tiny as you are. Even Oga normally doesn't finish everything in the warmer. I won't be surprised if your stomach starts to pain you."

Thankgod looked reprimanded. He lowered his eyes. She wanted to reach out and touch his shoulder, but she felt unclean, even though he was the one covered in grease and dust. They'd barely spoken to each other since the incident with Luka, but she'd sensed that he was avoiding her.

"If you start to feel any pain, come and tell me immediately," she said.

She managed to resume work but kept glancing at the doorway. Every now and then, Thankgod would cross the frame of the doorway and pass out of view, occupied with some task or mischief at hand. The hours passed slowly. With each that came and went, her hope grew bolder. Musty had said some things about the poison—that it could take a while to work, that she could get away before the effects became noticeable—but she wasn't so sure. When it was a quarter to five, she allowed herself the thought that perhaps she could get to the end of the day without incident. Just fifteen more minutes to go. Whatever happened afterward would be someone else's problem. She stopped moving suddenly, amazed by the fact that she had just thought that. It had entered her head so casually. Was this an indication that her true nature had begun to alter itself, to bend toward evil? She remained frozen in the wake of the thought, listening to its echo as it slouched away noisily, back into the depths of her mind like some hideous leviathan.

It was shame that made her pick up her phone and dial Paul. She could have tried going at it alone, but she knew she wouldn't be able to hold herself together if anything were to happen to that boy. She would need someone to help pick up the pieces of her. She put the phone down after speaking to Paul and raised her head. Thankgod was in the doorway, shuffling slowly toward her. He was hunched, clearly in some kind of agony. She went to him and helped him to an empty chair.

"What's wrong?"

"My stomach," he said quietly.

James appeared then. "What's wrong with him?"

"He said his stomach."

James leaned over Thankgod and touched his forehead. "Thankgod, how are you feeling?"

Thankgod was beginning to squirm. "Cikina!" He said it again and again. *My stomach. My stomach.*

"Don't worry," she said, "we'll go to the hospital. Paul is coming to take us."

"Do you have to take him to the hospital?" James said. "You don't know these children. He probably went and ate something he shouldn't, the greedy fool. Save your money. He'll feel better soon." He left.

Murmula hovered over Thankgod, afraid that his condition would worsen if she looked away, even though this was her doing. She picked up her phone and called Paul again. He sounded short when he said he was on his way. Her hands had started to shake again, and this time the shaking spread to the rest of her. Thankgod was ebbing before her very eyes. His writhing seemed to lessen even as his moaning increased. He slipped to the floor limply and continued to twist and angle his body there.

Paul arrived ten minutes later and entered the reception. When he saw Thankgod, he rushed over and looked at Murmula.

"What's wrong with him?"

"His stomach," Murmula said. She knew her face was wide open, revealing the terror that had taken possession of her body, giving away the fact that she knew more than she ought to about the situation. But she didn't care.

"Did he eat something?" Paul said, running his hands helplessly over the boy.

"We need to take him to the hospital!"

"Hospital? Is it that serious? Can't we go to a pharmacy and get—"

"If we don't take this boy to a hospital, Paul, he's going to die! Do you hear me?"

Paul stared at her, registering her words, parsing them. There was a crease in his brow that she knew meant he still had questions, but he turned and hoisted Thankgod into his arms. Murmula rushed to the door to hold it open. James was standing outside by the car.

"Open the car door!" she screamed.

Paul hurried across the yard and placed Thankgod in the back seat. Murmula sat there with him. She could feel her chest rising and falling uncontrollably. Tears rolled out of her eyes no matter how much she blinked them away. She cradled Thankgod's head in her lap as the car swayed. He had closed his eyes. He continued to grip his belly, rocking gently from side to side.

"We're going to Plateau Hospital," Paul said.

Murmula nodded. She kept her attention fixed on Thankgod, refusing to meet Paul's eyes in the rearview mirror. There was traffic on Tudun Wada Road. Paul hissed and turned the car right, and they passed through shaded streets that dipped and rose in roller-coaster fashion. Murmula's stomach leapt and dropped along with the car's movements.

"God is punishing me."

Murmula looked down at Thankgod's face. The words, faint like wisps of smoke, had come from his lips. She hoped he wouldn't try to speak again.

"God is punishing me," he said louder.

Paul flicked his eyes up into the rearview mirror. He and Murmula stared at each other briefly before he had to look at the road again.

Murmula lowered her head and said, "God isn't punishing you."

"God is punishing me for lying about Oga Luka."

She was sure Paul had heard it, but she still brought her lips to Thankgod's ears and said, "Stop talking. Save your strength."

He suddenly twisted on his back, leaned his head over her knee, and vomited all over her shoes. She felt the hot, slimy fluid seeping between her toes and stifled a shudder. The sour fumes punched her face immediately.

Paul raced through potholes and over speed bumps, gripping the wheel until his knuckles were pale and taut.

At Plateau Hospital, the security man offered the gate pass. Paul snatched it out of his hand, tapping his fingers impatiently on the wheel while the elderly man walked over to the barrier pole and raised it. Paul spun into the compound and swung the car around in front of the emergency entrance.

They dragged Thankgod suspended between them into the emergency room. He had lost his shoes, and his bare feet trailed on the floor. They stood in the poorly lit entrance for almost a minute, waiting for someone to approach them. Paul led them to a nearby bench, where a couple of patients were stretched out, napping. He looked down at her feet, and her eyes followed. Amidst the pale coating of undigested rice and other unknown matter on her skin were streaks of red. Blood.

"Let me go and find someone."

Murmula sat there, trying to stay alert. Thankgod's head was leaning on her shoulder. She realised that he had stopped moving altogether. She didn't move, too terrified to check if he was still alive. How could she? Paul came back a few minutes later with a nurse. She was slim and light-skinned, with a birthmark on her chin, very pretty. Stupid details that stood out and meant nothing at all.

"What is wrong with him?" the nurse said.

"His stomach is paining him."

The nurse retrieved a gurney that was idling against one wall, and they laid Thankgod on it. Murmula watched his face as the nurse examined him. His stillness unnerved her. The nurse felt his pulse, held a stethoscope to his chest. She raised her head and looked at Paul and Murmula.

"What did he eat?"

Paul started to speak. "I don't know but—"

"Poison," Murmula said suddenly.

The nurse looked at her. "You're saying he was poisoned?"

"Yes," Murmula said, and swallowed. An image of Thankgod's lifeless body had been like a developing negative in her head, taking on form and substance. She had to do everything in her power to see that it didn't come true. Fuck the consequences. "Yes. I think so."

"How long ago?"

"I'm not sure. Hours."

"What time?"

"I don't know. At least four hours ago."

"Any other symptoms?"

Murmula started to shake her head, but Paul said loudly, "He vomited blood in the car."

The nurse was joined by a colleague, and together they rolled the gurney away, into the bowels of the hospital.

Murmula turned and saw Paul looking at her.

"Poison?" he said.

Murmula didn't respond. She started pacing. She could feel the beginning of it, the unravelling of her seams. Perhaps she shouldn't have called him. Now she had to deal with his questions. Her sticky feet were like obscene objects that had been attached to her by some devious magic.

"Murmula, answer me. You said he was poisoned?"

She continued to scuttle back and forth across the room, the soles of her feet slimy against her shoes, lubricated by vomit. People were staring at her. If this boy died, innocent blood would stain her hands forever. There was no restitution she could make, no penitence to wipe it away. It would always be there, stacked against her, waiting to accuse her at Al-Qiyamah. She had poisoned a child. She had poisoned an innocent child.

Suddenly, Paul gripped her arms and held her in place. The look on his face told her his terror was deeper than hers.

"What happened?" he asked quietly.

He already knew, but he wanted her to confirm his terror, to break his heart, to give him a reason to begin to hate her. All she could think of doing was running. So she squeezed out of his grip and ran.

"Murmula!"

She could hear him coming after her. His footfalls were loud, like thunderclaps. She tore right across the path of an approaching vehicle, which screeched angrily at her. She ducked past the barrier pole at the gate and spotted the line of keke napeps waiting for their turn to take passengers. If she stopped there, Paul would catch up to her. She looked back and saw him reaching the gate. She kicked off her slippery shoes, scooped them into her arms, and bolted down the side of the road. She didn't know where she was going. A car tried to make a left turn across her path. She slammed a fist on the hood and cut right in front of it; more screeching of brakes, the driver's cursing fading away behind her. Her veil had slipped from her head, exposing her hair, her face, trailing in the wind behind her like a tail. What must people think of her? How had she come to this? Running barefoot in the streets. There were tears on her cheeks. Once she stopped needing her lungs for running, she would need them for weeping.

She didn't look back until she reached the entrance to Plateau Club, at least five hundred metres away. There was no sign of Paul. She sat in front of a clothing store and allowed her racing heart to slow down. There was a sharp pain in her chest. She hoped it was death, Allah's judgement descending on her. It would be better than what awaited her in Paul's eyes. Because Allah was merciful; He was her Creator. But what could she say about Paul? Musty had been right. He would despise her as devotedly as he had loved her. He would think of her as nothing but a filthy Muslim girl, deserving of death. What had she been thinking?

Of course it could have only ended like this. An innocent person hurt; Paul turned against her; Mr. Pamson, her target, unscathed.

The store had a mannequin out in front, just inches from her. It was displaying a woman's gown—white, with sequins down the side. She looked at its face, at the head tie that crested in a giant bow. She felt envious of it. It had no consciousness, and so felt no terror. She curled over her knees and wept, unaware of the passing of time or the existence of a world outside herself until she felt a hand on her shoulder. She raised her head. Someone was standing next to her. She looked up into the dour, worried face of a young man in cargo shorts and a white T-shirt. The door of the store was open behind him. He offered her a few wads of tissue. She took them and croaked her thanks.

Murmula chartered a keke napep home. Her phone was ringing—Paul. She turned off the sound and dropped it into her purse. The breeze blowing into the back of the vehicle helped dry her face. She used her pocket mirror to redo her makeup, concealing any traces of emotion. But there was little she could do about her swollen eyes. When she was satisfied, she put away the mirror and caught the driver watching her through his own side mirror. She ignored him and put on her sunglasses. She sat with her back straight, determined to look as dignified as possible.

She left her sunglasses on when she entered the house. Baba Karami was in the living room, reading a newspaper. She registered the unusual sight and how quiet the house was, but it didn't interest her.

"Murmula, how was work today?" he said.

"Fine, Baba." She tried to make her voice as clear and normal-sounding as possible.

"Toh, welcome back."

She greeted Gogo Hauwawu and Ishat in the kitchen and explained that she wasn't feeling well and would be going straight to bed. She ignored their looks of concern and went to the bedroom. She washed her feet, changed, and climbed into bed. Her phone now had nearly fifty missed calls from Paul. The message icon kept flashing as new WhatsApp messages and texts poured in. She turned off the phone and closed her eyes. But she didn't sleep. Ishat floated in and out twice. Murmula didn't know how far apart the visits were. She tried to speak to Murmula the second time, but Murmula only pretended to be asleep.

At one point she felt her cousin climbing into the bed beside her and pulling her into an embrace. Murmula could smell the rosewater scent on her, so delicate and pure. She started to cry again. Ishat rocked her like a baby, whispering to her that it was all right. They had barely exchanged words since Gogo Hauwawu had yelled at Ishat and compared her unfavourably to Murmula. But Ishat was willing to push past that so she could comfort her. It made Murmula cry harder.

Murmula heard the rain start to fall, but she kept her eyes shut. The sound grew louder as the rain grew heavier. Her thoughts continued to circle her mind like birds of prey—dark, brooding things of great scale. The rain grew so heavy she thought the roof would cave in. She wished it would. She wanted the rain to wash her away like she had heard rain floods sweeping people away in parts of Jos in the thick of the rainy season.

AFTER

15

Pamson changed out of his wet clothes and sat in the living room while, gradually, a new sensation of disquiet overtook him. He returned to the bedroom and stood by Rahila's side of the bed. He stared at the empty space for some time. Hours had passed, and he'd been unable to bring himself to touch any of it. The will finally solidified within him. He bent and pulled back the blanket. The nightgown was lying where Rahila should have been, but without Rahila in it. It was stretched out across its full length, the colour of sparkling apple juice. Silky and smooth if he ran his fingers over it. He didn't. His gut told him that whatever he was witnessing couldn't be undone if he touched her clothes.

The rain stopped nearly three hours later. In that time, he had sat at the dining table, running his mind through what he remembered. The vague sensation pulsing through the membrane of his sleep that Rahila had gotten out of bed. Waking up to thundering rain and weak daylight. The vacant space beside him. The morbid stillness in the house. Paul's empty room. Water falling from heaven like a judgement, pounding everything. Rahila's birthday meal was still spread out on the coffee table, arranged around the cake. The unopened presents were arranged around that.

He continued to sit, waiting for something to happen, for his wife to walk in with a joke and an explanation rolled into one, for the fog of quiet unmooring he was subsumed in to roll back. With the rain gone, there was now a loud hush. He sat listening to the slowing drip of rainwater from the eaves—tap-tap-tap-tap-tap-tap-tap-tap tap tap tap tap tap tap tap taptaptaptaptaptaptap

taptaptap

He got dressed but couldn't find the keys to the gate for some time. At last, he listened to the hunch that had been nudging him for the better part of an hour during his search. He went again to Paul's room, stood again beside the bed, stared again at the fucking clothes. A pair of red basketball shorts and that damn blue shirt with the words that had a new, mocking boldness to them:

SAY

¥£$

TO

THE

HUSTLE

His hand trembled when he raised the shorts and went on trembling when he found the gate keys in one of the pockets, the left pocket: Paul was left-handed. On many occasions he had gone to bed forgetting to leave the keys on the kitchen counter. But it had made no difference; he was the one who locked the gate and the first to be up. Had been. Was.

Pamson swung the BMW through the quiet roads and did a turn around the estate. Few people were on the road, but that told him nothing. And he didn't trust his own sense of things. He parked the car in front of the gate and held his phone, wondering if he had Reverend Dogo's number. The clergyman was his litmus test, if his suspicions were correct. There was movement in the rearview mirror, and when he turned, he saw Hajiya Kande standing with a man outside her gate. She was wearing a large grey abaya that covered her from head to toe. She and the man turned and looked at Pamson when he approached. The man had grey stubble and more than a passing resemblance to Alhaji Attahiru; Pamson recognised he was Alhaji Attahiru's brother. They had met sometime last year when Pamson had stopped to deliver Ramadan greetings and had been wrestled into joining them for the iftar.

Alhaji Attahiru's wife and brother said nothing now and stared at him.

"Did you wake up well?" he asked them.

"Lafiya," Hajiya Kande replied.

She said nothing more. They had the look about them of people who had clashed against some inexplicable presence and stood with its shadow hovering over them, marring their features, disfiguring their understanding of things; they looked the way he imagined himself to look, and he knew that they had encountered the same puzzle.

Back inside the house, he checked his WhatsApp notifications. Several forwarded messages had come in from different contacts; then he realised it was the same message, accompanied by a number of pictures:

> Rapture Has Happened!
>
> This morning (July 11th 2018), I woke up to an empty house. My husband was missing, my housegirl was missing, my gateman was missing. I was the only person in the house. I didn't know what to do, so I called my neighbour to ask if they had seen my family. But she was crying because her newborn baby wasn't there when she woke up. The more calls I made the more I understood what was happening. Then I remembered that the LORD had been speaking to me that the world was on the brink of Rapture and that when it happens

> people will be surprised about who is taken and who is left behind. If you have been left behind, it is time to go back to your God because He is giving you another chance—

Pamson stopped reading and scrolled to the bottom. The long message ended with a request to pass it along to ten other people, as it was a way to show God your repentance and start going back to Him so that you don't miss the next Rapture. Pictures were attached to the message: an empty bed with empty clothes, an empty car with empty clothes draped over the reclined driver's seat, empty shirt and trousers over empty shoes . . .

Pamson switched on the TV. A newscaster on AIT was discussing the strange disappearances that were being reported around the country—WIDESPREAD REPORTS OF PEOPLE DISAPPEARING. He switched to Channels TV—DISAPPEARANCES ON A MASSIVE SCALE: RAPTURE OR RUSE? All the national networks were discussing the same thing. Some of the TV presenters discussed colleagues of theirs who hadn't shown up for work only to be revealed to have also vanished. Pamson realised he had only been looking at local news channels. He flipped through CNN, BBC, Sky News—all the major networks, all covering the same thing. Whatever was happening—had happened—appeared to be on a global scale. The more Pamson sat there and listened, the more his understanding grew tumid with horror. If he was to believe what he was hearing, it meant that Rahila and Paul had just vanished into thin air while they were sleeping. And the baby too.

He switched off the TV and got the car keys and drove out again. This time he turned into State Lowcost Junction and drove up the main thoroughfare, scanning the houses. People milled about under the eucalyptus trees, but there was no purpose to their movement. They stood in groups, talking. Every now and again he would pass in front of a house where they appeared to be in the act of some kind of mourning.

His phone rang as he turned the car around in front of the Mining Corporation Quarters gate. It was Eunice, Paul's sister.

"Hello?"

"Hello, Uncle." She sounded subdued, muted. He could tell from her voice that she had been crying.

"What's wrong?"

"Do you know what's happening?"

"No."

"I called Aunty Rahila's number, but she didn't pick up. Even Paul too."

"How are your children?"

"They're fine, Uncle, but my husband . . ."

Pamson opened his mouth, but his tongue couldn't shape the words into being. Eunice was sobbing in a small, contained way, as though she was afraid she would wake someone up.

"What about them, Uncle?"

"They've . . . They're not around too."

"They also disappeared?"

He sighed heavily before saying, "Yes."

"Jesus."

After getting off the phone as quickly as he could, he decided driving wasn't a good idea. He went back home and lay sideways on the bed, staring at Rahila's flattened nightgown. When his phone rang again hours later, it reeled him out of a fitful sleep and into the shocking cold air of real life. He'd been dreaming that it was all a dream, but the shapeless nightgown was still there in front of him.

"Hello?"

"Dareng, what is happening in our world?"

"Mark," Pamson said groggily, then hoisted himself into a seated position. He hadn't checked the caller ID before answering. "How are you?"

"You're sleeping with all this madness going on?"

Pamson was silent.

"You've answered. That means you're still here. Your wife fa?"

Pamson shook his head, remembered that Mark couldn't see him. "No."

"She disappeared too?"

The word was stuck in his throat, but he forced himself to say it: "Yes."

"Wayo Allah. What kind of a thing is this? Even Solo."

"Even Solo ma?" Pamson shut his eyes. It was really happening. Had really happened.

After he ended the call, he started calling his contacts. He found Luka's name and pressed the dial button. Only after it had started to ring did he remember what had happened between them.

"Hello?" Luka said quietly.

"Luka. Have you heard what is happening?"

"Yes, Oga."

"Your mother fa?"

"Mama is gone."

There was silence. Pamson thought about what words of comfort to say, but how could you offer comfort when the tragedy was incomprehensible?

"My wife and Paul too."

Luka said nothing. His breathing crackled through the connection.

"I just wanted to check on you. At least you're fine."

"Nagode, Oga," Luka said, before hanging up.

Pamson called the other boys' families. Al'amis and Bala had also disappeared. He couldn't reach Thankgod's mother because her phone was switched off. But James was fine. He dialled Murmula's number, but it was also switched off. It became a gamble, deducing who was still alive based on whether they answered or not. Jonah, no answer. Maman Ivie, switched off. The last number he called before giving up was Philip's. But it also rang until it disconnected.

The coming days would reveal the depth and extent of the disappearances. People in China, Australia, India, Saudi Arabia, Papua New

Guinea, all calling into TV stations and describing how their loved ones had vanished in the middle of the night, while they were sleeping. No matter how much he listened to them speak, he couldn't bring himself to accept it. All that remained of his wife's presence and the child she carried were a crumpled nightgown and a far-off dampness long dried, the result of their final act of lovemaking, but he still couldn't believe it. The weeks passed, and he still refused to make the bed or sleep in it or wash the sheets. He spent hours thinking of the baby, the little girl who was fully formed, just waiting to be welcomed into the world. The house should have been full of voices and laughter and the crying of an infant. But all that remained were him and the bottles of stout he had turned to drinking nightly.

Of course the government didn't have answers. They never did. That buffoon of a president was somewhere out there, anywhere but in the country he had been elected to govern. The ministries kept dodging responsibility. The health minister said it was less a public health matter and more a justice matter. The attorney general said it had nothing to do with justice because there were no culprits or suspects. The interior minister borrowed from the same book but with a different twist: "Our internal security apparatus wasn't designed to counter spiritual forces."

The inspector general of police, ministers of finance and labour, and chief of army staff were missing. When the president returned, he instituted a presidential task force to be led by the secretary of the government of the federation, for whom a replacement had to be found because he was also missing. He had to fill the gaps made by missing heads of several agencies. It was the new chairman of the National Population Commission, a man younger than most expected, who served as the sole voice of logic and leadership. He talked about setting in motion a plan to create a registry of names, locations, and identities.

Pamson would put on CNN and BBC and drink his beer, watching not just his country but the entire world scrambling to make sense of it all. His mind a muddle of half-formed thoughts but just sharp enough to still catch the dissonance between the figures being tallied by the presenters and the headline in bold that remained permanently at the bottom of the screen: US President and First Lady Among the Vanished.

The numbers continued to pour in from the different countries tallying their vanished, converging into a global total that ticked up every hour or so on the screen. Thousands and thousands and thousands. The names of the vanished scrolled through his head, including the word *thousands*, as though to make up for the numberless mass of the lost that he didn't know.

Thousands.Rahila.The baby.Paul.Alhaji Attahiru.Thousands. Maman Ivie.Thousands.Jonah. Thousands.

On the night of 10 July or the morning of 11 July, hundreds of thousands of people were sucked into thin air while they were sleeping. Three weeks after that, Dareng Pamson continued to fall asleep in the living room with the TV on and a stout in his hand. Half of him was in a spiral of despair as he wondered whether God's judgement for his sins had finally caught up with him; the other half was still waiting for Rahila to walk in with that fucking joke and explanation rolled into one and maybe their newborn child to boot, and they would stay up into the night crying and laughing and marvelling at what the Lord had done.

16

The floor underneath Musty's bed was a giant ashtray. Murmula heaved her weight against the mattress until it stood upright on the wall. She tied a wet scarf over the lower half of her face and swept the room, sprinkling water from a bucket as she proceeded. After that, she wiped the dust from every surface. When she was done, she sat on the reset mattress and stared at her cousin's clothes on the table: a black jallabiya and checkered boxers. The last thing he had worn. It had taken Gogo Hauwawu a month to be able to cross the backyard and push open Musty's bedroom door. The broom in her hand had quivered, then dropped to the ground. She wouldn't be able to clean it herself, as she'd vowed. Murmula picked up the broom and told her aunt to go and lie down. She had folded the empty clothes, feeling like her two hands belonged to someone else. Her head didn't understand what her fingers were doing. She hadn't accepted what had happened, that it could happen. That people with flesh on their bones and blood flowing through them could disappear into thin air. Flesh and muscle and organs, all that matter and mass, gone without a trace.

The past month had been difficult. Both Gogo Hauwawu and Baba Karami were stricken in a way that seemed permanent. Murmula's best efforts to push past her own confusion and console them were useless. Try as she might, she couldn't get her mind to relinquish the memory of the morning after, when she'd woken up and accidentally rolled onto Ishat's flattened pyjamas. She'd raised the lilac shirt and trousers before her like the questions that they were, expecting an answer to drop out of them. Maybe the memory wouldn't have gotten its hooks so deep into her if nothing had happened. But something had dropped out of those clothes, and she hadn't been prepared for it: a bloodstained tampon, pinkish against the white parts of the bedsheets. She had flown out of the bed like a flustered bat, screeching and screeching until hands were holding her. The memory was still slinking by hideously when it occurred to her that it would be her companion until the day she died.

She dumped the sweepings of cigarette ends and ash in the garbage bin and hovered around the back door, wary of going inside, where Baba Karami was napping on the sofa. He had started going to the mosque every evening for a few hours, opting to perform his la'asr prayers there and stay behind for the tafsir. Murmula joined him at first, then started going on her own, at her own time. The women's section, though smaller, was less full, and she wished Gogo Hauwawu would also go with her. Murmula didn't speak to any of the other women, but she drew comfort from sharing the space with others who had also gone there because of the strange grief that held them all like a body of water. Murmula had never been intensely religious, but the imam's voice had become indispensable in this period of her life. She was reassured to hear things she had always heard and known from a voice that soothed her so much. It made them feel truer than they'd ever seemed. As though the voice was doing the delicate work of translating messages between her head and her heart. Until it wasn't.

In the kitchen, Murmula closed the door that led to the living room and started doing the dishes. She filled the water drum, then got on her knees and scrubbed the floor with a hard brush. A month's worth of mud, food particles, and oil drops were gnashed into a brown, frothy rage underneath her vigorous movements. The house had regressed into a ghostly version of its formerly impeccable self, and Murmula felt responsible. Apart from Musty and Ishat, she hadn't lost anyone she considered vitally close in the disappearances—a couple of distant cousins she barely knew had gone missing, but that was it; both her parents were safe and whole in the grave. What justification did she have for falling apart and letting the house descend into this state? She didn't know where the strength had come from today, but it was here now, and she would use it until the entire house sparkled again. Gogo Hauwawu must have heard her, because the door opened and she was there in the doorway. She asked her to come and stay with her in the bedroom.

Murmula washed her hands and changed. She found Gogo Hauwawu under the covers with only her head showing. She was lying on her side. For a moment Murmula thought she might have a fever, but her aunt's forehead was cool when she felt it with the back of her hand. Murmula sat holding her hand. Every few minutes she looked at her watch.

"Do you have somewhere to go ne?" Gogo Hauwawu said.

"It's almost time for azahar."

"The mosque is a good place. I'm glad you and your uncle are going there more now."

"Let's go together mana."

Gogo Hauwawu said nothing.

In the intervening silence, the call to prayer rose and filled the neighbourhood. But instead of saying she had to go, Murmula said, "Do you know any jokes?"

"Jokes?"

"The imam mentioned a hadith that says we should be playful with our family. He said jokes can help us in this time."

Murmula waited. Finally, Gogo Hauwawu said, "I don't care what the imam has to say right now. Go before you miss your prayers."

There were only six women in the mosque. Murmula joined the prayer line, catching the final raka'at. After she had performed her outstanding raka'ats, she picked up a copy of the Qur'an and placed it in the angle formed by her crossed legs. She opened to the first page and started to read out loud.

"Bismillaahir Rahmaanir Raheem. Alhamdu lillaahi Rabbil 'aalameen. Ar-Rahmaanir-Raheem. Maaliki—"

Thankgod.

The name had flashed across her mind, a sudden spark. Her voice faltered, and she blinked. Had she also seen it with her naked eyes, the way she could see the Arabic script that was in front of her?

She waited a few seconds. When nothing happened, she tried again. "Maaliki Yawmid-Deen. Iyyaaka na'budu wa lyyaaka nasta'een. Ihdinas-Siraatal-Mustaqeem . . ."

She managed to reach the end of the sura, letting her voice soar and dip with the vowels. She turned the page, cleared her throat, and began Suratul Baqarah: "Alif-Lam-Mim."

Thankgod.Paul.

She shut her eyes, shook her head, pressed on: "Dhalikal-kitabu la rayba fihi hudan—"

Paul

Thankgod.

The bunny.

No matter how much she tried to let herself go, the whispers were there, waiting for that moment when her mind would dip below the surface of the world and into concentration. This had happened each time she tried to read. It didn't matter what it was. A news article on her phone. A poem. It somehow seemed meaningful that it happened even with scripture. She replaced the Qur'an and looked around. There were more women in the room now than when she had arrived, many of them performing the azahar prayers they had missed. Long, dark robes that flowed with the gentle breeze that came in through wide open doors and swirled when they bowed for a ruku'u or a sujaddah.

There was a sermon ongoing, but it wasn't the customary voice. She realised her presence at this time was unusual, and that the imam was probably only available in the late afternoons and evenings. Through gaps in the partition that separated the men's and women's sections, she could glimpse the speaker. To her surprise, she saw the imam's red cap and his trademark checkered keffiyeh that was spread across his back. He was at the front of the congregation, listening. The speaker looked young, almost a teenager. Yet it wasn't his appearance that arrested her but what he was saying. He was speaking about jinn.

"They are like us. They eat, they marry, they have natural relations. They are able to know what is right from what is wrong. In Suratul Al-Dhariyat, Allah says," and he recited the verse in Arabic before translating back into Hausa: "'I created both aljannu and men to worship Me alone.'"

When it was time for questions, someone asked, "Is it possible aljannu are responsible for these disappearances?"

The young speaker smiled sheepishly before looking at the imam, who took the microphone from him. He turned his body partially to face the congregation.

"There is no mention in the hadith or the Qur'an that aljannu have abducted humans. We must remember that Allah has made it so that aljannu do not interfere in human affairs. But if perchance aljannu are responsible for what has happened, it is Allah who has allowed it, and we must trust in Allah's wisdom. 'You may dislike something although it is good for you, or like something although it is bad for you: Allah knows and you do not.' Reason has its uses, and if we are to use our reasoning combined with what we know from the scriptures, then it follows that this is something aljannu are capable of. But Allah knows and we do not. We must trust in Allah's will."

For the rest of the day, Murmula thought about the imam's answer. Reason combined with the scriptures. It was possible for Allah to speak through dreams, and a person who dreamed dreams that came true was said to have some traits of a prophet. She couldn't remember the hadith. If she put this alongside the notion that humans and jinn were of equal standing before Allah, then perhaps jinn also had dreams from Allah. Prophets had been sent to them, after all, and even the Holy Prophet

(Peace Be Upon Him) had gone and preached to jinn personally. Was it possible that there existed prophets among the jinn?

Yet at the same time, some part of her mind dismissed it all as superstitious rubbish. It was taking her back to the very foundations of what she had believed without question her whole life. Since the disappearances, she had been experiencing a disorientation each time she listened to grown men speak seriously and deeply about spirit beings with magical abilities. The same disorientation she felt when she considered the disappearances, but on a much smaller scale. It seemed that the more time she spent at the mosque, the more her mind devised counterarguments against what she was hearing. It had been a subtle process, hidden even from her. In the weeks that followed, once she understood that her reason for frequenting the mosque was to listen to the explanations and solaces offered about the mysterious tragedy and shoot them down like little birds, she stopped going.

She came to have only one conviction: that she had caused it all. She was convinced of it despite her awareness that it was as impossible to prove as jinn were. She had slept very little, staying awake and trying to unravel it all in her stuffy head. Thinking about Paul, about Thankgod, about Luka, about Abdulmajid, even about the chicken she had stabbed to death. She had told lies, caused damage, and—worst of all—plotted murder. She had even forced an innocent boy to lie, thereby dragging him into the orbit of her evil. In the process, he had been hurt, possibly killed. His poisoning had been a switch she had flicked without thought, and two and a half million sleeping people (the latest official count) had been sucked into oblivion. But more than anything else, what left her immobile was the hefty suspicion that Paul had vanished, too, and that she cared about him too much to try to verify.

17

There was an old desktop computer in Reverend Dogo's office that looked like it hadn't been switched on in the five years since the office building had existed on the church lot. It was on a table that stood against the wall, as if it had found itself there by accident. The computer monitor reminded Pamson of the thirteen-inch JVC television set he had purchased secondhand for two thousand naira in 1995. The first TV he had ever bought. This was five years before his wedding, when they had received a much larger Sony Trinitron television as a gift.

Pamson watched the clergyman, who was seated behind his desk. He was not the vibrant man he remembered who'd stood in front of the church and pointed sanctimoniously at the congregation. He had lost his wife and two of his children in the disappearance and was left with only one child.

Pamson had called the reverend the previous afternoon to ask if he could meet. The reverend had offered to visit Pamson at home, but he had blurted out before he could stop himself that he was happy to come to the reverend's office. Pamson didn't have the wherewithal to clear up the mess: the destroyed cake, the beer bottles stationed around the living room. They had fixed the time, and now here was Pamson, seated and listening to the man attempting to make small talk. He complained in jest about how the project expanding the church's parking lot had been indefinitely delayed because the contractor, the site engineer, and foreman had all gone missing. Now that the stewardship of the church had fallen to him (the reverend-in-charge had also disappeared), there was nobody to speak to about the project.

"Rapture, Rapture, Rapture," Reverend Dogo said, chuckling to himself. "Now Rapture has happened. Do you know how embarrassing it is for me as a pastor? For Rapture to happen and for me to still be here, dealing with problems like this? Who knew Rapture would leave behind headaches like this?" His laughter rolled out like a gale on its last legs.

Pamson smiled to humour him, but he wasn't convinced by his mirth. There was something about it that seemed obscene and also stretched too thin, as if it would snap at any moment and the man would crumble into his rightful state. Pamson didn't understand how someone could lose practically his entire family in such a way and remain whole. This all must be an act. How long would it last before his mask cracked, before he gave in to defeat? Now that Pamson thought of it, he wondered if his drinking had become so bad that he had begun to reek.

"I am making plans to start visiting all of our members who were affected," Reverend Dogo said. "In a congregation of over three thousand, almost a thousand people gone, just like that. Men, women, children. Sometimes up to five people in one family."

"And what about you?" Pamson said. "Who will visit you?"

Reverend Dogo considered this question meekly, his head lowered over his chest like a burden. At last he shrugged and looked up. "How have you been faring?"

Pamson nodded and pursed his lips. "Fine. Fine."

"Have you been coming to church at all?"

"I'm trying my best." It was a big congregation. Reverend Dogo couldn't possibly know that he hadn't gone in months, even before the disappearances.

Reverend Dogo smiled. "She used to drag you here, didn't she?"

Pamson acknowledged this by giving his own smile. Not that it mattered whether the reverend knew he hadn't been attending the Sunday services.

"What about now? After what has happened?"

Pamson's right leg was shaking on its own, rocking back and forth like the needle on a seismograph. What about now? What a question. Everything about his life had come to a standstill. He had lost his whole family. His business was all but dead, with any hopes of revamping and expanding it gone with people like Paul, Philip, Solomon. He had also started having bad dreams that he thought he had left behind over a decade ago. They were back now with a fury he didn't know dreams could possess. Images once restricted to memories that had now seeped into his dreams: those uninvited guests weren't only coming during the day; they had taken to barging into his head at night. He knew they were memories, and he had come to see that dreams and memories were essentially the same thing. What about now? He shrugged and said nothing.

"So after your wife and millions of people around the world have vanished, just like that," Reverend Dogo said, "you don't feel like you should draw closer to God?"

Pamson was right. This was a very different Reverend Dogo. There was no righteous anger, no condemnation in his voice. It was an honest question, asked in a tone that suggested a genuine interest in the answer. "No."

"So what do you think happened to all those people? To your wife? Your unborn child?" Reverend Dogo asked in English.

"I don't know," Pamson said quietly. "I don't think there's an answer."

"There's always an answer. Even if we can't see it."

"I'm sorry, Reverend, but this is all bullshit."

"It's okay to be angry with God. If you look at the psalmist—"

"Fuck the psalmist, and fuck God. That is, if He exists."

"Okay," Reverend Dogo said, and adjusted himself in his seat. "You don't believe God exists?"

"No," Pamson said, though that was an exaggeration. He had gone from implicitly trusting in the vague idea of God to now wondering whether the outline of that idea he had carried with him was nothing but a shadow cast by his imagination. Reverend Dogo was wearing a smile that he wanted to annihilate.

"Doesn't this miraculous event show you that the supernatural is real? That we're in the End Times?"

"Jokes aside, Reverend, is this Rapture or not?"

"I don't know. But God knows."

"If He knows, why hasn't He said anything to you?" Pamson said, biting down on a shriek. He wanted to rip off that stupid collar from Reverend Dogo's neck, wanted to tear down the miniature wooden cross that hung on the wall behind his desk. "And don't tell me to keep trusting. You and I know it's bullshit."

Reverend Dogo weighed his next words before speaking them: "Why did you come here, Pamson?"

Pamson cranked his head and looked out the window. Great cumuli were forming above the church building located on the other side of the courtyard. As August rumbled to a close, he could sense little changes in the air. The rains had reduced in frequency but not intensity. On certain dry days, he could smell from the verandah at home the faint beginnings of the dust-laden breeze that wicked moisture off skin and dried clothes in a matter of minutes. It was the descent into Harmattan and the end of the year. All would be cold and dusty. His lips would chap, and Rahila wouldn't be there to give him the lip balm she got him every year. His feet would begin to crack because he would fail to oil them before bed. He was already dreading the festive Christmas season.

With his eyes still pointed out the window, he said in English, "I came because I hoped you would have answers, Reverend." He looked at Reverend Dogo and switched back to Hausa. "You ask how come I don't believe in the supernatural. My neighbour is a Muslim man.

One of the nicest people I knew. He also disappeared. I saw on CNN a young woman who had lost her parents who were atheists. All kinds of people disappeared. There may be a supernatural dimension, but I don't think it belongs to a single religion."

"Dareng, let me ask you something."

Pamson waited for it.

"What has happened to all these people? To your wife. Your child. My family. Is it a good thing or bad thing?"

"How can it be a good thing?" Pamson said, clamping down on another surge of rage.

"So you're saying it's a bad thing."

"What else would it be?"

"If it's a bad thing, what you're actually saying is that the world is a good place and now they won't get to enjoy it anymore. But if it's a good thing, that means that the world is a bad place and they have been saved from its suffering. Are you saying that the world is a good place?"

"No, no, no. I'm not saying anything about the world. I'm just saying . . ." He let his voice trail off.

"But you are saying something about the world," Reverend Dogo continued with the same annoying, patient smile. "Which is it? Is the world good or bad?"

Pamson realised he had grown breathless. He remained as still as he could, but his leg started moving again, jerking to and fro rapidly. He didn't understand why the question irked him so. "There's nothing good about the world," he heard himself say.

Reverend Dogo nodded. "Exactly. It is our grief that speaks for us when we wish that our families were still with us. And it is selfish. Grief is selfish. But we know in our bodies that this world is a terrible place. The Bible tells us that the world is corrupted and fallen, and to be away from it is to be at home with the Lord. The End Times are here, and we have to make sure that we are not found wanting when the Lord returns."

Visiting Reverend Dogo had been a waste of his time, and Pamson steamed over the decision all the way to the garage. When he got down from the car, he saw that there was no padlock on the gate. James was probably inside. He stood for a moment and stared at the cement block Maman Ivie had used as a seat, at the ashes that dusted the ground. He didn't know what had become of her children or whether her husband still worked out of town. In the yard were three cars whose owners hadn't come back for them. He and James had tried to reach two of the owners without success, but no one knew who the third belonged to, a golden Ford Focus with a Mikang license plate. The person who stood on the verandah and stared out at the yard wasn't James. It was Luka.

They watched each other for some time. Finally, Pamson walked over to the building, squeezing past the young man to unlock the door and go inside.

"Where did you get the key?" Pamson said with his back to him.

"I forgot to give it to you. And you forgot to ask."

"There's no longer any money here." The door clanged loudly and creaked open, and Pamson stepped into the reception. Luka followed him.

"I didn't know I'd meet you," Luka said. "I just came to drop something."

Pamson entered the office and sat behind his desk. "Sit down," he said gruffly.

Luka dragged the single chair to the desk and sat. Pamson could see he was uncomfortable, but there was also some defiance in his eyes, around his mouth. His wounds had healed, but he had scars on his forehead and lower lip.

"What did you bring?" Pamson said.

"I want to confess something first."

"If this is about the money—"

"I did not take the money, Oga!" Luka shouted. "I swear on my mother's head, I didn't touch your money. I would never steal from you."

Pamson stared at him. The young man quivered with emotion, then pushed a tear out of the way. Pamson realised he believed him, and that he was now trying to wrap his mind around the new meaning that was unveiling itself between them. He supposed he owed him an apology.

"What do you want to confess?" Pamson said quietly.

"You remember when you gave me three days to come and tell you if I was the father of Helen's baby or not?"

Pamson nodded.

"And I told you I wasn't?"

Pamson watched him.

"I lied. I'm the father. When I refused to take responsibility, she left me alone. She just ignored me. I thought she would badger me until I accepted. But she just said she would leave me with God." Luka cleared his throat. "When the disappearances happened, I gave up hope. Especially after I heard about your wife and how . . . I'm sorry, Oga. But I thought Helen had also disappeared with the baby. When I found out she was still here, I felt like it was a sign from God. I was scared I had lost her and the baby. I realise I love her, Oga." Luka placed a yellow envelope on the desk. "We're going to get married."

Pamson picked up the envelope. Inside was a folded sheet of yellow A4 paper with black ink letters. Someone at a random business centre had literally typed it and printed it out:

The families of Nde John Jonathan Kangdim
and Mr. Edward Bala
cordially invite you to the wedding
solemnization of their children
Luka John
&
Helen Bala
Venue:
St. Moses Catholic Church
Tudun Wada Ring Road, Jos

"The date is two weeks from this coming Saturday," Pamson said.

"You saw what happened, Oga. I'm not going to waste any more time. This life is short."

Pamson smiled. "Congratulations."

"Thank you."

"If you didn't take the money," Pamson said, "who did?"

Luka lowered his head, arranging the words before he spoke them. "Strange things like that never happened in this garage before that girl came, Oga."

Pamson listened, weighing the import of it. "So you're saying she took it?"

"I don't know. What I know is that she had a hand in it somehow."

"Thankgod said he saw you."

"She convinced him to do it. You know that boy, not very smart, always playful. Maybe he tried to take the money and she caught him and made him say it was me."

"But why would she do a thing like that?"

"She despised me."

"Why?"

"I didn't trust her. She knew it."

Pamson sighed softly. "Did you hear what happened to Thankgod?"

Luka nodded. "James told me. That he was poisoned, after eating your food. Like I said, Oga, things like this never happened until this girl came here."

So much was unclear to Pamson, but Luka's words resonated in him like the beginnings of an answer to a puzzle he had failed to solve that now lay forgotten in a corner of his mind. Why had Murmula come into his life in the way she had?

"Oga, why do you think some people were taken and others were left?"

"I don't know, Luka. Even so-called men of God don't know the answer to—"

He stopped suddenly. A song had started playing. At first Pamson thought it was coming from outside. But he hadn't opened the window, and there was no one in the yard. It was coming from the room—from his pocket, he realised. He took out Paul's phone and stared at the screen. The ringtone was a 2Face song he didn't recognise, but he recognised the name that was flashing on the screen.

"When did you start listening to 2Baba, Oga?" Luka said.

"It's Paul's phone."

"Aren't you going to answer it?"

Pamson waited for the phone to stop ringing. He didn't know when it had come on. He switched it off and returned it to his pocket. "No," he said.

18

When Paul didn't answer, Murmula released a sigh of relief and thumbed her way from the phone app to Facebook, where she had been watching a video by an Indian conspiracy theorist who claimed that the lost people had been kidnapped by a vast network of rich and powerful people working together with tech companies and private military contractors. He was asking why the disappearances had happened only at night. He claimed that no one could execute something like this on a global scale without staggering the abductions, hence the fact that people in places like New Zealand and China had started reporting the disappearances before anyone else. That was what he was calling them: abductions. The video had over fifty million likes. Many comments were in agreement, but some were asking how a whole president and the first lady of the United States could also have been abducted.

"Just say it was the Illuminati, idiot," she said with a hiss, and switched apps yet again. On Instagram she got stuck watching an endless string of videos of people vanishing out of their clothes. The clothes would crumple on the ground when they disappeared, like a house of cards imploding. Some of the effects were seamless and impressive, but in many she could see the strings that held the clothes up or weird, jerky gaps in the edit. Everybody was doing them. She found the videos bizarrely comforting, as if the world had agreed to come together and make fun of its shared misfortune. After twenty minutes of this, she clicked the phone off and stood up. She had dressed up, prepared to go out nearly an hour ago but had lost her nerve. Then she'd made a bargain with herself that if Paul answered the call, that was her sign. Yet she knew she was only after an excuse not to go.

As she approached the junction, she half expected to see the road completely deserted. It was with a slight swoop of delirium that she watched a keke napep pull up in front of her mere seconds after she had stood beside the road. The driver wore a red shirt and black trousers. He had a wedding ring on his right hand. Her usual fascination with the mystery of strangers had been deepened by recent events. She found herself wondering if every person she encountered had also been directly affected. She stole glances at the driver's eyes in the side mirror—pale eyes with reddened whites that could have been the result of any number of causes and not necessarily grief. The city outside the keke seemed unchanged. Things proceeded as before, adjusting to the sudden gaps in the physical world that the lost had left behind. There was the fruit vendor on Domkat Bali Road, wearing the same white hat, under the same umbrella, spraying water on his fruit with the same plastic bottle. There was the place farther down the road that sold butane gas, cars pulling in and out of the compound, a security guard in a navy-blue uniform waving them through.

The first thing that seemed touched by what had happened was the sawmill by the junction to the garage. It was quiet, its stacks of lumber idle under the open shed. No one was around. From a hundred metres, she saw that Maman Ivie wasn't at her spot. The gate to the garage was closed. She was ten paces away and was about to turn around when she noticed the smaller pedestrian door ajar. When she pulled closer, she froze. Luka had his back to her and was trying to lock the reception door. She was still far enough away that she could turn and leave without him being any wiser. But she had come here looking for a way to begin to make things right. She wasn't going to run again. She stepped through the pedestrian entrance and watched Luka across the yard struggle with the lock. He bent and shifted his weight against the door, jiggling the key one way first, then the other. She moved closer still, her thudding heart the only thing she could hear, and cleared her throat.

"You have to release the door and push it inside just a bit," she said.

Luka turned. When he saw her, his body grew taut, his hands folded into fists, the muscles in his face became alive with hate. It reminded her of watching a chameleon change its colour. He moved toward her. At first she remained standing. As he drew closer, he snatched up a wheel spanner that was lying on the ground. The same one he had thrown at Bala's head. He didn't need to speak to convince her that he would use it. She ran back to the gate. She could hear his footsteps behind her. The padlock hung from a hole in the pedestrian gate, with the key still in it. She slammed the gateway closed, snapped the padlock shut, and took out the key. The gate was now between them. Luka glared at her through the bars. He glanced at the padlock, fidgeted with it, stared at the key in her hand for a moment, then turned and ran back to the reception door. He came back with the keys.

"Luka, you have every right to hate me," she said quietly. "I just came to look for Paul. I wanted to find out about Thankgod's health."

Luka reached through the bar with the key, trying to slide it into the padlock. "Just let me open this thing; you'll see what I'll do to you."

"Luka, because of God."

The first key didn't work. Luka tried another one.

"Luka, I'm begging for your forgiveness. I just want to know how Thankgod is. Please. Can you tell me?"

Luka stopped moving and watched her for a few seconds. "So you really did it. You really poisoned him."

Murmula was breathing hard. She stared back, unable to speak.

"Why?" Luka said.

"It wasn't meant for him."

"Who was it meant for? Oga?"

Murmula didn't answer.

"Wai who are you really? Why did you come here?"

Murmula could feel her tears sneaking up from behind. She shook her head. "Please. I'm not a bad person. Wallahi tallahi I'm not a bad person."

"But you tried to poison Oga. You forced a small boy to lie so that Oga would send me away. You almost destroyed my relationship with someone I consider my father."

Murmula shook her head, willing her defence into existence because she didn't have the words. Everything he was saying was true. She had said it to herself many times in the days since the disappearance, a kind of self-flagellation, a penance for her actions. But she had secretly hoped that they weren't true. Hearing Luka list out her crimes undid that illusion, and she watched it dissipate. He hadn't even mentioned the lies she had told, the ways she had deceived Paul, Mrs. Pamson. Innocent people, all of them; they didn't deserve to bear responsibility for another man's sin. She had convinced herself she was after justice. Instead, she'd only used it as a pretext to commit unconscionable crimes.

Luka had given up trying to find a spare key for the padlock. He stretched his hand between the bars. "Give me the key."

"I'll give it. Just tell me how Thankgod is doing. Because of God. I want to know that he's fine. That nothing happened to him." She knew her tears had escaped and were running freely down her face. She knew her voice was pathetic, whiney. But it was the only voice she had.

"Thankgod is dead," Luka said quietly.

Murmula stood there, breathing, trying to decipher the three words he had spoken, as though there was some deeper meaning to them, some code that she had to unlock. Somehow her hand floated upward with the key into Luka's reach.

He snatched it and unlocked the gate. He was still holding the wheel spanner when he stepped through the opening, but he didn't try to use it. Perhaps he could see that he had already defeated her with those words.

He pointed a finger in the direction of the road and said, "Go back to those that sent you and tell them the person they want dead isn't here.

You people do not like peace. I'm warning you now, if I ever see you here or anywhere around Tudun Wada again, I will kill you myself. Go."

Murmula inched backward slowly, trying to remain awake to the world. She turned to start going, then stopped and faced him again. Luka stood, barring the way like a sentry.

"I'm sorry for what I did to you," she said softly.

Luka bent forward in a smooth motion and scooped up sand in his hand and tossed it at her. The spray of dust and grit pelted her face. She clawed at her eyes.

"Didn't I just warn you? You've caused enough trouble here. That man has lost his wife, everything. Just leave him alone. I said if I see you around here again, I will kill you with my own hands. Leave this place before I change my mind."

As Murmula hurried away, she tried to dam her tears with what remained of her will.

Little boy dead.

Little boy dead.

Little boy dead.

Little boy dead.

Every few paces she would glance back to see if Luka was following her. She heard her phone ringing, but she didn't look at it until she was safely in a keke napep headed back home. It was Beatrice. The sight of the name on her screen left her breathless for a few seconds. When she finally answered, the sound of Beatrice's voice kindled a warmth in her chest. Beatrice still worked at Mrs. Manuel's shop. She wanted Murmula to come over. Murmula asked to come down from the keke napep and caught another one heading into town. She alighted at the intersection of the FirstBank and the Mobil filling station and walked down to Beach Road. She stood at the gate to the property, amazed at the silence. The itinerant DJ and his wheelbarrow were nowhere to be seen. It was the first thing she asked about after Beatrice had hugged her and brought her a cold Fanta.

"Na wa for you o," Beatrice said in mock remonstrance. "You won't even ask me how I am, if I am alive and well. It is that jobless human being you're interested in."

Murmula pushed down the news about Thankgod and screwed her face into smile. She had missed Beatrice's sardonic joviality. "I can already see from your fat cheeks and full bumbum that you're alive and well." It was true. Beatrice's skin glowed. There was an air of prosperity about her that transcended her woody perfume.

"Abi you have a secret crush on him ne?" Beatrice tapped Murmula's knee. "You for tell me since, I for arrange am for you."

"The place just feels quiet, like someone died."

"Me, I like it that way. For once, a person can hear herself grumble and complain."

Beatrice was still speaking when the glass door to the tailors' room slid open and a tailor named Muazu appeared. He and Murmula had hit it off when he learned she was the only other Muslim who worked in the shop. He had started calling her Diyar Afonja when he heard she was from Ilorin.

"Diyar Afonja," he said with a smile. "Today you remember us."

"Speak English, my friend," Beatrice interjected. "How do I know you two are not planning to sell me?"

"If we sell you, it's your fault," Murmula said. "How long have you been in Jos and you don't know Hausa?"

"Abeg, I don't have the gift of cramming languages up and down," Beatrice said, and squeezed her face. "I'm a typical Igbo woman. My gift is understanding money. That is the language I can speak very well."

They all laughed. Muazu said he was on his way to the mosque and asked Murmula if she would join him. She said she wasn't staying long and thanked him for the invitation.

"It looks like everyone is around," Murmula said after he left, realising what she meant as soon as she'd said it.

"Everyone except Talatu."

"What happened to her?"

"Hmmm, my sister." Beatrice shook her head. She didn't speak for a moment.

"Did she also disappear?"

Beatrice raised her brow and looked at her. "Disappear?"

"Yes."

"Don't tell me you also believe in that nonsense."

Murmula stopped moving. She felt like she was suspended inside something other than air, something viscous and slow-moving that muffled her hearing and altered her vision. She noticed that the Fanta bottle was slipping out of her hand. She put it on the floor and drew her spine into a straight line.

Beatrice noticed her new iciness. "Ah, sorry o. I didn't know you're one of them. Let's change the subject—"

"No. I want to talk about it." Murmula didn't bother concealing the anger in her voice.

Beatrice looked at her.

"People have lost loved ones. How can you act like nothing ever happened?"

"Me, I haven't seen proof o."

"You don't have anyone that disappeared?"

Beatrice shook her head.

"Nobody in your house?"

"I live by myself."

"No relatives?"

"My parents are dead. I am an only child. Even both my father and mother were the only children. My grandparents are dead. The rest of my family is in Enugu. As far as I know, they are all around."

"What about your neighbours?"

"I don't talk to my neighbours."

"Your church?"

"I'm a Catholic, but I haven't gone to church in a long time."

As Murmula watched Beatrice, her friend seemed to shape-shift before her eyes. Murmula was seeing herself in Beatrice, or at least the potential for a version of herself. She had no friends here in Jos or back in Ilorin. Her father and mother were dead. She was an only child. But for Baba Karami and his family, she might have been cut off from the world beyond herself. Beatrice's refusal to accept what had happened puzzled and infuriated her, but she could see how easily she herself could have been just as isolated.

"What about Talatu?" Murmula said, trying to locate a crack in Beatrice's screen of denial. "Why isn't she here?"

"Talatu died."

Murmula's mouth fell open.

"She was killed by her fiancé. He put her head in the toilet and drowned her."

"Inna Lillahi wa inna ilayhi raji'un."

Words that had failed Murmula when she heard about Thankgod now came readily to her lips. She cradled her head in her hands and lowered it gently toward the floor. It stopped between her knees and remained there like a star suspended between the heavens and the earth. Something heaved its way from the bottom of her stomach and up through her body. It came out of her unmanacled and naked and wild. She didn't know Talatu well, yet something in the incongruous details of her death was the killing stroke in a deterioration process that had begun with the poisoning. It had been worsened by the disappearances and then further compounded by the news of Thankgod's death. Murmula raised her hands to heaven, placed them on her head, tried to grab herself at the seams so she could rip herself asunder—

—still warm to the touch, like she slipped out of bed seconds ago to use the bathroom but also left her clothes behind and that blood-tinged wad of cotton that shouldn't be so terrifying but is for reasons that are beyond Murmula. Baba Karami and Gogo Hauwawu standing as dark statues in the dark dawn, marking what she has seen as real, standing inside Baba Karami's arms and all of them together, staring at the space that Ishat used to occupy with every ounce of her flesh, and one of them going to call Musty—no longer matters who—and returning with clothes clutched strangely in hands that belong to them all and they stare together with eyes that belong to them all—Ishat whispering something softly about dinner from the door and being ignored because the world just then has become a bit too much for Murmula and she just needs a moment, a night to herself, and will attend to the burgeoning guilt of lying with her body to her little cousin and make up for it in the morning, sweet, little Ishat, already a woman though they don't discuss but probably will at some opportune time, and a pure sweet little boy dead and poisoned and sweet Ishat who is too pure to hold a grudge for too long and holds her like the big sister she herself never had and so could never have known that that is what it means to sister someone to hold them on a night of rain like they are all that matter and a little boy dead in the atmosphere in the world and—

—pressed to her forehead. Murmula sat up and took it out of the hand doing the pressing and saw then that the hand belonged to Mrs. Manuel. She was stretched out on the sofa in the shop. Beatrice, Muazu, and the other tailors all stood around and watched her with silent, worried expressions. There was a damp cloth in her hand. She dropped it and sat up. She made to get to her feet, but Mrs. Manuel stayed her with both hands. Murmula looked at her again, but Mrs. Manuel had turned her face to bark something at the ogling crowd. When she looked at Murmula again, her face relaxed into something warm and soft.

19

He had been swearing a lot, but it wasn't helping. Words like *fuck*. Actually, it was just *fuck*. He thought it might let him loosen steam from his head. Instead, all it did was make him think of what Rahila would have said, how she might have looked at him. But the beer did help. It made the world feel softer against him, as if there was an all-pervading cushion between him and everything that was happening. Even with the TV turned on and the news cycling its way through the hours. The world had moved past its initial shock into deduction mode. The new chairman of the National Population Commission had become the face of the government's attempts at restoring calm and confidence to the public. While a detailed roll of the disappeared was being put together, with survivors encouraged to provide full details on a widely disseminated website, the chairman was working in tandem with the new inspector general of police and the new secretary to the government of the federation to engage in a forensic investigation of all claims of disappearances. Family members were also encouraged to preserve the last-known clothing of the lost and maintain patience while members of the Nigerian police worked their way through the communities under their watch.

Pamson had no intention of complying. He changed the channel.

On CNN, two scientists, a physicist and a chemist, were debating what the disappearances meant for the laws of matter. It was all gibberish to Pamson. He flipped the channel again. Al Jazeera had a political commentator discussing the missing heads of state and repercussions for strategic interests and the global balance of power. More gibberish, but he left it on and picked up Rahila's phone. It lit up with a beep. He had been dreading this for weeks, but with his mind sufficiently fortified against any onslaught of anguish, he got past her screen lock with a single guess (her birthday) and scrolled through her messages. He found the texts from him—that was really all he was after. They were all brief and to the point, often typed with one hand while he drove, riddled with incomplete words or the absurd impositions of autocorrect. He released an amused grunt at *I'm not hugging* that was a response to *Paul is making semo*. He had always been in a hurry when communicating with her by phone, as if something of the utmost importance was waiting for him on the other end of the exchange. But there had been nothing except what had always been—the grime of his fucking life. Now she was gone and he was still here, surrounded by it, the same old grime. He opened her drafts to see if there were any unsent messages with his name on them, but the folder was empty. It hadn't been much different in person either, he had to admit. Hence his attempt to fix it, to save his marriage—but God or whoever the fuck was up there wouldn't have it. His mind had just started to spiral again into the depths where his uninvited guests had taken up permanent residence—he really thought he had escaped them for good—when the phone chimed multiple times in quick succession. A slew of messages had just come in.

Many of them were from Rahila's colleagues. Work-related questions sent late at night. An inquiry about the definite delivery date for a grant application. Rough financial projections by someone who was bad at math and needed her input. Gossip about an office romance. And a greeting from Murmula: Good evening ma. I hope you're well. Just wanted to say hello. I hope you haven't been affected by what is happening. It had been sent earlier that evening. He skipped up the screen with the tip of his forefinger, scanning the history of their communication. Inquiries about the day, about a training, about health, about family. A profusely worded text thanking Rahila for her generosity and her kindness and wishing her all the blessings of Allah and Firdausi. He hadn't given the girl much thought since his discussion with Luka. Was she really involved in the poisoning incident? At any rate, the business was all but dead. Would he be able to actualise the vision for Pamson Motor Care without Paul? Without Philip and the infusion of cash he had promised? And knowing what the business could have been, would he ever be able to contentedly return to what it once was? The thought of closing the garage continued to hover before him like a buzzing insect intent on gaining his attention.

He picked up Paul's phone from the coffee table and turned it back on. Murmula's text message entered almost immediately: R u there?

He started to scroll up the chat, then sat up, the better to see. He suddenly wished he could adjust the world properly into focus. He didn't understand at first what he was reading. He muted the TV, and the house fell into silence, as if that would help him see better.

Murmula, where are you? Please pick up.

Murmula, they've taken him into the operating room.

M. What the fuck?!!

Why aren't you answering?

Is there something I need to know?

How did you know about the poison?

What did you give him?

Did you poison him?

Its late and I'm here with this boy, worried hes about to die.

His mother is here with me now. They doctor was asking questions. I had to make something up.

I haven't told Uncle Dareng or Aunty. I want to hear from you first. Call me.

Murmula, whatever it is, we can sort it out. I'm sure it was just a mistake.

I just got home. Call me. I'll leave my phone on.

That was the last message. Pamson had found the phone under Paul's pillow nearly two days after the disappearances. There were missed calls from Eunice and other names he didn't recognise, presumably Paul's friends. Pamson had driven to her house to see how she was coping. At the sight of him, she had wept into her hands and remained inconsolable even when he stood up to leave. The tragedy was so ruthless and complete in its ubiquity that it had transmuted the process of shared mourning he was used to. Everybody had been touched. He had resisted the whispered offers of those intending to visit or drop off a meal. He sensed in them a half-hearted desire to rise to custom despite the weight of their own sorrow. He ignored calls from Mark Miner and others he considered friends. More than once, someone had knocked at the gate, and he had stared at the TV, unmoving and unwilling. Reverend Dogo had said Rahila and all the disappeared had been spared the fate of having to exist in such a wicked world. He said that this was the true meaning of the Rapture, that perhaps God had to separate those who had the stamina to withstand evil from those who didn't. That the Rapture was mercy and not reward. But he still couldn't explain why it affected people irrespective of creed. Pamson thought it was all rubbish. He had torn up his baptismal card upon his return home from seeing the clergyman.

Pamson checked the time on the text from Murmula. It had been sent two days ago, the same day she had called Paul's phone. Perhaps within minutes of calling, while he was still with Luka. He flicked his way to the top of the messages and started reading.

The first message was from Paul:

Hi, this is Paul.
My number.

Her reply:

Thanx

Days later, from him:

My uncle and aunt are having a thanksgiving in church.
Would you like to come?

U want me to come to ur church?

No, not that.
People usually come to the house after.

U're inviting me?

Yes

Owk

A day after the thanksgiving:

That was nice

Thanx for inviting me

I enjoyed the chicken

Thanks for coming
My sister makes the best chicken

I don't feel like ur uncle likes me

Oh, really, is it like a secret family recipe?

What makes you say that?
It's her own secret recipe
Lol

I keep wondering why he won't give me a chance

I'm sure he has nothing against you personally
But put yourself in his shoes
What would you do if a complete stranger came from nowhere
and asked you for job?

U're right

It would just mean so much

Aunty definitely has an interest in you
She's been asking questions
If you stand any chance in working for uncle, it's with her

A couple of weeks later:

Did ur uncle like the idea of expanding the business?

I've given him the proposal
Still waiting

The next day:

Any good news?

Still waiting . . .

A few hours later:

Good news
He loves it
We talked about it this morning for like 2 hours

Masha Allah

That's great

Thanks for striking the match
You're such a genius
Lol

Just remember me in ur kingdom

Trust me
I've got you

Pamson didn't move for some time. It wasn't a lot to go on, but it seemed quite plain that Murmula had gently steered things in her favour. There had to be more to her than she'd claimed. He took his phone and called James.

"Hello, Oga."

"James, tell me everything you know about the day Thankgod was poisoned."

There was silence on the other end for a few seconds. Finally, James said, "Oga, I didn't want to tell you because . . ." He allowed his voice to diminish and then die out altogether.

"What happened?"

"He started complaining that his stomach was paining. At first no one paid any attention, you know how he likes to eat everything. The girl took him inside—"

"Murmula?"

"The receptionist."

"Yes, Murmula."

"Yes—she took him inside and stayed with him. After some time, Paul came and they went to the hospital. When I talked with Paul on the phone, he said that it looked like Thankgod had been poisoned."

"Did she go with them?"

"To the hospital? Yes. She was even the one that called Paul and told him to come."

"But how did they know it was poison?"

"The girl said it. Paul said she told them at the hospital."

"How did she know?"

"That's what we're all wondering, Oga. Maman Ivie said she was the one that came to collect your food in the warmer. I remember when you gave it to Thankgod."

"Are you saying Murmula put something in the food?"

"It explains everything, Oga. Did you eat from it?"

"No."

"See? That food is the last thing Thankgod ate before he went to the hospital. I tried to call his father, but his phone was switched off. I had to go to the house . . ."

Pamson listened to the disturbing details with his ears, but his mind was undergoing something far more unnerving: sudden clarity. He felt like a juggling pin in midair with the wrong side up, but with a kind of devastating perspective. Someone had tried to kill him. Someone had entered his life under pretext and tried to administer a foreign substance into his system that would affect his bodily functions and end his life. That required a certain dedication. It wasn't an accident. With cold-blooded intention, someone had looked at him and concluded that he deserved to die.

He didn't ask why she would do such a thing. Should it matter when his sins were so stark against what he had been trying to cover them with for the past two decades: being a decent, hardworking man? Who was he to think he could escape? Those uninvited guests, they would be with him forever because they actually weren't uninvited; he had opened the door and let them in, and he couldn't change his mind all of a sudden and expect things to return to normal. It didn't work that way. They were faceless, featureless, bound by a single trait, his guests, his ghosts: he'd slaughtered them all with his own hand. But there was one face, one figure among them whom he remembered. It hovered over his left shoulder from time to time. In his boyhood he had often tried to determine the shape of clouds and, unlike his friends, had been bad at it. The clouds all seemed inseparable, homogenous, indistinguishable. But one day he'd looked very hard, and one image pounced up out of the cumulous mass: a shapeless head with a long beard. Each subsequent attempt yielded the same image: a bearded head. The contours shifted in small ways, but it was the same head, one he had come to believe belonged to God. God's head followed him around into his teens, and then it disappeared. The face he remembered was like God's head fore-grounding itself against the other clouds. The face of a young man—a boy, really—topped by a flaming-orange beanie, bottomed by a purple hoodie. Pamson didn't remember where he had killed him or why. But he remembered the shape of the bullet hole he had put in his cheek. Had he been a member of a rival gang, a tool deployed from some other politician's arsenal? Or had he just been at the wrong place at the wrong time? Pamson had thought about that face many times, wondered about those who had called him beloved, how they were getting on without any answers as to his whereabouts. It wouldn't be far-fetched to imagine Murmula as that young man's avenger. He'd considered the possibility many times, that someone might come after him. Now here he was. Whether she was related to that young man with the orange beanie or any of his other guests, she was here now, after his blood.

"Oga? Oga?"

He still had the phone pressed to his ear. He thanked James and turned off the TV after he had hung up. He stared at the destroyed cake, wishing he could put it back together so he could do it all over again. If he stayed any longer in the house, his hands would find something else to dismantle. He got the car keys, and when he had backed out of the compound, he screamed the car down the street without stopping to close the gate. A cloud of dust rose in his wake.

Murmula had tried to kill him.

He turned into State Lowcost Junction by some impulse and didn't stop turning until he had parked in front of St. Monica's Catholic Church. The building stood, three-cornered and majestic with its cross pinnacle and reddish-burnt bricks.

She had emotionally manipulated Paul into helping her to get hired, under the pretext of wanting to learn about cars.

At the gate he asked where he could find the confession room. The guard pointed him to a building behind the church, at the edge of the property. He walked the grounds, noting that he was not alone, that people were streaming in and out of the building to which he was headed.

Using her charm and beauty and seeming innocence, she had gained access into his life and begun to undo it from the inside. Like some sadistic predator that toyed with its food, catching and releasing it over and over.

He entered a corridor that had a long bench against one wall. A square window at the end of the corridor allowed the day's waning light in. About six or seven people sat along the bench in what appeared to be a queue. He was the eighth.

She had won the trust of his wife. Had injected confusion into the garage's atmosphere, forcing people to turn on each other. Because of that, he had used his own two hands to beat up Luka for a crime he had never committed. He had fallen right into her trap.

Every few minutes someone would come out of the confession room and a new person would go in. The line moved, and he shuffled his weight up the bench.

She had tried to hurt him but only ended up poisoning an innocent boy in the process.

At last, it was his turn to go in next. He waited at the edge of the bench as the confession-room door shut behind the woman in front of him.

Murmula had burrowed into his life like a worm and had begun to destroy it bit by bit, and he deserved it. Every last thing she had done to him.

The woman came out of the confession room, and he stood up, taking note of her for the first time. She was young and wore a colourful silky scarf with a flower pattern. Her eyes were moist. She bowed her head in greeting when their eyes met and walked away. Pamson turned the door handle and went in.

He was in a small dark room. The only light came in from under the door. A wooden screen partitioned the room into two, effectively its own wall. There was a cushioned seat in the middle of the screen. Pamson sat in it and noticed that his ear was now level with a small mesh opening in the wood. He opened his mouth but didn't know what to say.

"Is anyone there?" a smooth male voice said.

It was impossible to tell the age of the speaker, but there was an unmistakable youthfulness in it.

"Yes, I'm here," Pamson said.

"You can go on."

"I want to share something with you. I've never told anyone this thing before."

"You're supposed to say, 'Bless me, Father, for I have sinned,'" the voice said, burdened by a strain of patience.

"Yes, okay, sorry. Bless me, Father, for I have sinned."

"When was your last confession?"

"Um, I don't know, Father."

"You don't know?"

"I've never confessed."

"Are you sure you're a Catholic?"

"I'm COCIN, Father."

The voice sighed wearily. "This isn't how we do things."

"Father, please. My soul is heavy. I need someone I can talk to."

"Go and see a counsellor."

"The things I want to confess, I can't tell a counsellor. I have to tell someone or else . . . or else I don't know what will happen."

There was a pause. "Well, I'm sure the Lord would not be pleased if I sent a sinner away. Catholic or not, this is the house of God. What is your sin, my son?"

"It isn't just one, Father. They are many."

"Go on."

"I cheated on my wife with another woman."

"Go on."

"I agreed to help a House of Assembly member embezzle money. I gave him permission to use my company."

"Is that all?"

"I have killed people."

"Go on."

"Many people."

"My son, there are people waiting. Don't keep breaking your words. Say it all at once."

"I used to work for one politician in town. Maybe you even know him. We were his boys. Anytime he wanted to cause trouble or kill someone, he sent us. He paid us money to start fights and intimidate the supporters of his rivals. We started many fights, and we used bottles, knives, guns. I killed a few young men at the time. They would have been my age today, maybe with their own families."

The voice started to speak. "My son—"

"When the first crisis happened in 2001, I had already stopped working for the man. But in our area in Angwan Rukuba, when there were clashes between Muslims and Christians, I used to join the fights. I claimed I was defending my people. I had a gun that I used. I killed many young men, Father. Many young men. We would load their bodies into the back of cars and go and dump them in a lake somewhere, or bury them in mass graves where we were sure nobody could find them. I stopped cars on the road; if a person was a Muslim, we pulled the person out and hacked him to death. I shed so much blood, Father. So much blood."

"My son, you—"

"Now my entire family has disappeared, Father. Everyone I love. They were among the people that disappeared. And I just found out that one of my workers tried to poison me. I think I'm paying for my sins, but I don't know who is punishing me. I don't know if it is God or somebody else. I know I deserve it. But I can't sleep. I can't eat. My business is dead. I don't know what to do. I don't know what to do, Father. Please tell me what to do." Pamson's voice had become tremulous and he was weeping.

The voice didn't speak for a long time. When it finally did, it said, "The disappearances have left me as confused as you. I lost my only son. Let me be honest with you, man to man. Do you speak Hausa?" The voice had lost its grandeur and self-seriousness. It was now looser, more uncertain.

"Yes."

The voice switched to Hausa: "Everything you're seeing me do here, I'm doing it because I need to survive. I still have my younger ones and parents to support. If I stopped being a Father, where would I start from? God is dead to me. I wish I could tell all those people waiting to come in that this is a waste of time. But I have to keep on doing it because I need to survive. None of it matters. Everybody must continue to do what is in front of him. If it helps you, if it puts food on your table, clothes on your children's back, fine. But if not, find something else. Don't waste your time worrying about your conscience. Nobody is going to judge us or save us."

The voice ceased and didn't speak again.

Pamson stared at his hands in the dimness. Nothing was going to remove the blood from them. Not the years of grease and soot stains he had imprinted on them in the name of hard work, not baking a cake in the name of love, not coming to a stupid confessional. There would be no mercy for him. He was who he was, and nothing would ever change that. He would have to find his own way forward.

20

A pall had settled over the city. She knew it was the departed rainy season and the gradual shift toward Harmattan, but it felt like a haunting, still. In the mornings on her way to work, she would sometimes alight from the keke napep in front of the Mobil filling station by the FirstBank. The drivers often refused to go straight through because it meant risking fewer passengers on that lonelier stretch of Beach Road. When she came down, she would walk the three hundred metres to the shop, dwarfed by the buildings and the trees that loomed over her all the way from their roots on adjoining streets. She would stare at the moving, indefatigable world and marvel at its merciless efficiency, at its insistence to continue as it had always done. She was complicit in this, for here she was on her way to work, getting on with her life, living. As though Ishat and Musty and two and a half million others hadn't spontaneously ceased to exist. And she had caused it. Not death, something else. Something far worse.

And Paul. It had been three days since she had texted him. He was gone, too, she was sure of it. That had to be the only explanation for his silence. Or was it? Could he still be angry about the hospital? Could she blame him? How would she react if he had abandoned her at the hospital with a dead boy?

Mrs. Manuel's car was parked in front of the shop. Murmula paused at the door, bracing herself for yet another encounter with the woman's relentless exuberance, before pulling it open and going inside.

Mrs. Manuel was seated on the sofa, drinking a cup of tea and reading a fashion magazine. Her reading glasses were balanced daintily like a small bird on a small branch. She looked up, and her face broke into a giant grin.

"Hello, my dear! Come, come and sit with me."

"Good morning, ma," Murmula said.

Mrs. Manuel almost pulled her into the seat beside her. Her body felt warm and full and maternal through her sunset ankara gown. Murmula was overcome by the inexplicable urge to lean into that warmth, to let herself be swaddled by motherly affection. Mrs. Manuel held out an empty mug to her.

"It's ginger tea with lemon and honey," Mrs. Manuel said as she poured the steaming amber liquid into Murmula's mug. "This dry weather is my worst time of the year."

Murmula raised the mug to her lips more out of a reluctance to speak than out of thirst. Since Mrs. Manuel had walked in on her the other day having a breakdown, she hadn't let up in this coddling behaviour. She had conducted a casual cursory interview on the spot, taken a pancake-thin summary of Murmula's work experience, and offered Murmula a job within a half hour. Murmula owed it largely to Beatrice, who had stood by and interjected with mildly exaggerated claims about Murmula's expertise in computing and data management. In the end, Murmula took the job because it would let her spend more time away from the house, away from Gogo Hauwawu's insistent melancholy. She would also get to be around Beatrice, who had grudgingly changed her mind about the disappearances after witnessing Murmula's meltdown.

Beatrice had texted that morning to say she would be late because a tanker had flipped over and was blocking the road out of Apata. After Mrs. Manuel left, Murmula sat with Beatrice's handwritten account of the previous day's earnings and transferred them into the new laptop that Mrs. Manuel had procured at her request. It was painstaking work, but her brief stint at Pamson Motor Care had prepared her.

She'd had time to think in the one week she had spent here. As though occasioned by some vague quality inside the shop—with its rolls and rolls of women's fabric, its steady train of bejeweled customers streaming through with children and maids and the occasional husband in tow, and the hush that often claimed it while Beatrice napped or went to make a delivery—certain things began to come into stunning focus. The major revelation was that her life had no direction. Avenging her father and getting justice was not the purpose she had believed it to be. It had taken over her life and robbed her of all clarity. In the wake of everything, the idea of killing a man, or even taking apart his life, suddenly seemed foolish, a waste of time. And too costly. She already knew what it felt like to have blood on her hands; she didn't want to extend that feeling. She had also made the mistake of believing she could be selective, discriminate in her vengeance; now she saw that it was impossible not to touch others in the process. Had she succeeded in killing him, what, then? Would she have been able to insulate his wife from the pain of losing a husband? Would she have been able to help his unborn child grow up without feeling like the lack of a father was a gaping hole in its life? Would she have been able to extract Paul's grief out of his soul like a poison so he wouldn't have to miss his uncle?

Paul. He seemed to be shadowing her, even in this place he'd never been to. She felt his presence constantly, though he was snubbing her, dead or alive. She suspected that the mobile DJ had also disappeared, but whatever the reason was for his absence, Murmula was glad he wasn't there to play songs anymore. What if he played the wrong song—Runtown's "Mad Over You," for instance—and derailed her day? She missed the sense of fulness Paul had given her, the way he had coloured in the negative spaces left by her parents' demise and her own general sense of unmooring. Without her even realising it, he'd become a bulwark against the meaninglessness that had plagued her for years. She'd been blind to it when he had been right in front of her. Now he was all around her, following her everywhere, underscoring how empty her life really was.

Using what she remembered of the systems Paul had created for Pamson Motor Care, she organised the data so that the numbers could provide a story at a glance of the business's performance. Her goal was to figure out a way to completely digitise the financial accounting of Eldoba Stitches so that Mrs. Manuel could make more strategic business decisions. When she was done with it and had taught Beatrice how to use it, she would quit and probably leave Jos for good. She couldn't continue to wait around for confirmation of Paul's absence. For all she knew, it was possible that the entire Pamson household had also been lost. Mrs. Pamson hadn't returned her text after all, which was unlike her. The truth was that she didn't want to know.

The rest of the day passed without incident. She had started bringing her prayer abaya with her to work, folded into her handbag. But it had been merely a formality: she never used it. She made another excuse when Muazu asked her to go to the mosque. After he left, she once again was unable to account for refusing to simply take the abaya out, perform the ablution, and pray. She barely remembered the last time she'd offered salat or even any du'a. She ate her lunch outside under the mango tree beside the building, where the fruit that dropped from the branches, littering the ground in rotting piles, made her think of her missed salats piling up, waiting for her to remember them. None of it seemed like it mattered now.

She closed at a few minutes after five. The keke napep trip back was one of those rare chains of occurrences in which the driver was taking the exact route she would have followed home and failing to find any passengers along the way. It was nonstop, and she had the back seat of the vehicle all to herself. Feeling a little guilty at her pleasure in such a smooth ride, she gave the driver two hundred naira instead of the one hundred naira he was expecting. His thanks followed her all the way around the bend.

When she walked into the house, Baba Karami and Gogo Hauwawu were in the living room. *Ratatouille* was playing with the volume turned off, but nobody seemed to be watching it. Murmula stopped in her tracks as she remembered Ishat with a sudden flutter of memory. *Ratatouille* had been her cousin's favourite cartoon. Animation. Movie. Murmula tore her eyes from the screen and greeted her uncle and aunt. Gogo Hauwawu managed a tiny grunt and nodding of her head while Baba Karami looked around and asked how her day had gone. From the way they leaned forward in their seats, as if waiting for something to enter their lives and bring about change, any kind of change, she could tell they had been having an argument. Was she the thing they were waiting for?

"What would you like me to make, Aunty?" Murmula said.

"I'm not hungry," Gogo Hauwawu said without looking at her. "Don't worry about me."

"And what about me?" Baba Karami said. "Wato I should starve because you're not hungry ko?"

Gogo Hauwawu raised her face as though to get a good look at him. "Don't you have a mouth? Tell her what you want and she'll make it for you."

Baba Karami turned to Murmula. His brow was stretched taut, his nostrils flared. She had never seen him so angry. "Sit down, Murmula."

Unsure of what this meant or where exactly she should sit, Murmula took the farthest seat from them, the one closest to the front entrance.

"I want you to be the judge between us," Baba Karami said. "And speak the truth. We all live in this house. Since the thing that happened, happened weeks ago, this woman hasn't done anything in this house. When it comes to food, if you're not around to make something, I have to go to the kitchen myself and find what to eat while she's in the room. She stays home all day. I'm your witness; you're the one that cleans, cooks."

"You talk as if many years have passed," Gogo Hauwawu said. "Your children ceased to exist two months ago. I'm sorry if my grieving process is too slow for you."

"Everybody has been affected by this, Hauwawu, but they're not hiding in the room. Even Murmula here has started working again. That is how you cope with something like this. You've refused to go to the mosque or to see the imam."

Murmula lowered her face. She wished her uncle—or anyone else, for that matter—wouldn't raise her as an example. What would he say if he knew all that her hands had wrought? The hypocrite she was. Munafiqun. Munafika.

"Murmula, say something mana." Baba Karami turned to her.

Gogo Hauwawu kept her eyes glued to the screen, where a ghost and a rat were scaring the life out of each other. "Stop dragging her into this. This is a case between me and you."

Murmula cleared her throat. "Baba, the truth is that everyone is different. You can't expect two people to have an injury and heal at the same time. We each heal differently. You have to stop comparing Aunty to other people. Not even to you or myself. She needs to go through the process of her own recovery. Aunty, as for you," Murmula said, propelled by a gush of confidence, "stop staying in that room alone. You can at least go to the mosque and perform du'a. The imam's tafsir has helped me. You can ask questions, and others can benefit from the answers too. And none of your friends come here anymore. Even the ones that came, you've refused to see them." Murmula stopped there. She had just told another lie, but surely this was different. If it got Gogo Hauwawu going to the mosque and socializing again, wouldn't it be a good thing? But as the silence stretched on, she wished more and more that she hadn't spoken.

"Thank you for telling us the truth, Murmula," Baba Karami said. "I will try to be more understanding with your aunt. Will you forgive me, my baby?" He reached over and took Gogo Hauwawu's hand. She released a tiny, grudging smile, then pulled her hand away.

"Thank you, Murmula," Gogo Hauwawu said.

A few seconds later, Gogo Hauwawu made to get up. Maybe it was the panic of a rare window of peace and harmony quickly closing, or a vague sense of the amount of effort it would require to have them both together before her again, or her desire to start speaking more truthfully to them. Whatever it was, Murmula, despite her better judgement, found her mouth moving again, heard her voice speaking plainly.

"Baba, I wanted to ask you about something. I'm sorry to have to bring up the past."

Gogo Hauwawu stopped moving and looked up.

"Of course, Murmula. What is it?" He leaned forward.

"What do you know about my father's land? The one in Federal Lowcost?"

"The one he sold?"

Murmula wasn't sure what he meant, but she said, "Yes."

Baba Karami sank into the chair, shaking his head, turning his gaze on the floor. "That was a painful matter. When your father told me he had decided to sell it, it made me sad. But things were very tight for him. He died shortly after, so I never got to know much about it. Your mother was very private; she kept everything to herself."

Murmula stared at her uncle, gutted by how much her mother had kept him in the dark. Why hadn't she shared the burden? Instead, she had left it to her to be the avenger. Something that should have been a man's responsibility. Mama hadn't been fair to her.

"Why do you ask?" Baba Karami said.

Murmula shook her head and said, "It's nothing. I was just wondering about it." Then she took a deep breath and added, "I'm planning to go back to Ilorin."

Gogo Hauwawu, who had stood up, sat back down as though she had been dropped. She turned her gaze on Murmula. Murmula recoiled under its intensity, understanding then that this was not a thing that should have been said out loud.

"Go back and do what, exactly?" Baba Karami said.

Murmula knew she couldn't take back what she had said, but she tried anyway. "I don't know yet. I haven't finished thinking through it. I may even just decide to remain here. Let's see."

"Or are you engaged to someone we don't know about?" Baba Karami said.

Murmula recognised the levity in his voice. It was small and strained and barely perceptible, but it had been in her father's voice, and now it was in his, too, trying to help her. She smiled at him to convey her gratitude.

"I know what has happened is difficult," Baba Karami said. "But you don't have any other family anywhere. Your mother, God rest her soul, would have wanted you to stay with us. Look how far you've come. Less than six months here and you've already gotten two jobs. You don't know what next Allah will bring along."

Murmula hadn't quantified the time she had spent in Jos, but it had felt longer than six months. She had been quietly measuring the weight of recent events in years. It had felt like years.

Gogo Hauwawu spoke suddenly. "I'm not the one that breastfed you, I'm not the one that carried you in my womb. But I had hoped that you would have at least started to think of me as your mother. Especially in the last two months, after what happened. But clearly you've shown that you have no place for me—"

"Hauwa!" Baba Karami barked.

"You call him Baba, but you call me Aunty. If he is Baba to you, doesn't that make me Mama? Allah has taken away my children. Allah has taken away your parents. Instead of you to begin to think of us as one family, parents and daughter, you want to leave—"

"I said, that's enough!"

"Is it because we have nothing to give you? If your uncle was a wealthy man and could give you a job, would you be saying you want to go back to Ilorin?"

"She said she was just thinking about it!"

Gogo Hauwawu stood up and pointed at Murmula. "She's lying! If she was going to change her mind, would she have said it?" She was shouting now. Her thick, short arms bludgeoned the air, her sleeves trailing behind in dark streaks. She snapped at Baba Karami, "Leave me alone, Baban Mustapha! You ungrateful girl! You wicked girl! How can you decide to abandon us after something like this? After everything we've done for you!" Murmula tried to bury her head in her arms, but it was no use. Gogo Hauwawu's voice pursued her into the pocket of solitude. There was no hiding place. In her black, flowing gown, she looked like a vision of maternal terror unleashed upon the world.

Murmula stood up with the intention of getting away, but Gogo Hauwawu seemed to have straddled the room, like she was everywhere at once. She pushed her back into her seat. Her strength was horrifying, and Murmula hid her face again. "You're not going anywhere! Do you hear me? How many days have I spent alone in that room! If I was your fucking birth mother, would you abandon me like that? Leave me alone like that? Do you know what it means to lose a child? Look at me! I said, fucking look at me!" Murmula felt her leaning in. She didn't know what she would do, but she waited. Instead, she heard quiet jostling.

When she raised her head, Baba Karami was holding on to his wife's arm, trying to pull her away.

"Baban Mustapha, I said leave me alone!"

Gogo Hauwawu's palm connected with his face. A resounding crack split the room, and Murmula flinched. There was a horrible pause that felt like the dying of something. When Baba Karami slapped his wife back, Murmula flinched again. And then she was on her feet, planting herself between them. But in doing so, she realised she didn't know who she was trying to protect.

"Go to your room, Murmula," Baba Karami said quietly.

Avoiding their faces, Murmula obeyed and sat on her side of the bed, her back to the door. Sleeping on the bed had been difficult, and she had managed it by completely avoiding Ishat's side. As though her cousin would come along shortly to lie down and whisper *Sai da safe* in her tired, tiny voice. Those were the very last words she had heard from her. Murmula held her breath and kept still, waiting to hear more yelling from the living room. But there was only silence. That, too, proved unbearable for her. She peered through the curtain: the living room was empty. Wrapping her veil around her head, she closed the front door gently behind her and walked away from the house.

She thought she might go to the mosque, see if she could find something there to help her deal with the whirlpool of emotions that was stirring in her. But when she reached the mosque, she kept on walking. Save for one or two worshippers, the ablution station next to the well was empty, the array of colourful plastic kettles stark and almost beautiful in the fading light. The smell of wet earth around the place was strange and welcoming to her. A woman she passed was setting up a hearth to make and sell masa, the transparent buckets of batter pale and bland against the vibrant earth. A girl of about ten was sweeping the ground while arranging a couple of benches that would receive the clients. Murmula skipped a river of a puddle and continued down the alley, which soon hit a wall and branched into two opposite directions. She'd never come this far into the neighbourhood before. She went left and soon came to a small intersection. There was a tiny market spread out in each arm of the crossroad, slowly winding down for the day. Tables, some barer than others, laden with little pyramids of tomatoes, onions, and bell peppers. Someone was frying awara behind some nearby wall, the oily and rich smell of the cheese curds heavy in the air. She went straight through the intersection, ambushed by the stray thought that her mother had made awara a lot with red pepper seeds ground into yaji, ginger, and lots of maggi.

From five hundred metres, she saw that she was approaching a fairly busy alley. Traffic flowed perpendicularly in both directions. The alleyways were fully in shadow by the time she reached the road. She took another left, realising it would take her to Last Gate. She was going in a rectangle. She had always had a good sense of direction, and it had made her proud because it unnerved the men in her life. All the guys she'd dated, all of them needing to be needed, to feel indispensable. But she had always been fine on her own. As she joined the flow of bodies coursing up and down the sidewalk, she felt like a trickle cascading into a creek. The sidewalk was too busy and lined with obstacles in her path—vulcanisers and their equipment, sellers of hardware, a fruit vendor selling oranges and lemons from a wheelbarrow. She stepped off and onto the street itself. Vehicles flew by, some so close she felt their wind brush against her arm. She still expected the streets to be much less crowded after the disappearances, but it all looked and felt the same. She walked against the flow of traffic—she had pedestrian sense. Cars, trucks, keke napeps, motorcycles. Everything loud and busy and purposeless. Movement for the sake of movement. Taken as a whole, this was what a city road with traffic was. It existed to be traffic, to serve as an essential part of the city, for what was a city without traffic? What was it without its buildings and its network of roads? What was it without its hordes of humanity to populate it and make it feel lived in? To make it be able to say about itself, *I am a city*? Like a toy city needing to prove that it was a city, with its little cars and people and roads. But taken apart, the different components began to take on individuality, take on purpose. As she was now, walking this darkening street in the glare of headlights that grew harsher with each passing stroke of dusk, she existed to add to the flow of bodies, to move along. It didn't matter if the bodies were Muslim or Christian or whatever else—all that mattered was that they were bodies moving in a strange, convoluted, deranged choreography of chaos, bodies that could perform the miracle of evanescing. But once she got home and entered her room, her purpose would wake up, raise its head, and sniff about hungrily, a terrifying question in search of a terrified answer.

As she stood outside the house forty minutes later, wondering if she had any right to call this or any place home, her phone made a sound. She had forgotten it was there. She had been gone perhaps an hour, though it had felt longer. Baba Karami hadn't looked for her or tried to call her. The cuts Gogo Hauwawu had made with her words were still fresh; Murmula preferred to treat her as a blacked-out figure in her mind for the moment.

She unlocked her screen and looked at the text, a response to the question she had thrown into the sea nearly a week ago and then given up hope she would ever hear back.

R u there?

Yes.

She started typing.

21

What a relief.

Why are you relieved?

I thought u disappeared

I'm here

U left me in suspense . . .

Maybe I deserve it

Yes

U didn't want 2 talk 2 me?

No

U were angry?

Would you have been happy in my position?

I'd have bn mad

Why did u answer my text?

I don't know
Why did you text me?

I dnt know

How is your aunty?

Or your cousin?

Mrs Pamson?

She isn't here.

What do u mean?

She's gone

Audhu billahi

She disappeared?

Yes

Inna lillahi

Am so sorry

Dat explains her silence

I texted her but she didnt answer

What does that mean?

Inna lillahi?

Yes

U dnt remember?

Remember what?

I once told u what inna lillahi means . . .

I'm sorry
I don't remember many things nowadays
Everything is strange
Remind me what it means

It means we belong 2 Allah and 2 him we shall return

My cousins also disappeared

I'm sorry about that.

How is Mr Pamson?

He's also gone

What?

He disappeared 2?

Yes

There was a long pause here for at least three minutes. Finally:

Am sorry Paul

Thank you

So u r by urself in the house?

Yes

Can I see u?

Okay

I want 2 apologise and explain everything

But I want to do it face 2 face

I want to see you too

I tot u wld neva want 2 see me again

I do
I miss u

I miss u 2

Where shld we meet?

You can come to the house
There's no one here
We can talk here

When?

Tomorrow

Owk

I have 2 go 2 work

But I can come when I close at 5

Okay
I can drop you at home after

Owk

Thanx

The city in the bluster of Harmattan was not the city in the rain, and the city in between was a different city still. There were confusing signals. There was enough dust to bathe the cars in the driveway overnight, yet the scent of rain would linger in the air like a stray detail that had been forgotten when the rainy season was being removed. Sometimes, in the late afternoons when he stood on his unpaved street just outside his gate, Pamson would see the low-hanging sun behind a wall of disturbed dust—a perfectly round, perfectly orange celestial fruit.

The neighbourhood, for all the sense it produced of being insulated from others, felt that much emptier after Hajiya Kande and her children's departure. As far as Pamson knew, nobody had been left in the house. The conversation in that confession room had triggered a certain repose that enveloped him. It was frightening in its simplicity, how starkly everything stood before him. As though the world had been stripped of all pretenses and laid bare before his eyes. Everyday objects took on a violent, otherworldly brilliance, and this effect was merely intensified when they were struck by sunlight. He swept the house and mopped the tiles, got rid of the unopened birthday presents, made the beds, started sleeping in their room again. He was slowly waking up to the way things truly were. He didn't know if he'd ever been awake before.

Despite the government's appeals for survivors to preserve and not tamper with the clothing of the lost, he washed Rahila's and Paul's clothes and folded them away into their respective wardrobes. Only a fool would wait for the Nigerian Police Force to follow through. Besides, what would they do with evidence? For all he knew, it was a desperate attempt by the government to be seen doing something. He listened to a retired policeman, a former DSP, on AIT asking how exactly this intervention was related to forensics. Did the NPF have a lead on the suspects? What did they know that US intelligence didn't, especially since their commander-in-chief had also been lost? No nation had a bigger reason to solve this mystery than America, and everybody knew America didn't play when it came to its intelligence. Yet they had come up with nothing. In the world of hard logic, there were theories of alien abductions, the involvement of certain governments (including the United States), and outright denial that such a thing could have happened.

Pamson had deliberately refused to wash the bedsheet, but each day his wife's scent and the musk of their lovemaking were that much less perceptible. She was gone, but she was also fading away. He worried that his memories wouldn't be strong enough to hold on to the small details that had made her who she was. He started to read the novels she had favoured, the Danielle Steels and Karen Kingsburys, taking note of the places she had marked, trying to decrypt the cipher that was her handwriting. At Luka's wedding, he watched the young man in a grey suit and his heavily pregnant bride dance on the reception ground, remembering the boy who had wandered onto his lot and offered to do any kind of work in exchange for food. Remembering the bride, then just a newly pregnant slip of a girl, coming to him with eyes full of tears to report Luka. Now look at them. Coupled for life, their vulnerabilities to sorrows untold greatly multiplied. Each flower that bloomed was a promise of death unfurling. Each triumph of love was a tragedy-in-waiting. Pamson wasn't so sure anymore if it was worth the risk.

◆ ◆ ◆

Good morning

Gd mrng. How was ur night?

Fine.
There's a change of plan
I can't meet today

Sorry
Something came up

Owk

When wld u prefer?

I'm not sure
I'll get back to you

Owk

Have a nice day

◆ ◆ ◆

Murmula no longer thought a jinn was punishing her, but she still found it hard to concentrate on a passage of text. While there were no distressing interruptions that hijacked her vision, her mind kept drifting to the fact that Mr. Pamson had disappeared along with the others. She still wasn't sure what to make of it. Was it a kind of justice that his final fate wasn't unlike her father's: a disappearance? Only now had she made the connection. If Mr. Pamson's fate was the justice she had sought, what did it mean if there was no one to miss him? And it seemed unfair that oblivion would be his comeuppance when he deserved to undergo what she had been forced to endure all these years. Furthermore, he had been unaware of his crime. Was it true judgement if the culprit missed the opportunity to see which particular crime the punishment was for?

She had no trouble reading numbers, and spent hours poring over Beatrice's handwritten figures, which were like a magnet for her mind, allowing her to focus intensely. She noticed that Beatrice did her best to avoid mentioning the disappearances when she was around Murmula. But when it was brought up in some transient fashion, her tone appeared to be that of someone coming around to consider alternative points of view. The more time Murmula spent in Mrs. Manuel's shop, the more she realised how glad she was to be there. Her encounter with Gogo Hauwawu had unsettled her so much that she hadn't given further thought to the question of returning to Ilorin. She was also waiting to meet with Paul, and the waiting was a torment she had begun to suspect he was using to punish her.

Three days after their row, Gogo Hauwawu followed Murmula into the bedroom and asked her to sit with her on the bed. They had been avoiding one another, despite Baba Karami's entreaties. He eventually gave up and stopped talking to both of them. He shunned the food either of them made and went to bed without eating. It remained a mystery where he got his meals from. When Gogo Hauwawu entered the room and sat, their knees almost touched as they faced each other on the bed. Gogo Hauwawu was wearing a plain, straight jallabiya and had wrapped a beige scarf tightly around her head. Murmula couldn't bring herself to look at her for the first minute or two, but when she finally did, she saw that she had lined her eyes with tozali and touched her face up with rouge. The effect was uneven. The sight of it stabbed anguish deep into Murmula. Ishat had been adept at applying makeup—she had often teased her mother for refusing to take advantage of her expertise when people were paying big money for such services.

"How was work today?" Gogo Hauwawu asked quietly.

"Work is well. How was your day?" Murmula found herself echoing her aunt's tone.

"I cleaned and did your uncle's laundry. Then I tried to look nice for him, but he isn't back yet. Maybe it's a good thing, because I hope you can tell me if I look silly." Gogo Hauwawu smiled, rolling her eyes.

Murmula couldn't conceal her laughter anymore. Gogo Hauwawu joined her. It was like a heavy blanket had been pulled off the room's atmosphere. Murmula breathed more easily after that. They went to the master bedroom, and Gogo Hauwawu sat on the bed while Murmula knelt in front of her. She gently wiped her face clean and started over. As Murmula applied the makeup, Gogo Hauwawu talked.

"I didn't come to apologise before now because I was too ashamed. I'm still ashamed. I didn't know where those words came from. I think I was a different person."

"You were," Murmula said. "But grief changes us all."

"I hit my husband," Gogo Hauwawu said. "I've never hit my husband before. To be fair, we slapped each other. But there has never been violence between us."

"You've also never had to deal with the loss of all your children," Murmula said. When Gogo Hauwawu didn't respond to that, she said, "Did you apologise to Baba Karami?"

"That very night. He apologised first. I was the one that started it, but he apologised first. Can you believe it?"

"He sounds like his brother. My mother used to say that sorry was like saliva on my father's tongue."

"Your father, God rest his soul. I never knew there was a gentler man than my husband until I met him. He was such a good man. A truly good man."

"Tell me a story about him."

Gogo Hauwawu chuckled immediately, as though the anecdote had been waiting on her lips. "One day, he came to our house because he and your mother had had a fight. We were living around Masallacin Juma'a then. This was before you were born; your mother was pregnant with you. He was so angry. When he told Baban Mustapha what it was about, they decided to switch clothes for the evening and pretend to be each other."

"What? Like a couple of creeps?"

"No, it was nothing like that at all. Baban Mustapha went to your house and had a conversation with your mother, and she calmed down and came around. Meanwhile, your father was wearing Baban Mustapha's clothes, pretending to be him. I didn't know that that was what they had planned. You know he liked to enter the kitchen. So, I was preparing to go and make dinner, but he told me to relax, stay with Mustapha in the parlour. He went in and cooked one delicious fried rice. Baban Mustapha came back, and they exchanged their clothes and he went home. He didn't tell Baban Mustapha he had made the rice. For almost a week they didn't say anything, but one day I asked Baban Mustapha what he had put in the rice because I wanted to make it. That was when I realised what had happened. Your father, he was gentle, but he was also very mischievous."

Murmula's shoulders shook from the laughter. "What did my mother say when she found out?"

"We were both very angry with them. We promised to get back at them, but we never found a way to do it."

"What was the argument about?"

"It was about you."

"Me?" Murmula said, shocked. "I thought you said I hadn't been born yet."

"It was about your name. Your mother didn't like the name, but your father, once he had an idea, he didn't know how to let it go. None of us had heard the name before. But here we are today, you're bearing it, and what a beautiful name it is."

Once Murmula had evenly applied the foundation to Gogo Hauwawu's dark skin, she started with the rouge, slathering it in short, widening swaths.

"You're free to go wherever you like," Gogo Hauwawu said. When Murmula met her eyes, she saw that she was looking at her face. "Whatever you decide, I want you to know that this will always be your home and we will always be your parents. Do you understand?"

Murmula nodded and said nothing more. She silently fought the tears that rushed forth, hoping she could finish in time to make an excuse so she could run to the bathroom and hide.

◆ ◆ ◆

Can you come tomorrow?

Owk

What time?

It is the weekend
What time is fine for you?

Give me some hours

Let me see

I will come arnd 1pm

Okay
The gate and front door will be open
Just come in

Owk

I've missed u

◆ ◆ ◆

Pamson had kept putting it off, wondering what he was doing. But now that he had committed himself, he needed to ensure there was no way to back out of it. There were also things he needed to do before then. When Luka and Helen mentioned their intention to visit him, he added seeing them as one of those things. He then realised it was the only thing. Of all the ties he had, all the relationships he had tended over the years, the one that mattered most to him among those that remained was what he shared with Luka. And he finally understood that Luka had been a kind of son to him. It was why he had sat in the privacy of his office and wept quietly the day he had nearly killed him at the garage.

He hosted Luka and Helen with soft drinks and cake, all remainders from Rahila's birthday celebration. Helen was demure and soft-spoken. They were the only guests he'd had since the disappearances. He felt like he was watching a replay of a scene from his previous life, when it was a normal thing for the living room to be full of voices and laughter, when people didn't permanently sublime into the ether. Their baby was due in a month or so, and Pamson watched them across the living room, the way Luka was serving his wife and reaching over for things on her behalf and being an eager, helpful husband. He remembered how he and Rahila once were and what they had become and how close they had come to fully reclaiming what they once had. Silently he hoped that Luka and Helen might be saved the trouble of losing it all only to have to fight to win it back.

"Oga, we will be going now," Luka said, standing up. He touched Helen's elbow softly as she hoisted herself up in increments. An action of no practical value but endearing all the same. They walked in front of him through the doorway, and he watched their hands brush against each other. Luka held each door open for her. Her braids from the wedding were still in full display, and they swung freely around her head and shoulders, the cowrie shells at the tips clinking like gently falling hail. When they had passed through the pedestrian opening and were standing on the street, they turned to say goodbye. Pamson removed the envelope he had been keeping in his pocket and gave it to Luka.

"Don't open that until I tell you to."

"What is this, Oga?" Luka said, turning it over in his hand.

"You'll know one day. For now, go and keep it somewhere safe. Make sure he doesn't open it."

Helen smiled and snatched the envelope out of his hand. "No problem, sir."

He waved one last time at them as they walked away hand in hand, then went inside, locking the doors as he went. In the bedroom, he pulled out the drawer at the foot of the wardrobe. It was supposed to be a receptacle for his belts and the ties Rahila had kept buying for him that he'd never used. Over the years, Rahila's own things had gradually overrun the compartment: handbags and purses, shell necklaces and bracelets, an implausible number of rubber bands. He slid the entire drawer out of its hole and put it aside. There was a gap in the concrete underneath that appeared deeper than it really was. He had specially requested when the wardrobe was being installed for the mason to leave the hollow there. He pulled out the black plastic bag and took out the heavy, clunky object inside that was wrapped in an old T-shirt. He hadn't seen the black semiautomatic pistol in years. He had forgotten its existence. He had tried to file it away with the part of his past it represented. But Mary was right: you couldn't just act like the past had never existed. Even though he could see the magazine resting beside the pistol, he still checked the chamber to make sure it was empty. The hammer slid back effortlessly, and when he tried the trigger, it clicked satisfyingly. He sat at the dining table and took his time loading the cartridges, as though he were passing the beads of a rosary over his finger. He snapped the magazine into the stem of the gun and placed the loaded weapon on the table. He sat there staring at it and thinking about the voice in the dark room that had spoken to him.

◆ ◆ ◆

Am on my way

Okay

22

At a quarter to one, Pamson went outside and stood against the rear wall of the house. He had full view of the gate if he peered around the corner. His repose no longer surprised him. Not since the day he had picked up Rahila's silky nightgown and hand-washed and stretched it on the clothesline, all with steady hands. But for the breezy coolness that clung to the shadows, the day was hot and dry, the sky entirely bereft of clouds. He could almost taste the dust. A field was burning somewhere in the area, its scent heavy in the air. Years had rolled by, and he hadn't followed through on his intention to start a vegetable garden. The unpaved section of the compound was a beige bareness. He hadn't even planted a single tree.

When it was exactly one o'clock, he watched her push the pedestrian gateway open and step into the compound. He had a vague impression of her standing outside and waiting for the clock to reach its mark. She carried a richly patterned light-blue wrapper and blouse along with a matching veil that looped over her head tie and around her shoulders and under her chin. She was the colour of the sky. She was carrying a black plastic bag. Closing the gate gently behind her, she passed out of sight, the heels of her shoes clopping gently against the pavement.

Pamson waited a moment longer before walking to the gate and inserting the key and locking it. He tugged one last time at the padlock of the main gate, as he had done that rain-drenched morning while searching for Rahila and Paul—secure as ever. He went back the way he had come and entered the house through the kitchen. He locked the door behind him.

◆ ◆ ◆

Murmula stood just inside the door of the living room. The house was quiet. Everything looked neatly arranged in a way that she didn't remember, as though it were a showroom and not a house where real people lived. Even the throw pillows had been placed in a way that accentuated their diamond shapes, equidistant across the sofa. It all made her uneasy. She hadn't been back here since the day the Pamsons had their thanksgiving celebration. Each step she took on this ground that was her stolen inheritance felt momentous, uncanny, the way she imagined walking on water might feel. This sensation would never go away, she realised. The land had been permanently stained in her consciousness, tied up inextricably with the memory of her father. What violence had been done to him? Had it happened here?

"Assalamu alaikum?" she called, with a downward inflection so that it sounded like a question.

The waina and alkaki she had spent much of her night making felt like they were growing heavier in the plastic bag. The bag's oval grips were starting to dig into her flesh, hurting her fingers. She went over to the coffee table and placed the bag on it.

"Paul?"

She heard movement in the kitchen; then someone came into the room. But it wasn't Paul. It was a jinn.

As Pamson stepped into the living room and into full view of Murmula, he had the heady sensation of crossing from one state of being into another. There was no turning back now. He registered the way her body recoiled, as though a bullet had slammed into her. While she remained frozen, he crossed the room and closed the front door and locked it. He had placed all the house keys on a single ring, and he slipped them into his pocket and turned to her. She was backing away into the room. He pointed at the single seat nearest the door.

"Sit down," he said in English.

He skirted the edge of the room and took his own seat. She sat down, and he realised they had taken the exact same spots they'd sat in the first time they met on that rainy afternoon months ago.

The jinn looked alarmingly like Mr. Pamson, except for a few alterations. The hair on either side of his bald pate had grown out. He now had a full beard, which gave him a scruffy appearance, made him seem at odds with his surroundings. He almost looked deranged. She felt like she had stupidly entered the cage of a wild animal. When he started across the room, she wanted to run, but he moved with such speed and silence she wondered if it was at all possible to outrun a jinn. He told her to sit. His tone was flat, his voice hoarse as though from lack of use. They sat and watched each other in silence. The seconds avalanched into an eternity. She tried to reconcile what she knew with what she was seeing, but her fear overpowered everything, stuck to her like a million burrs that she couldn't brush off. Still, she tried. What did she know? Did jinn have the ability to appear as humans? She didn't remember the answer; she hadn't been paying attention in islamiyah. A part of her had only believed in jinn the way one believes in the never-witnessed act of creation, or in a hereafter; they came pre-attached with the plain fact of life or death. Yet here was a jinn, an actual aljanni. He stared at her with dark, shimmering eyes. The fact that they could push through into the physical realm was something she had never considered seriously. She remembered learning about their awesome power. A slap from a jinn could twist her head 180 degrees; her face would look backward permanently. Information taken for granted that now had too much meaning.

Just as she had presumed without question that it was impossible for physical bodies to sink into some unseen place. What could she believe? How could she take any fact for certain now? How did she know that she hadn't also vanished into some other realm?

When the jinn pulled out a black gun and placed it on the coffee table, she realised jinn did not need guns. Her terror shifted then. She understood at last that she hadn't been brought here to be haunted; she had been brought here to be murdered.

◆ ◆ ◆

After he had placed the pistol on the table, Pamson watched her. Her fear was palpable. He could see the ways she was trying to appear calm and failing. Every minute or so, a tremor made its way down her throat. He looked at the bag.

"What did you bring for Paul?" he said.

It took her a while to find her voice. "Waina and alkaki."

"You made it yourself?"

This time she couldn't speak. She contented herself with nodding instead.

"You came expecting to see Paul," he said. Paul's phone was beside the pistol on the table. He raised it for her to see and put it down again. Then he picked up the folded blue shirt on the arm of his chair and let it unfurl. "This is what he was wearing when he disappeared."

Murmula stared at the shirt in Mr. Pamson's hands and wondered if it was a joke. Did he remember that it was what she had worn the day she had been drenched in the rain? There was no sign of amusement on his face, but he was enjoying this, wasn't he? From the way he sat there, tormenting her with his gun, with his silence, with his otherworldly presence. She wasn't going to cry. She wouldn't give him the satisfaction of seeing her break up into pieces. But she was distinctly aware of trying to do too much at once—pretending to be unafraid, pretending to be unsurprised, pretending to be undevastated—and her concern that she might buckle and fail spectacularly under the strain of it all became one more object to be juggled.

She swallowed and tried to speak, but the strain had squashed her voice flat. Her chest rose and fell. Rose and fell. Rose. And falling.

Rising.

And falling.Rising.

And falling.Rising and.Falling.

Pamson didn't take his eyes off her. He could practically see her lungs, her diaphragm overworking, as though he'd been granted X-ray vision. She went very still for the longest moment, and it seemed the world had gone still too. He heard a heart beat in the silence, and it took him a few seconds to understand that it was his.

The girl's sobs exploded like a train crashing through a brick wall. She flew nearly clean across the room, propelled by some unknowable force. She landed on the centre rug and shifted the coffee table. He had never seen anything like it. The gun slid gratingly to the edge of the glass surface and fell over. Pamson snatched it before it hit the floor. One aimless finger started to move the trigger—good thing he had left the safety on.

The girl wept so loudly that he wondered if he had ever seen true weeping before now. She was mumbling her despair in three languages. Her veil had snagged on the rug as her head moved from side to side. Her head tie came off. Strands of her hair slipped out of the bun she had tied them in. As he watched her, he felt a slight softening right below the surface of his resolve.

◆ ◆ ◆

Something touched her from beyond the orbit of the blackness that smothered her. She suddenly remembered where she was. She whipped her head up, saw him stooped over her, and scrambled away from him. He straightened up and looked at her.

"You can go and wash your face in the guest toilet," he said in Hausa.

She picked up her veil and head tie and closed the door behind her. She checked if there was a key. There was none. A small round mirror hung over the sink. The person who stared back at her wasn't the person she had seen in the mirror before she left home.

Paul Paul*Paul* Paul

She had been witnessed in such a state by none other than he, the killer of her father. She wet her fingers and used them to brush her hair back into place. She took a few more deep breaths, opened her makeup purse with rattling fingers,

Paul Paul*Paul*

and set about the task of restoring her dignity.

Pamson waited so long that he regretted letting her go in there. Did she know that the more time she wasted, the more likely his resolve would start to crumble? Was she doing it purposely? Maybe he had been callous in the way he had revealed the truth about Paul. The poor boy had been completely taken by her, which was why she could control him so easily. But Pamson hadn't anticipated the feeling being mutual.

When she finally came out, she was reset to her former self. Every grain of hair, every swoop of fabric, was perfectly in place. It was as if her breakdown had been erased from the record of this encounter. She sat down, and Pamson felt obliged to say something appeasing.

"I am sorry," he said in English. "I didn't know you felt that way about him."

Murmula kept her eyes averted, aimed at the lower regions of the room. She said nothing in response.

"Should I give you some cake and tea?" he said. "I baked the cake myself." When she didn't answer, he added, "It was my wife's birthday cake. Her birthday was the day before the disappearance."

"I'm sorry," Murmula said quietly. She remembered now that Paul had mentioned Mrs. Pamson's birthday to her. In the midst of her plotting, she had forgotten. That was the same day Thankgod had died—the same day she had killed a little boy.

"You and Paul were dating?"

Murmula paused before shaking her head. "It wasn't official."

"If you had more time, would it have become official?"

"Maybe."

"Were you planning to get married?"

She frowned, then shook her head. It was the first time she raised her eyes and looked at him.

"So why were you dating? What were you hoping to achieve?"

The question caught Murmula off guard. In the beginning she had interrogated again and again her intentions for getting involved with Paul, even after acknowledging that he was merely a means to what she wanted. This obsession had faded along the way with increasing time spent with him. Her intentions became a puzzle even to her own mind, and she soon gave up trying to understand them. She had wanted Mr. Pamson dead, but she had also wanted to remain in Paul's life. Somehow she had fooled herself into thinking it was possible to have both. That it was possible to continue to love someone while at the same time wilfully harming someone they cared about. The question had come up for her. What would she do if Paul asked her to marry him? She most likely would have said no, but it would have been a soft, pliable no; a no that was a maybe, let's see; a no that had a mouth of its own and said yes confusingly, annoyingly.

Pamson was beginning to think she wouldn't answer the question, but finally she said, "I don't know."

"You poisoned an innocent boy," he said.

She exhaled loudly, said softly, "It wasn't meant for him."

"It was meant for me."

Murmula nodded. She seemed to have found some boldness in that toilet, because she didn't avert her eyes. And for the first time he saw it—the thing whose absence confused him, the thing that had always been supplanted by a disarming emptiness in her gaze when she looked at him. He saw it then, her hate, and remembered that he'd seen it before: the day they'd first met when she had used her eyes to scan not just his form but his entire being. He was convinced that she had meant to kill him.

"You must be wondering why I asked you to come here."

"I know."

"Tell me."

Murmula couldn't say it. She wasn't prepared to die, that much was evident. But he was surprised by the pleasure this gave him. He stood and picked up the pistol.

The sight of the gun in his hand dismantled the self-possession she had cobbled together from makeup, mental fortitude, and a spruced-up costume. Her vision seesawed horribly. She was going to be sick. She shut her eyes and took a deep breath. When she sank to her knees, she didn't know if it was to beg for her life or to pray to her maker. But a moment later she found out:

> *Inna lillahi wa inna ilaihi raji'unInna lillahi wa inna ilaihi raji'un*
> *Inna lillahi wa inna ilaihi raji'un*
> *Inna lillahi wa inna ilaihi raji'un*
> *Inna lillahi wa inna ilaihi raji'un*

Her tears flowed again freely, but her weeping was silent this time. Her voice had taken on a will of its own. While she quietly dissolved, it raised the supplication over the room. All her life had been lived, all her choices made so that she would end up here, on her knees before the man who had destroyed her family. Now he would see to her own destruction.

When the cold mouth of the gun touched her temple, her voice quit and returned to her. Her eyes sprang open without her bidding. Her body betrayed her and released a horrible whimper.

"This is where you will put it," Mr. Pamson said in Hausa.

Murmula turned her face to him, and the gun fell away with his hand.

"What did you say?" she asked.

"In your thinking, I brought you here to kill you," he said. "But I wanted you to come and finish what you started." He took her hand and placed the gun in it. It dropped suddenly when he took his hand away, but she raised it at the last second and got slowly to her feet. It was heavy and cold. She looked at Mr. Pamson. He was standing there, watching her, waiting.

"You want to kill me," he said quietly. "Toh, here I am."

"You don't want to know why?"

He shook his head.

She was confused. She also felt foolish. She looked at the gun again. Finally, she shook her head.

"You don't want to do it?"

"You really don't want to know why I tried to—"

"I don't care."

She rummaged in her bag with her free hand and came away with some tissue. She blew her nose and wiped her face.

Pamson watched her with growing impatience. He was beginning to feel silly standing there, waiting for this girl to fulfil his death wish. He suddenly sensed the profound dissonance between his living room, the place of so many memories from his life, and this situation that was unfolding within its walls. But it wasn't unfolding fast enough. Plotting his own death had been easier than he'd expected. Now, with all the necessary elements assembled—the weapon, the would-be killer, the privacy—the smooth effortlessness he'd so far experienced was about to encounter resistance. He might lose his nerve.

"It should look like I did it to myself," he said, and took a step toward her. She flinched, then raised the weapon. The fact that it was now pointed at him was progress, but there were still a few more steps. He reached over and gripped her by the wrist and pulled her closer to him; she tried to resist but was no match. His own strength startled him. The moment stretched to its limit. "The safety is on." Without taking the pistol from her, he reached his finger, brushing hers as he did, and shifted the latch out of position.

Each time he touched her, she wanted to shrug her skin off and disinfect it. But when his finger slipped against hers in what was the lightest of touches, she nearly screamed. He had pulled his hand away for what she assumed was the last time, and she still didn't understand why she had raised the gun. He reached out again, beginning to say something, tugging her closer still.

"You have to put it directly—"

The gun went off, ending his words. In the small room, it sounded louder than anything she had ever heard. The shock of the blast entered her body, and she dropped the weapon. It didn't come out the other side of her. She shook all over. She ran without thinking into one of the bedrooms. The key was in the lock. She slammed the door shut and locked it. She backed away from the door.

Slowly it dawned on her that she was in Paul's room.

23

Pamson touched the burning place at the back of his neck. His fingers came away bloody. A trace, pink. As though the wound had remembered as an afterthought to bleed. He was still deaf from the gun blast—the weapon had gone off right next to his head. He had dropped to one knee at some point. He stood up and pushed his hands against air for balance. His eyes searched the walls. Where had the bullet gone to? He picked up the pistol, clicked the safety back on, and emptied it. Then he started searching the bedrooms.

Murmula stood in the middle of the room, shell shocked. Had she just killed a man? Had she just taken another life? A little dead boy, and now this?

—the door handle turned, squeaking softly—

she backed away from it. She needed to distract herself: the posters! She started looking at them, aware of an encroaching grief that she was afraid would flatten her. If she ignored it, it would pass. Ice Cube, Ice-T, Ice Prince: they were all present, arranged in a triangle. The Ice triumvirate. She almost smiled at the thought of Paul's obsession with detail and how he took pride in his ability to tell bad jokes

—the door rattled in its frame—

Wyclef Jean, Lauryn Hill, and Pras as the Fugees would have taken up nearly an entire wall but for the window. The poster had been snipped in its corners and in the places between the rappers' bodies to make it fit

—*"Open this door!"*—

She had only been in here once, the day she had come to change out of her wet clothes, the day she had met Paul, the day she had set it all off. But she hadn't been in any state of mind to notice, let alone be interested— She had hurt him, hadn't she? Mr. Pamson. She had hurt him, but she hadn't killed him. Thank God—Thankgod

Thankgod

She had overestimated her ability to inflict damage, but in doing so had ended a little boy's life. How cowardly, how lazy in effort and imagination and courage to attempt to kill a man by poisoning him, failing to look into his eyes, failing to point out to him which sin he was paying for with his life. She sat on the edge of the bed and laid her hand on the last place in which Paul had slept. Oh, Paul. He had been lying there, his head full of questions that she had cruelly raised and refused to answer. He had to have been sleeping, otherwise he'd surely still be here. Were any of those who disappeared awake when it happened? Or had their minds all been distracted by their dreams when their bodies were stolen? She ran her hand over the flatness of the bed. The synthetic skin of the mattress was rough against the pads of her fingers.

PaulPaulPaulPaul
PaulPaulPaul
PaulPaulPaulPaul
Paul

Her hands were still shaking. Oh, Paul—

The door crashed open to the sound of splintering wood.

She flinched so hard she slipped off the bed and struck her rib on the edge. Pain crackled through her. Instantly, she pushed it aside and raised her head. Mr. Pamson stood in the doorway.

"Come to the parlour," he said gruffly.

He resumed his seat and waited for her to arrive. When she did, she had her hand on her right side. She stood before him, staring back in some pitiful display of fearlessness. He had seen frightened faces, and hers was up there with the most frightened of them. "Sit down," he said quietly. The groove the bullet had gouged in his neck stung like pepper. She sank into the same place on the love seat, and he said, "Tell me why."

Murmula was certain she had broken her rib. The pain was getting harder to ignore. Now that he had asked, she realised she couldn't say, "You killed my father," and expect that to be enough. She needed to qualify it. She needed to tell a story, which was the last thing she wanted to do. Her reluctance to explain was tinctured by her pain, but mostly it stemmed from how desperately she didn't want to be pitied. There was no way she could fully explain without surrendering to tears. She didn't want Mr. Pamson's pity; she wanted him shattered to bits at the foot of her misery. If there was any pitying to be done, it should come from her. But he had the upper hand. With the doors locked and the gun back in his possession, she was truly at his mercy. There was no power her voice could wield that would alter things as they now stood. She cared less about leaving this house alive and more about sowing in him a guilt that would taint his days. Her interactions with him over the past few months showed him to be humane—he really believed he was a good man. Perhaps compassion was her ally, the doorway to guilt. With this in mind, she decided upon the unthinkable. She put her hand in her bag and pulled out the white envelope she had taken the trouble to buy from a bookstore in State Lowcost Junction on her way here.

Pamson watched her slide the long white envelope from her handbag, like a sword being unsheathed, like a writ of condemnation with his name on it. She struggled across the room. He remained still, petrified by the same fear that lurked in the shadows each time he wondered why she had targeted him. One among the many people whose lives he'd taken had to have a connection to her. It was the only thing that made sense. A male relative of some kind—an uncle, a brother, maybe a father. She gave him the envelope and returned to her seat. He turned it over. It wasn't his name. He was about to eavesdrop on a conversation.

Murmula nearly cried out when she sat down. It was getting more difficult to breathe, so she kept her inhalations shallow. She raised her head when she heard the rustling of the paper. Mr. Pamson opened the envelope and withdrew the letter within. She had written it on a whim, convinced that her voice would fail her when she came face-to-face with its intended recipient. So she had put everything into it.

24

Dear Paul,

There's no excuse for what I did. For leaving you like that with that boy in the hospital. For ignoring your calls and messages. I won't say that I didn't see them or that my phone was dead. I saw them and I ignored them. Because I'm a coward. I didn't know how to face you. I was ashamed of what I had done. I was afraid of seeing the disappointment in your face, in your eyes, when you found out. I was afraid of seeing how hurt you would be when you found out about my real plan, my true intention. How can I show you that I and my intention aren't the same thing in this situation? According to Islam, Allah judges actions according to intentions. So maybe what I'm trying to say doesn't make sense, maybe it sounds like I'm contradicting myself. But I'm not my intention when it comes to this particular situation.

Before I talk about my intention, I want you to see where I've come from in my life's journey to get to this point where I am today. You know how I was born in Jos and grew up in Jos. You also know my dad disappeared during the crisis of 2008. These are the beginning point and the end point of my Jos story as a girl growing up.

You don't know the middle. I will tell you everything in the middle.

My parents were living in Nassarawa when I was born. We lived on a long street called Gaskiya Avenue that wasn't very far from Sarkin Mangu Street. I remember how we grew up with our neighbour's children. We didn't care who was a Muslim or a Christian. My best friend was a girl named Chundung David. I don't know where she is now. Our families didn't keep in touch after what happened. But before that, our parents used to send us to each other's house during Christmas and Sallah. During Ramadan, my mother used to send me with kosai and kunun tsamiya in the evening to Chundung's house and some of our other neighbours. Sometimes they would make me stay and eat dinner with them even though my mother was waiting for me to go back so she could give me my food. That was how I learned to eat and love gwaten acha with groundnut, gauta, and biscuit bone. Our mallam used to come and teach me and some other Muslim children on the street after la'asr prayers. After lessons, we went out to play soccer and ten-ten with the other neighbourhood children. In the rainy season, we made boats and sailed them down the puddles when it rained. In the dry season, I remember how the dust used to rise in the evening and it would look like gold dust was falling on everything and everyone. I miss those times a lot.

When the first crisis happened in 2001, we were still living there. It was scary. I was about eight at the time. We used to stay inside and lock the doors because we didn't know if people from other parts of Nasarawa would come to our street. But we didn't worry about the people living on our street, whether Muslim or Christian. We believed that we would protect each other. Our street was long and we had yan banga that used to patrol at night, made up of both Muslims and Christians. That also helped. We heard many terrible stories about people that were killed or betrayed by their neighbours, both Muslims and Christians. But our street survived it.

My parents really believed we were safe on Gaskiya Avenue even though many Muslim families in Nasarawa left the area. There was one family on our street that left even after the mai unguwa reassured them. My parents thought about leaving because my father had bought some land in Federal Lowcost and was already building, but their landlord, a Christian man, begged them to stay and even reduced the rent money for them. So, we stayed in Nassarawa. We thought everything was fine after that.

When the crisis of 2008 happened, we weren't surprised. But it still took us by surprise. My dad was working for Hill Station Hotel as a manager, and they were having financial problems. They stopped paying their staff, and it affected his building project. Things became very bad for us financially. After the crisis, when the city was still very tense, my dad decided to sell the land and the building he had started. He had used all his savings, and my mother wasn't working. I still remember the last time I saw my dad. I just came back from school. I was attending a secondary school at the time that was around Dogon Dutse. He dropped me at home and told my mother that he was going to go to the land to meet *with someone who wanted to buy it, but they wanted to see it first. I remember how my mother told him to wait a few days because there was still tension in the city, and it meant he was going to be driving through areas that were dangerous because he was a Muslim. He said she shouldn't worry, that he was going to be careful and pass through Farin Gada. We never saw him again. My mother and my father's twin brother searched everywhere, but they never found him or his car.*

Months later, my mother went to Federal Lowcost to see the land, but it had been fenced with a padlock on the gate. My mother found out from the neighbours the name of the man who claimed to own the land. My father's death really affected my mother seriously. We had no money. She was hoping to sell the land and pay for my school fees. After what happened, she didn't have the energy to chase it. She didn't know how to investigate it. She told me my father hadn't paid for the land documents, so the land had no deed. She decided to go back to Kwara State, where her family lives. My grandmother and aunty lived there at the time, even though my grandmother died shortly after we got there. Then my mother. But before she died, she told me the name of the man who had killed my father and stolen his land. She made me promise to get justice. But I had already made that promise to myself, even before she asked me. My father didn't have a son to avenge him, so it was going to be my responsibility. I saw how badly my father's death affected my mother, ultimately leading to her death. She became very sick and depressed. It also affected me because I was very close to my dad. After my mother died, I could blame only one man for the death of both my parents, for destroying my family's life, for destroying my life. I miss them so much, especially my dad. Sometimes I start crying suddenly just like that when I think about them and what my life could have been. When you lose your dad, it's like the world turns against you, like you no longer exist, because there's nobody to protect you and provide for you. Imagine when you lose both your parents. So you have to learn to be strong for yourself and to take care of yourself.

Anyway, to cut a long story short, the name my mother gave me was Dareng Pamson. And the house is the house you live in, No. 27, 14th Avenue, Federal Lowcost. It was Dareng Pamson who killed my father and stole his land and brought this curse on my family. That is why I did what I did.

This is the most honest letter I've ever written. I've never told anyone this before. I've been writing my thoughts and feelings in a diary for almost ten years, since my dad died, and I've never written anything that's this frank. The reason I can be this honest is because of how I feel about you. I know that whatever was between us can never go anywhere because I don't expect you to forgive me. I don't deserve your forgiveness, because the way I feel about your uncle hasn't changed. And now I'm so confused about it. I saw Luka the other day; he told me what happened to Thankgod. I killed that poor boy, and I will have to live with the guilt for the rest of my life. I don't deserve your forgiveness, and maybe I never will. When I think about your uncle and how he disappeared, too, I feel angry and regretful because I wish he could have been around for me to carry out my revenge as planned. But maybe that's just my wishful thinking, because now that I know what it feels like to be responsible for someone's death, I'm not sure I can take another life. But I still would wish him death. Does that confuse you? I know it confuses me. The poison wasn't originally part of my plan, but it seemed like the easiest way. Instead, I killed a poor boy. I don't know how I can pay for this sin, but I will continue to seek Allah's forgiveness.

This is why I did what I did. If I leave before you read this, know that I have never loved anyone more than I have loved you. We never dated, I know. I don't know if I can be able to love as deeply as I have with you. I didn't realise this until I became afraid that you had also disappeared with the others. Sharing music and food, going hiking, watching your amazing mind work and solve problems. All of it were the happiest days of my life since my dad's death. I have accepted the way I feel about you as my burden to carry. Maybe it is what I deserve for what happened to Thankgod.

I'm very sorry.

xoxo
M

25

When he finished the letter, Pamson took a deep breath, aware of several things at once. A floral whiff of perfume that floated off the pages (there were four leaves of paper), the same as the scent that Murmula wore; the conviction that this exquisite cursive, rendered in deep-purple ink, was the most beautiful handwriting he had ever seen; a strange, dreamy sensation that the ground had been pulled like a rug from under his feet and he had lost his balance.

Murmula watched him fold up the papers and put them back in the envelope. With his face averted in what she assumed to be shame, she felt her anger mounting. She was surprised by the steadiness in her voice when she asked, "Do you remember?"

Pamson raised his head at last and looked at her. The question he was dreading. How could he begin to answer it? At length, he shook his head and said, "No."

"You don't remember killing my father and stealing his land?" Murmula said in Hausa, her voice spiking righteously, the pain in her side peaking along with it.

Pamson felt a twinge in his chest. How could he sit there and explain it all away, after all that she had carried across the years to get to this point? Hate was such a heavy thing to bear, and it seemed unfair that she had carried it so far and so long for nothing. No, he couldn't explain it away. He was complicit, though not in the way she understood. He felt his own anger surging within—anger on her behalf but also anger for the position he occupied. "I want to tell you how I got this land," he said, "but it seems like you're in pain."

Murmula was bent over. She wanted to shake her head, but there was no use. The pain would continue to grow worse. Had she really broken a rib? Was she in danger of puncturing a lung? When Mr. Pamson asked her where exactly was hurting, she touched her rib and shuddered from the movement.

While he waited in the lobby of the diagnostics clinic, he wrote his letter by hand. It was less a letter and more a statement. He skipped the formality of salutations and addresses and got into the business of what had happened. He'd written a statement for the police once, and this seemed like one of those, necessary for proper investigation and the eventual dispensing of justice. He didn't know what she would do with it once she had it—he didn't care.

The details, worn and faded by years, came to him like small objects glimpsed through rain. But he pressed on, determined to commit as much as he could marshal from memory onto the page. He had brought a small exercise book, the kind favoured by primary school pupils, and the recollections demanded nearly seven pages. But then, his handwriting was cumbersome and wasteful of space to begin with. He wrote quickly because he hoped to finish before Murmula came out.

In the consulting room, the doctor, a middle-aged woman wearing a hijab and thick reading glasses, raised Murmula's X-ray to the light and looked at it for some time, bringing it closer every few seconds. She put it away and said there was no indication of any breakage in the imaging. She said it was possibly a hairline fracture and would heal itself in a month of two. She recommended rest and dedicated home care.

When Murmula came out, Mr. Pamson wasn't where she had left him. She looked up and down the waiting area. At the front desk, she found a roll of stapled pages with her name on it, and some cash. There was also a note that said *I hope you get better quickly. I'm sorry for all the pain I've caused you.*

◆ ◆ ◆

Pamson stopped the BMW in front of the Mobil filling station on Ahmadu Bello Way and bought two tins of boiled groundnuts. He cracked them expertly with his thumb as he drove pensively through the business district, through the GRA, up Yakubu Gowon Way, down the endless slope that connected Old Airport Junction to Domkat Bali Road, where the elevation switched up and required him to use the accelerator. Past the vast bushes of Wildlife Park that uncoiled anonymously and menacingly to his right. A hyena had once escaped and crossed the road into Federal Lowcost, terrorising the dogs and the chickens. So the reports had claimed. There had been enough accounts of sightings that he believed them. The groundnut shells were a neat pile in the passenger's seat by the time he drove into the compound and closed the gate, his thoughts much clearer than they'd been when he started eating.

Murmula told her uncle and aunt that she had slipped and struck her side on a step, and a kind person who had witnessed it had driven her to the hospital and paid for her bills. As they swallowed this without questions, without resistance, she remembered the overpowering guilt that always accompanied the act of lying to them. She had forgotten about it in the wake of the disappearances, and she had probably assumed in some unconscious fashion that it was now only a relic and would soon be buried deep under freshly spun good deeds and piety. Presently she felt it growing in bulk and circumference, felt it squashing her into the ground just a little more. In the weeks to come, while her aunt busied herself with house chores and nursed her in a sustained flurry of head-scratching ebullience, Murmula poured words into her diary. She was the oldest she had ever been, and the world had never confused her more.

26

Pamson sat in his car, waiting outside Haruna & Miner Attorneys-at-Law. The firm was just across the road from the Old Government House junction. It occupied the top floor of a modest, yellow-painted duplex that had a bakery on the ground floor. Pamson had bought bread from the bakery and its other branches many times, the best bread he had ever had in Jos until Jonah had opened shop. The last time Pamson had driven past Jonah's Baked Delight, the sign had been taken down. The entire property appeared to be undergoing some kind of renovation, most likely for a new tenant.

Mark's light-green Honda Civic peeled away from the road and slid into a parking spot under a mango tree beside the building. He got out and walked down the verandah and up the staircase. He was wearing shorts and a light sweater that seemed insufficient for the prevailing chill. He had either failed to notice Pamson's BMW or assumed he had already gone up and was waiting for him by the door. No doubt he was upset for being dragged out here so early on a Sunday morning. They hadn't spoken since that day he'd learned of Solomon's disappearance.

Pamson waited five more minutes before going up. The law firm had been partitioned into two offices for Mark and Solomon, a reception and waiting area, and a small boardroom. Mark was behind his desk, performing some vague action on his phone. They shook hands and Pamson sat in front of the desk. He had witnessed how the offices had changed over the years. They had transitioned to whiter furniture that looked more expensive, more comfortable. The bookcases had become fronted with glass, a lush handwoven rug had appeared along the way. All indications of a growing clientele. The room was very quiet. Apart from the vehicles that thundered past and the distant swells of worship songs from multiple churches, there was very little noise around. They were probably the only two people in the building. This was why Pamson had chosen the location and the time. There was very little likelihood of being interrupted.

"Pamson, Pamson. Is this your face?" Mark began in Hausa. He smiled and shook his head. "I won't lie, coming in here sometimes, especially on a day like this. When I remember Solo—sometimes I just leave. I go and work in a place where there are people. If not, I just feel like it's the whole world that has disappeared."

"If you had gotten married like we advised, you wouldn't be so lonely." Pamson said it without smiling.

"Rather, it's a good thing I didn't marry. What if I lost my whole family?"

"You would have had children. The chances of all of them disappearing would have been low."

"But it's been known to happen ai."

Pamson fell silent and nodded at this.

Mark shook his head again. "Do you know, one of our clients—her husband was beating her. Very rich man, but he got married in his forties. Beautiful young woman. But he used to beat her. One time he broke her arm. She decided she wanted to divorce him. We were going to get her as much money as we could. But that guy, he was just difficult; he refused to give her an inch of anything. He wouldn't divorce her, and he made her life miserable. She ended up having to leave the house, but he wouldn't let her take the children. For almost two years, she was living in her parents' house. Then it happened. He was among those that disappeared too. Just like that, the guy was gone, as if someone rubbed him out with an eraser from the woman's life. Now she has her children back, and all of the properties are now hers.

Her in-laws—you know how our people can be—they wanted to start saying that she was the one who made him disappear with jazz. But they couldn't when it wasn't just him, even the president of America. So they had to shut up. The man that was making her life hell just disappeared. Today she's a happy woman with a lot of money. Can you imagine?"

Pamson took this in. "It's very convenient when your problem just disappears, ko ba haka ba?"

"I'm telling you," Mark said with a chuckle. "Anyway, what can I do for you? It's like you've been hiding. Lafiya, this one that you're not smiling this morning?"

"Lafiya," Pamson said, then corrected himself. "Actually, ba lafiya."

"You have me worried fa. Has something happened?"

"Nothing has happened. I'm fine."

Mark looked at him again, then leaned back in his seat. Another smile curved his lips. "So, this is how I finally get to see you." It was both a question and a charge. "When are we going to continue with the company registration? You know that life must go on ko?"

Pamson shrugged. "It has been strange for everybody. None of us understands what happened. Maybe we will just continue to be strange to each other until we get used to the way things have become." He stopped himself—the task at hand. "How are you coping without Solo?"

"It has been strange, like you said. It had been very hard for his wife."

"How is business?"

"Business is okay. It's hard without him. But we continue to push on."

"I remember that he was the one that mostly handled things when I bought that land where my house is. Right?"

Mark jiggled his head from side to side as he weighed this submission. "Maybe. It was a long time ago, but you know we did everything together. Maybe he was the one you were talking to. But when we were in the office, we did everything together."

"You know I never met the man who sold it to me. I was just wondering about him yesterday. I was supposed to meet with him, but the day of the meeting, I decided not to go out. It was during that crisis of 2008. You remember?"

Mark nodded.

"It wasn't a safe time to be moving around anyhow. But the man sounded like he needed money. I never spoke to him. Solo and I were supposed to go together so that we could be introduced. But I decided not to go and told Solomon to conclude the matter because I had already seen the land and liked it. You remember, he had built to lintel level ko?"

Mark nodded again. Pamson noticed that his movements were becoming measured, less fluid.

"I checked the man's name on the land agreement. I noticed that the only thing that was written there was *Mr. Denge*." Pamson reached into his back pocket and pulled out the document. He unfolded it and pointed to the name. "But there was no signature. I didn't notice it until yesterday."

Mark raised the document and studied it, then looked up. "Like I told you, it was such a long time ago. I don't think I can remember."

"Solo would have been the best person to remember ko?"

Mark nodded again.

"Unfortunately, he isn't around to help us."

Mark's lips curved wistfully. "That's Solo for you. You know that his memory was so sharp? He never forgot anything."

"Let me tell you a story. Maybe it will unlock your memory a little. If it doesn't, we can always try something else. About six months ago, a young woman came to my house and said she wanted to work. Her name is Murmula Denge. To cut a long story short, she started working for me. You've met her. I found out later that she tried to poison me. When I finally got the chance to ask her why she would do such a thing, she said that I killed her father and stole his land. Can you imagine this kind of thing?"

Mark had no response this time. In the dim room, his face had taken on a dismal look.

"She said in 2008, her father left home to go and meet me at the land, and they never saw him again. They never received any money for the land. When they went to see the land, a fence had already been built. Does that remind you of anything?"

Mark released an expansive sigh and pushed his chair away from the desk. It seemed the room itself had become too small for him all of a sudden. "That was a long time ago, Pamson. It has passed. Solo isn't here to explain."

"Do you think she could be related to this Mr. Denge, as she claims? They have the same surname ai."

Mark shook his head. "I don't know. It happened in the past. Can we just leave this talk?"

"You say it is in the past, but did you hear what I said? Someone tried to poison me because she thinks I killed her father. When I don't know anything about it. What I know is that I paid money for the land and got the agreement and built my house. I was told that everything was fine. And for ten years I believed that everything was fine."

"It's in the past, Pamson. I can't help you. You have to let it go."

Pamson leaned forward and pulled out the pistol that had been tucked into his waistband, its coolness burning into the small of his back all the while. He flicked the safety off and pointed it at Mark.

"Jesus!" Mark jumped several inches in his chair. It rolled back into the bookcase behind him with a loud thud. Pamson grabbed the pistol and chambered a round, then held it steady and trained it on the man who used to be his friend. "If you lie to me again, I swear I will shoot you. Tell me everything you know about this land."

"Dareng, have you lost your mind? Put that thing away!" Mark was beginning to stand up.

Pamson pointed the gun at the bookcase and fired. The weapon roared and spit flares. The entire front of the bookcase crumbled into a rain of glass. By the time the pistol found Mark again, he was standing in the corner beside his desk. He had nowhere to run.

"I paid one point five million naira for this land, plus the five percent agent commission. Did you give it to the owner?"

"No."

"Why not?"

"When Solo went to meet with him, he didn't show up. He wasn't answering his phone. He kept trying him for several days after, but the phone was eventually switched off. Since you already paid, we decided to keep the money until we heard from him."

"Did you kill him?"

"No!"

"Did Solo kill him?"

"I swear to God, Pamson. How can you even suggest something like that? We didn't do anything to him."

"So what happened to him?"

"Wallahi I don't know. There were a lot of silent killings going on around the town. People just kept disappearing. Maybe some people followed him and killed him."

"What did you do with the money?"

"Haba, Dareng. That was a long time ago—"

Pamson stood up and advanced on Mark until the pistol was inches from his face. "What did you do with the money?"

Mark shook his head—not denial, desperation.

"You ate the money, isn't that so? You collected five percent from me and just ate the money."

"Pamson, please, I'm begging you. You don't know, but I have a small daughter. Please. I swear I have a daughter, she's seven . . ."

Pamson moved in and pressed the mouth of the gun to Mark's chest. He pushed him until Mark's back was flush against the wall. He could feel the quavering flesh vibrating through the gun's metal, the crazed rhythm of his pulse. It was like cradling a baby chick in the cage of your hand, the fluff of its yellow fur a tiny puff against your palm, its heart a flimsy percussion. Deep in Mark's eyes, the overconfident, obnoxious man he'd always known had vacated the premises—only a frightened child remained.

"The man you cheated also had a daughter. You're going to return that money minus your agent fee. You're going to return it in today's money, with interest. You have two weeks. Call me when it's ready. Unless you want me to pay you another visit. And if you prefer to deal with the police, I will be happy to tell them everything I know and invite other witnesses."

The pistol was all that remained of the years Pamson had spent working for Senator Garba. He had made the decision to keep it after the 2001 crisis, when fear and mistrust were still reverberating through the city. He had always liked its effective, compact size. Small enough to conceal but large enough to intimidate an opponent. And he hadn't used it ever since—not even the night armed robbers had attacked a house on their street and kidnapped one of the tenants who lived there.

When he got home, he dismantled the pistol and placed the pieces on the ground. The power within it scared him now. He didn't want to be responsible for such a thing any longer. On his way home, he had found a hardware shop that was open and bought half a bag of cement, a hammer, and some nails. He went to the generator room and found his old mixing pan and shovel from his mason days, all crusted over with hardened cement. He added cement and sharp sand to the pan, made the requisite hole in the centre, and poured water. When the mix was ready, he laid out the wooden frame he had hammered together around a skeleton of copper rods. He fit the pieces of the pistol so that they were suspended between the rods; then he poured the cement mixture. He stepped back and surveyed his work, not unlike admiring the gleaming consistency of cake batter before sliding it into the oven. When the slab was ready, he would slot it into the depression underneath the wardrobe. He had taken precise measurements. That would be its final resting place. He looked at his watch. It wasn't yet 10:00 a.m. He could still make it to church in time for the Hausa service.

27

Nov. 2nd, 2018

Thankgod is alive. Mr. P explained in his letter. Luka lied to me, but I understand. I still wonder if my actions caused all of those people to vanish. But when I told Beatrice everything, all she said was that I'm not that important. She didn't judge me, she just gave me another bottle of Fanta to drink. I know, very funny. Her tone is changing, it's like she's beginning to accept that people really disappeared. The fact that the American president was also affected and hasn't returned maybe opened her eyes?

In Mr. P's letter, he gave me two options. Get #27 back or receive money for it. I don't want the house. Too many memories associated with it, Mrs. P, Paul. At first I said I didn't want the money. Then I regretted sending the text after a few minutes, after I realised that money is the best form of justice. Especially since he said the money would be with interest. Because if I say I want justice and I refuse the money, then what is it that I really want? I can't say blood because I'm not interested in that kind of thing anymore. Plus, if anyone deserves *to die, it's not him. Maybe the lawyers who duped my father? Maybe the actual person that killed him. That person may be out there, may be among the lost people. Allah knows. Allah will judge that person.*

In any case, after I sent the text, Mr. P replied and insisted that I had to take the money or the house, because he wasn't going to keep both of them. So, I finally accepted. Today, less than two weeks later, I received the money. I was sitting in the shop, working, when the alert came in. It's why I decided to write this—I haven't written since Ishat's and Musty's disappearance.

Seeing such an amount drop into my account didn't give me the kind of satisfaction I expected. I thought that getting justice for Baba and Mama would take my pain away or reduce it. But it's still there and I still don't know what to do with it. Maybe justice needs time to do its work of healing? Maybe, maybe, maybe. Maybe all we have is maybe.

My rib has healed very well. The pain has been reducing so much that sometimes I don't even feel it at all. It is Gogo Hauwawu that will remind me to take it easy. Left to her, I'd never leave the house at all. But I would lose my mind just sitting there. We had already started arguing with her about the house chores. She kept saying that if I want to clean so badly, I should bring a husband so I can do it in my own house. I know she's joking, but maybe she's half serious.

Thankgod is alive, the little boy is alive. Alhamdulillaah.

◆ ◆ ◆

The disappearances had compounded her grief, there was no question about it. They had taken the hollowness that was linked to her father and mother, something small but intense but all hers, and morphed it into an ungainly massiveness that wanted to squash her. Nights with her uncle and aunt, eating dinner in front of the TV, had become a balm, a centring force. Before they started a movie, Baba Karami would switch to Al Jazeera for a half hour, listening to see if there had been any progress in the search for the vanished US president. He kept saying that if the Americans could bring their president back, then there was hope for the rest of the world. But Murmula wasn't so sure. They had no chance of succeeding; no one did. Or what if they did and decided to keep it a secret?

Months on, the disappearances continued to dominate the news cycles across many channels. At work, when Murmula looked up at the silent TV on the wall, with either CNN or BBC playing, the bulk of the text that scrolled across the screen had to do with the fallout. Iceland was erecting a glass monument inscribed with the names of all those who vanished within its borders, about two thousand people. A Zimbabwean billionaire who had lost his wife in the disappearances was privately investing in a research project that aimed to channel nanotechnology toward investigating the phenomenon. Nigerian news stations, on the other hand, seemed to have grown bored and moved on. Beatrice joked that Africans already believed in a spiritual world, so the novelty factor for something like this would be quick to wear out. Although one time, a pristinely dressed Yoruba man in white traditional dress had been interviewed on Arise News, claiming to have chanted the incantation that led to the disappearances. He offered to bring the lost people back, but on the condition that he be paid a ransom of a hundred million naira. A few days later, Murmula heard that he had been picked up for questioning by the DSS.

Tonight on Al Jazeera, three panelists were discussing the disappearances from different philosophical positions. A quantum physicist, a Native American spiritual leader, and a Mormon bishop. They were all dressed in suits and sat around the table—it would have been impossible to tell their points of view based on appearance alone. The Native American, Mr. Summers, was speaking about the spirit world and how the reality couldn't be explained strictly from a rational point of view.

"The hubris of humanity is that we think we can trap everything and dissect and analyse and describe. But what happens when three million people dissolve into the ether?"

"And that's the million-dollar question, isn't it?" said the interviewer. "What happens? How do we account for that?"

Baba Karami ate the last bite of his chips and eggs and put the plate on the floor. He pointed at the screen and said that Allah had given these white people a riddle they couldn't solve. "Everybody should go home and rest," he added.

When Murmula sat with them like this, the absence of her cousins was a fact that filled her mind. At the same time, she couldn't help feeling a striking inevitability, like she was exactly where she was meant to be. There was still so much they didn't know, but she would tell them everything. Why she had come to Jos. What she had tried to do. She would tell them about the money.

On TV, the interviewer turned to the quantum physicist. "Can quantum physics give us any answers?"

The man cleared his throat. "We learn more and more about the world each day. Our knowledge is catching up with our reality. What this suggests is that there is something in our reality that allows for the dissolution of human bodies. You have people disappearing and leaving behind braces, fillings on their pillows, false teeth. All sorts of strange things. To put it another way, Arthur C. Clarke said that all sufficiently advanced technology is indistinguishable from magic. Whether you want to call magic science or science magic, I don't care. But things once impossible have been known to become possible. Now, when it comes to quantum mechanics specifically, while the quantum realm introduces captivating phenomena like superposition and entanglement . . ."

"Murmula, you're an engineer," Baba said. "Please, what is he saying? I'm not understanding his English."

Murmula laughed. "Baba, even I am struggling to understand it."

"Toh, why are we watching it?" Gogo Hauwawu said. "Murmula, what are we watching tonight?"

"There's a new film my colleague gave me. It's called *Coco*. It's an animation, the kind Baba likes."

"Bring it," Baba Karami said.

Murmula registered the previous day's bookkeeping, moving with ease through the financial software's interface. She was only required to come in three times a week, but she still came every weekday and spent half days instead. She preferred to upload each day's transaction to the system rather than waiting till the end of the week, when there would be significantly more work to do in one sitting. Beatrice had gone down the street to buy them lunch, and the tailors were in the inner room. The store was quiet but for the clacking keyboard. Then she heard the call to prayer. Barely a minute passed before the door to the inner room slid open and Muazu stepped out.

"Diyar Afonja, sallah," he said, tapping his watch.

Murmula nodded, but before she could answer, the main entrance opened to a woman's laughter. Two shoppers entered. Murmula stood up.

"I'm alone; Beatrice will be back soon. I'll catch up with you."

Muazu nodded and headed out. Murmula went around the glass display box that hid her desk from the rest of the shop. She froze when she saw Mary, who was standing with her back to her. She would have recognised her figure anywhere. Today she wore a tight black dress that flared at the knees, revealing her shapely legs and accentuating her thighs. She was accompanied by a tall, greying man. He might have been in his fifties. She turned around, revealing a generous bulge in her belly. Her hand instinctively moved to it as she walked up to Murmula.

"Good afternoon," Murmula said.

"Good afternoon. Is your madam around?"

"She didn't come today. Is there anything I can get for you?"

"I came to pick up a lace. It has my name, Mrs. Ojo."

"My colleague who usually handles these things went out, but I'll see if I can find it."

"Thank you," Mary said with a smile.

While Murmula searched the drawers in Beatrice's desk, Mary and her companion conversed in soft voices. Murmula wasn't sure if Mary recognised her or not. It had been hard to read her expression. At the bottom of the second drawer, Murmula saw a white plastic bag that contained a gold-coloured brocade lace. The amount on the receipt made her eyes widen. It was made out to Mrs. Mary Ojo, paid in full.

"Is this it?" Murmula said, holding out the plastic bag.

Mary inspected it. "Yes, thank you very much. Please greet your madam." She collected the bag and turned to leave.

"Thank you for shopping with Eldoba Stiches."

At the door, Mary stopped suddenly and turned. "Please, can I use your bathroom?"

"Yes, ma. It's in the back." Murmula pointed in the direction of the bathroom.

Mary handed the bag to the man. "I'll meet you in the car, baby."

The man nodded and left.

Mary walked back into the shop, but she went up to Murmula instead. She wore a smirk. "So, we meet again."

Murmula stared back at her, amazed by her transformation. She seemed relaxed, radiant. Without her makeup, she looked even more beautiful than Murmula remembered. She had even lost the edge in her tone, as though she had previously been decked out for war against anyone that had the misfortune of encountering her. This was clearly peacetime.

"You remember me?"

Murmula nodded and smiled.

"You're no longer with Pamson?"

Murmula shook her head.

"How is he? Do you know?"

"It's been some time."

"Did his wife ever have the baby?"

Murmula frowned. "Why wouldn't she?" Her eyes dropped to Mary's belly.

Mary looked down at it, too, patted it, shrugged. She dropped the hand. "You never called me."

"I'm sorry. I lost my phone not long after we met."

Mary nodded and, switching to Hausa, said, "I hoped we could help each other. But the world has changed since the last time we met ko?"

"Yes, it has kam."

Mary stood there, as though waiting for Murmula to say something. Finally, she said, "My husband is waiting for me. Thank you." She turned and walked to the door.

Murmula loosened her tongue and called, "Congratulations!"

Without turning around, Mary raised a hand and wiggled her fingers, emphasising her wedding band. "Thank you." She passed through the door and was lost from sight.

Murmula stood for a moment, unsure of what had just happened. She shook her head and picked up her phone, all the while smiling to herself. In her phone book she scrolled until she found the name—*Mary (Pamson)*. She pressed "Delete."

Outside, she stood under the mango tree, wearing her prayer abaya, ready for the mosque. Her face, wet from the ablution she'd just performed, was upturned to the sky. There wasn't a cloud in sight. A cool breeze scurried in the shade, swaddling her, drying her wet skin in seconds, leaving as though having fulfilled an assignment.

Acknowledgments

My deepest gratitude goes to:

Selena James and the entire Little A team who worked behind the scenes, forming this book into a real object.

Chris L. Terry, for helping me to see this project better.

Andrea Somberg, for being there.

Naima Nasir, Doug Kaze, Bilkisu Arabi, and Sokshak Shikse, for being such fresh eyes.

My family, for putting up with this madness.

About the Author

Umar Turaki is a writer and filmmaker from Jos, Nigeria. He holds an MFA in creative writing from the University of British Columbia. *Every Drop of Blood Is Red* is his second novel. For more information, visit www.umarturaki.com.